MW01449416

FOREVER GUARDED

FOREVER BLUEGRASS #10

KATHLEEN BROOKS

Created with Vellum

Bluegrass Series

Bluegrass State of Mind

Risky Shot

Dead Heat

Bluegrass Brothers

Bluegrass Undercover

Rising Storm

Secret Santa: A Bluegrass Series Novella

Acquiring Trouble

Relentless Pursuit

Secrets Collide

Final Vow

Bluegrass Singles

All Hung Up

Bluegrass Dawn

The Perfect Gift

The Keeneston Roses

Forever Bluegrass Series

Forever Entangled

Forever Hidden

Forever Betrayed

Forever Driven

Forever Secret

Forever Surprised

Forever Concealed

Forever Devoted

Forever Hunted

Forever Guarded

Forever Notorious (coming January 2019)

Shadows Landing Series

Saving Shadows (coming October 2018)

Women of Power Series

Chosen for Power

Built for Power

Fashioned for Power

Destined for Power

Web of Lies Series

Whispered Lies

Rogue Lies

Shattered Lies

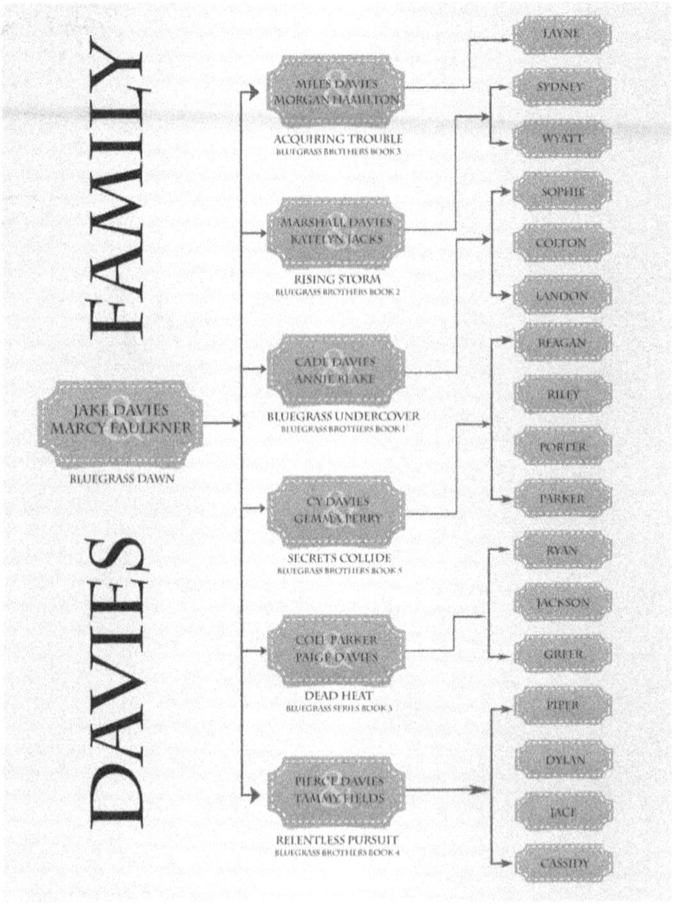
DAVIES FAMILY
JAKE DAVIES & MARCY FAULKNER
BLUEGRASS DAWN
MILES DAVIES & MORGAN HAMILTON
ACQUIRING TROUBLE
BLUEGRASS BROTHERS BOOK 3
MARSHALL DAVIES & KATELYN JACKS
RISING STORM
BLUEGRASS BROTHERS BOOK 2
CADE DAVIES & ANNIE BLAKE
BLUEGRASS UNDERCOVER
BLUEGRASS BROTHERS BOOK 1
CY DAVIES & GEMMA PERRY
SECRETS COLLIDE
BLUEGRASS BROTHERS BOOK 5
COLE PARKER & PAIGE DAVIES
DEAD HEAT
BLUEGRASS SERIES BOOK 3
PIERCE DAVIES & TAMMY FIELDS
RELENTLESS PURSUIT
BLUEGRASS BROTHERS BOOK 4
LAYNE
SYDNEY
WYATT
SOPHIE
COLTON
LANDON
REAGAN
RILEY
PORTER
PARKER
RYAN
JACKSON
GREER
PIPER
DYLAN
JACE
CASSIDY

DAVIES FAMILY FRIENDS

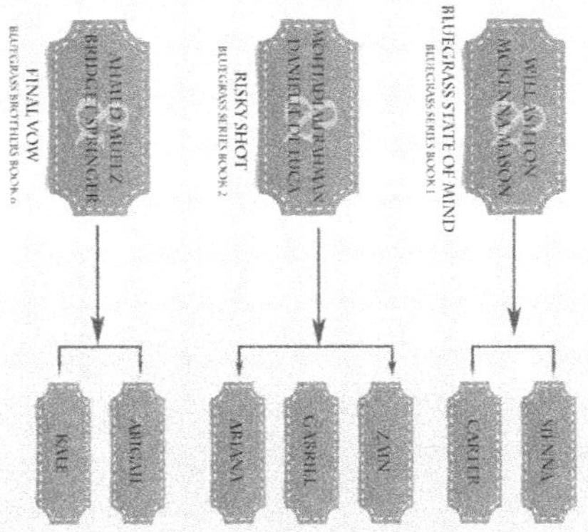

1

Piper Davies was alone in her laboratory in Lexington, Kentucky, as she worked her way through the day's mail. It was night and she'd put in a long day of work as a fall storm lashed out. Her nerves were frayed. Someone had broken into her lab a month ago and again at her home earlier that week. Piper was starting to think every shadow, every flicker of the light, and every man she passed on the street was a threat.

Taking a deep breath, Piper put the electric bill in the pile of other bills and tossed her copy of *Viruses Monthly* into the trash after skimming through it. She pulled her long, unbrushed, dirty-blonde hair into a sloppy bun on the top of her head as she listened to the low hum of the refrigerator used to store some of her viral strands mixed with the deep rumble of the thunder from the storm pounding the outside world. Around her, the rows of black-topped lab tables and stools stood empty. Her employees had left for the night some time ago. Piper sat on her stool at a lab table, slid her finger under the envelope flap, and tore it open. She pulled the single piece of paper out and unfolded it. It took a second for the words to come to her as Piper stared at the note in her hand.

Give me your project or die. This is your last warning.

SHE KNEW who had sent it. Well, kind of. Piper had been getting mysterious "Caller Unknown" calls from a man for a couple of months now, asking to buy her secret project. No names were mentioned, no identifiers of any kind were given, and no number was available.

Piper wasn't used to failing. She'd flown through her undergraduate work, majoring in engineering and biology with a specialty in viruses before earning her Ph.D. in nanotechnology. She'd wanted to help people. And she'd received a massive grant to do just that. The grant was to use nanotechnology to stop virus pandemics, but she'd failed on her project named FAVOR, which stood for Fast Acting Viral Outbreak Response. And worse, someone not only knew about FAVOR, but also about her failure. And this wasn't failure as in she would throw her project away and start years of work over again. No, this was a failure that could lead to the development of a bioweapon in the wrong hands. Instead of saving people from a pandemic, she could be the person who made it possible.

But Piper was close to a solution. It felt like she was one tweak to a nanopartide or one adjustment away to the nanostructure, and then it could work. She just didn't know the tweak or adjustment she needed to make. And that was messing with her mind more than anything. She really didn't know where to start. So she'd sit in the lab late at night and review her procedure or run experiments.

Piper looked over to check that the green light was on for the security system Nabi and Nash had installed. The alarm was also set. Nabi was the head of the Rahmi security in charge of protecting Prince Mo and Princess Dani Ali Rahman and their children and spouses. Nash, his second-in-command, had upgraded the system after the last break-in. The small island nation of Rahmi near the Persian Gulf was where Piper had started an international lab with Mo and Dani's son, Prince Zain. She never called him prince. No one from Keeneston did. They were simply the Ali Rahman family: Mo and his wife, Dani, their son Zain and his wife, Mila, their son Gabe and his wife, Sloane, and their daughter, Ariana.

Nabi and Nash had set up a state-of-the-art alarm system at both her Lexington lab and the secret lab her father, Pierce, had helped her set up in Keeneston. No one but her father, Nabi, and Nash knew about its location. Her father had ordered her a pre-constructed steel modular cleanroom, and they'd put it on a piece of land they'd bought under a company name far out of the way in Keeneston. And they didn't just put it on the land. They'd buried it. And that was where she spent long hours every night working. And where she'd go that night after she finished her administrative work.

But now she stared down at the threat and knew she was on a timeline to solve the issues plaguing FAVOR, for her life was in the balance. It was an easy choice for her to make. She'd given her life—one life—for the billions she could save by not handing FAVOR over to this man. Whoever he was, she was sure he wasn't going to use it to save people. Instead, he could mix it with Ebola, influenza, or one of the many other deadly viruses and spread it across the globe. In its current setup, FAVOR would deliver the virus to the healthy cells instead of protecting the cells and capturing the virus.

Piper slipped forward on her stool so her feet rested on the ground. She had to get to Keeneston and check on her project. When she stood, she instinctively looked at the door. The green light of her security system was no longer green—it was red.

Piper stopped breathing. She was no longer alone. She wasn't trained in combat like many of her cousins. Her uncles were former Special Forces, law enforcement, and even a former spy. Aunt Paige could shoot better than anyone and Aunt Annie was also a badass former undercover agent with the DEA. They'd all taught their children how to fight, how to shoot, and how to kill. But Piper's father, Pierce, was a farmer and inventor. He'd taught her how to engineer things, not how to throw a punch. And her mother, Tammy, was a little fairy of a woman who, while feisty, was one of the least violent people Piper knew.

Piper moved to stand behind her stool as her hands squeezed the seat of her metal stool while she began to slowly scan the room. There was a back door, a connecting door leading to the lobby with large windows overlooking the street, and a front door. If they came in the front door or lobby windows, she could race to the connecting metal lab door and lock it. But if they came in through the back . . .

The question was answered on a yelp as a leather-clad hand slammed against her mouth from behind, pulling Piper's body tightly against his own. The leather hand imprinted on her face as the fingers squeezed her cheeks. Piper struggled, but the arm imprisoning her around the waist was very strong.

"I see you got the boss's note," the husky foreign voice hissed into her ear. He sounded amused by her panic. And panic was definitely what Piper was feeling. Her heart was pounding and her lungs were burning as she struggled to drag air in through the sliver of space left open from the gloved hand over her mouth.

"Give it to me now and the boss says you can live."

His accent struck her as European, but it wasn't easy to place. It didn't matter because she was going to die. It was strange the things that went through your head, like trying to figure out the nationality of the man who was going to kill you, because one, you didn't have the project with you and two, Piper would never hand it over.

Piper had a decision to make as the fingers tightened painfully against her cheek and jaw. She could just let him kill her as she stood there crying, or she could die fighting. She might not be trained like her cousins, but that didn't mean she didn't understand the physics of fighting. Such as the pain a metal stool could inflict when smashed into a man's head.

The man screamed and dropped his hands from Piper as she slammed the stool into his head. Not sparing even a glance at the man, she brought the stool back over her head, dropped her hands down the legs, and then spun around, swinging the stool like a golf club right into the man. He was dressed in black jeans and a black jacket. His face was large, square, and covered in a thick beard. And that was all she saw before he fell to the ground, cursing her in whatever his native language was.

Piper looked at her assailant and over at the nearest door behind her. She decided to make a run for it and scream for help. She grunted as she hefted the stool back and threw it at him. The stool caused a cringe-worthy sound as it banged against his arms that he'd crossed into an X to protect his head.

Piper ran then. She heard the stool clattering to the polished concrete floor and the man scrambling to his feet as he continued to threaten her in his native language. She didn't need a translator to know he was going to kill her regardless now.

Her hand slammed into the chrome metal bar as she flung the door open. The lobby was small. There was room for a receptionist's desk and a loveseat with a small coffee table in front of it. Colorful artwork from local artists hung on the walls, and two large plate glass windows framed the dead-bolted front door made from matte steel.

Piper was almost there. Less than ten feet and she could flip the dead bolt and shove the door open. She never got the chance. Her body was hit hard from behind as the man tackled her. She screamed as the momentum slammed her onto the coffee table. Wood splintered as it gave way to their force. The air whooshed from Piper's lungs as he fell on her. She panicked as she could no longer breathe. Her face was mashed against the rug and magazines that had flown from the table, now broken under her body. The weight of the man behind her kept her stomach pinned to the ground and her arms outstretched as he wrapped his hand around her bun and yanked her head back.

He was breathing hard as he maneuvered himself to jab his knee into her kidney. "You bitch!" Piper didn't have the breath to scream as he banged her head against the floor with enough force that she saw stars—stars that were suddenly red and blue.

The man cursed again in the language she didn't know as the sounds of tires screeching to a halt outside reached them. He wrenched her head back once again. Her neck protested as hair ripped. "I'll be back, and I'll make you pay. Not because I was ordered to, but because I want to."

He shoved her head forward, her nose smashing into the rug as the weight of his body against hers lifted. Police were banging on the door and lights streamed in through the window as Piper pushed herself onto wobbly knees and began to crawl forward. Blood dripped into her eye as she struggled to reach up and unbolt the door. As soon as she did, it was flung open. Piper collapsed onto her back with a strangled cry. Her whole body shook with fear and pain as police flooded her lab.

"We need an ambulance," she heard an officer order a second before a worried face peered over her. "What's your name?"

"Piper Davies," she murmured as she wiped at the blood streaming from a cut on her eyebrow. "This is my lab."

"I'm Officer Edsel. You're a brave woman," the young officer told her as he grabbed a medical kit someone handed him. He pulled out a pair of latex gloves and slapped them on before pressing gauze to her cut.

"It's all clear. The suspect went out the back. We're canvassing the area," Piper heard someone say.

Officer Edsel nodded his crew-cut head and looked back at Piper. "It appears you put up quite the fight. Can you tell me what happened?"

"He broke in the back, wanting one of my projects," Piper said, trying to be as vague as possible. There was no way she wanted the details of her project FAVOR to become public record.

"Edsel, I found this."

The threatening note appeared in front of her as Edsel read it. "Want to tell me how long these threats have been going on?"

"The EMTs are here," another officer said from the doorway, saving Piper from having to answer.

Edsel looked annoyed at the interruption, but he nodded and backed off the line of questioning. "Is there anyone you want me to call for you?"

"Lord, no. If anyone from Keeneston finds out—"

"Sir, there's a helicopter landing in the middle of the street," the officer who had told them about the EMTs arrival shouted over the sounds of helicopter blades. Piper groaned as she closed her eyes in horror.

"Miss?" Piper opened her eyes as two EMTs looked down at her. One began hooking up a blood pressure cuff as the other lifted the gauze to check her wound. "What hurts?"

"Overbearing family and friends," she groaned as she heard Nash Dagher shove his way through the door.

"Piper!"

"No, no, no." Piper almost cried tears as Nash came into view. "You brought the helicopter? Now the entire town is going to know something happened to me, and I won't be able to do what needs to be done."

"I'm more worried about the fact that a clump of your hair is on the floor, your face is cut, and there are bruises forming on your face. What happened?"

Nash bent down and slipped an arm behind her. Piper let him help her sit up as the EMTs worked. "We can glue this cut shut. It'll heal on its own."

"Okay," Piper said absently as Officer Edsel quietly observed her.

"Is it the same threats as before?" Nash asked, not letting it go.

"Yes, but can we talk about this later?"

"I'd like this information for my report," Edsel finally said.

"Well, you can't have it. No one can!" Crap. Piper felt off kilter as the adrenaline from the situation began to dissipate, leaving her feeling like a wet rag. Piper sniffed and Nash began to look uneasy.

"Please tell me you didn't tell anyone you were coming to my lab," Piper begged Nash as the first tear trickled down her cheek.

Nash grimaced and backed away. "Just Sophie."

Piper sucked in an unsteady breath as the world crashed around her. If Sophie, Nash's wife and Piper's cousin, knew, then the *all* her cousins would know by now and probably three quarters of the town. By the time she made it back home, the entire small town of Keeneston would be asking her what happened. And right now she couldn't deal with that. Her life was in danger and the world was in danger, all because of her failures. And she didn't know how to fix it.

Tears flowed and Nash leapt up as if they were contagious. Officer Edsel leaned forward and clasped her shoulders in his hands as he leaned her toward him. Piper buried her head in his chest and cried all over his uniform as he patted her back. "Let me help you, Ms. Davies."

"Doctor," Nash corrected as Piper rolled her eyes. She didn't care about being called *Doctor*. She never had. And right now she didn't even feel worthy of her degree. And that made her cry even more. She was in full self-pity mode, and she didn't know how to turn it off. All these months she had stayed strong. She just couldn't do it anymore.

"No one can help me," Piper sniffled as an EMT shoved a clean gauze square in her hand for her to wipe her eyes.

"Let's get you to the hospital," one of them said from behind her. Piper shook her head.

"I think I'm okay. I'll have my own doctor look me over when I get home."

"I'll have Dr. Emma meet us there," Nash said, feeling a little more confident now that Piper's tears were drying.

"No, have it be Ava," she said of Dr. Emma's daughter. Ava had just graduated from medical school and Piper had been friends with her their whole lives. And there was a smaller chance of Dr. Ava calling Piper's parents.

"I need to finish taking your statement," Officer Edsel said kindly as he helped her move to stand.

Piper nodded her head. "Tomorrow?"

Officer Edsel didn't look pleased but agreed anyway after Nash promised to bring her back to Lexington to meet at the police station.

Nash slipped his arm around her as Piper wobbled. Damn, her head felt as if it had been scrambled. "Do you need anything before we leave?"

"Can you get a picture of the note? I'll put it with the rest of the notes I've received. And my purse is in my office."

Nash helped her to the couch and went to ask Officer Edsel for a picture of the evidence. Too soon, Nash had her strapped into the small helicopter, and they were flying over the dark rolling hills of the bluegrass back to Keeneston. Back to her family. Back to her friends. And back to questions she couldn't answer.

2

Piper didn't have to wonder where her house was as Nash flew the helicopter back to Keeneston. It was the house with cars completely lining the driveway and a steady stream of headlights heading that way like a big neon arrow.

Nash cleared his throat and tried to distract her from the fact half of the town was either at her house or on the way to her house. "Keep flying," Piper told Nash. "Or better yet, take me back to Lexington and I'll stay at a hotel."

"Sophie said it was just your cousins and they're worried about you."

"I'll remember this. You're supposed to be this big soldier who can keep his mouth shut and do what needs to be done and here you blabbed my situation to everyone! I was handling this, Nash. I don't want to talk about it five hundred times. I don't want to hear Ryan offer FBI assistance or for Sophie to hand me weapons. I don't want Deacon offering to investigate, and I don't want Matt making Cody sit in his sheriff's deputy car outside my house all night. And I don't want Layne telling me I could have beaten this guy up if only I'd worked out with her more."

Piper was becoming hysterical. Tears pressed against her eyes as her throat tightened.

Yes, she was part of a big family. She was the oldest of four children, soon to be five children as her mother accidentally got pregnant when she thought she was in menopause. And she loved her family. The second-oldest was Dylan, and if she wanted anyone's help it would be his. He did something secretive that involved plenty of danger. That's all she knew. But Dylan never judged. He never commented on what she should or shouldn't be doing. He was the steady presence in her life who called every birthday just to tell her he loved her. And right now that's all she could handle. She didn't want to be judged for failing when she was supposed to be so brilliant. The youngest, Cassidy, would do that and not even realize it.

Cassidy was sweet as pie, but her mouth could sometimes run away from her—in multiple languages. Luckily, Cassidy was away at college, but Jace wasn't. Jace was similarly kind, but he'd seen the bad that people had to offer too. He'd spent a couple years traveling to countries that needed help and building schools. Now he was in medical school and, like Cassidy, was going through that *I know everything* stage. And they didn't. Heck, Piper had a Ph.D. and right now she felt like she knew nothing.

But that wasn't all of her family. No, she had more cousins than she could shake a stick at. And they would all be there because, for better or worse, privacy wanted or not, they were family. It's what she both loved and hated about her family. Her other cousins were more outgoing. They loved girls' trips to Nashville and so on, but Piper was never comfortable in larger crowds. She'd rather host dinner for her cousins at home and sit in the living room drinking wine all night than dance in a packed bar on Broadway in

Nashville. And now, when all she wanted was to be left alone, she would be smothered with love.

"Are you hurt?" Nash asked. "You groaned."

"No, I just realized I was being unkind wanting to be alone. They're all here because they love me."

"We all do. But I understand. I'm a lot like you. I prefer to work alone. If it gets too smothering, then I'll fly you out. Deal?"

Piper winced when she tried to smile. Everything hurt. But Nash was a good friend. Her cousin Sophie was very lucky to be married to him. Nash landed the helicopter in her backyard and before they even touched the ground, the backdoor to her house opened and her cousins and siblings flooded out. At least her parents weren't there, or her aunts and uncles. Maybe there was hope that it hadn't gotten all around town yet.

"Piper!" Jace called out as he rushed toward her. Two brothers had never looked so different. Dylan was tall, with thick muscles and dark brown hair. His face and his body screamed, *don't mess with me*. Jace, on the other hand, was narrow-hipped, broad-shouldered, with light brown hair and a face that said he cared. While Piper was sure both Dylan and Jace helped people, Jace healed to protect people when Dylan probably killed in order to protect others.

"What are you doing here? You should be at school," Piper said when she met up with Jace. He had spent the summer in Chicago helping in the free clinic until fall term had started.

"Piper, you're more important than school. You need family, and right now I'm the only sibling around. Dylan is who knows where and Cassidy's school is a lot farther away than Lexington." Jace reached up and helped her from the helicopter. "Oh, sis. You need a doctor. Ah, that's why Ava is here."

And just like that, Ava was by her side. She was in scrubs with her curly hair pulled back and there were dark circles under her eyes. "You look worse than I do, and I just came off a thirty-hour shift."

With Jace on one side and Ava on the other, they escorted her through her cousins all standing with worried looks on their faces. Reagan, who had just been married a month before to her childhood friend, Carter Ashton, nibbled on her lower lip. Reagan had had a secret herself. She'd been secretly dating Carter and had known something was going on with Piper when she'd caught Piper receiving a threatening call. Ever since then, Reagan had been extra protective. By the crushed look on her face, Piper could tell Reagan felt responsible, even if she shouldn't.

"Piper—" Reagan's hazel eyes, like most of the Davies cousins, were filled with guilt—"I wish I had known. I . . . I . . . I could have done something to help."

Piper took a deep breath as she saw everyone had the same look. "It's not your fault. I'm fine now, really. I wanted to handle this myself. I should have said more. I thought I was doing the responsible thing by upgrading my security. I thought that would solve everything, but I was wrong."

Sophie's eyes went wide before she narrowed them at her husband. "You knew and didn't tell me?"

Nash shook his head. "Let's not forget, not all of you have turned to each other for help. Reagan and Carter had their secret relationship. Riley," he said, looking at Reagan's twin sister, "with your political killer. Ryan and Sienna with a murderer after her. Sydney and Deacon with finding those missing girls. Layne and the mysteries surrounding Walker. And last but not least, me. I didn't let any of you know where I was when I was undercover. Just like it took time for Sophie to ask when she was in danger. But we turn to each other when we're ready. And when we do, everyone is ready to help. Until then, it's private."

Piper looked gratefully at Nash as her cousins mumbled their agreement to what he was saying. It was both the blessing and the curse of a small town. And right now Piper finally felt able to take a breath.

"Let's look you over and then you can tell us however much you want," Ava said with a very professional smile. "Jace, can you grab my bag from the living room and meet me in Piper's bedroom?"

A path cleared as her cousins made room for her to walk into the house. Ava angled her into the bedroom and closed the door. Taking a deep breath, she turned and looked Piper over with a medical eye. "Take off your shirt, please. Let's see what damage there is."

With fingers that still shook, Piper pulled off her top. "Ouch," Ava said, taking in Piper's bruised chest and stomach. She looked around and saw another bruise on her back.

Piper hissed when Ava touched her stomach. "Any chance you're pregnant?" Ava asked as she examined the contusions.

"She better not be. Having Mom pregnant is bad enough. I can't imagine what our father would do."

"Jace," Piper said, rolling her eyes as her brother stepped into the room with Ava's medical bag. Piper noticed that Jace gave her a quick glance, his jaw tightening when he saw the bruises before dropping his eyes to the floor. Seeing his sister in her bra wasn't something either of them wanted to deal with.

"It's a medically necessary question," Ava told her as she pulled out her stethoscope and a pair of latex gloves.

"No. There's no chance I'm pregnant."

"Thank goodness," Jace murmured as Ava continued her exam.

"I'll be done in a second. Why don't you make some tea for Piper, and we'll meet you all in the living room," Ava said nicely to Jace, but Piper didn't miss the command in her voice.

Jace escaped and Piper let out a breath she was holding as Ava cleaned her up. "There will be no lasting damage. Put vitamin E cream on your face and try to rest for a few days. Are you ready to face the firing squad?"

Piper wasn't, but it was time. There was no hiding her failure now.

3

"Can you fix it?" Jace asked as everyone stood or sat quietly around Piper's living room while she told them what was happening.

"Of course she can. She's the smartest person I know," Wyatt Davies said with a confidence Piper didn't feel. Wyatt's sister, Sydney, and her husband, Deacon, nodded their agreement. In fact, when Piper looked around the room, everyone was nodding.

"I don't know," Piper finally confessed.

"What if you have more time to work on it?" Layne asked.

"Yeah, I could keep you safe while you worked on it," Walker, Layne's husband and former Navy SEAL, offered.

"I don't want to put you in danger. You've already been through so much. And then there's also the building of the Davies Training Center for the military and law enforcement. I know you're actively involved in that. And if you suddenly have to watch me, all the aunts and uncles will know what's going on, too," Piper said with a sigh. The idea of them smothering her was sending her into a panic attack already.

"Some things are more important than our parents knowing what we're doing," Reagan admitted. "Plus, Pierce and Tammy are way cooler than my dad. They never put GPS trackers on you. They support you no matter what."

Carter shook his head at his new bride. "Cy supports us. He's just overly involved. But it's done with love. At least that's what I tell myself."

Reagan smacked her new husband as everyone snickered. Cy was overprotective to the nth degree and then some. But he'd turned a corner with Carter when he took a bullet for Reagan and was now trying to be BFFs with his two sons-in-law, Carter and Matt. It turns out the friendship angle was even scarier for the two than when Cy was threatening them with bodily harm.

"Then I'll hang out with you," Layne offered. "I'm sure Sophie can spare some time, too."

"I can as well," Nash offered as everyone murmured their agreement to this plan, but Piper shook her head.

"No, I wouldn't be able to live with myself if something happened to y'all. And all y'all have lives of your own to lead. I refuse to have any of my family or friends in danger because of me. I'll run away in the dead of the night and face it on my own if I have to. It's bad enough I'm being pitied now, but I won't have the people I love hurt."

Piper jumped as the front door was flung open and Aniyah ran in on her spiked heels. Sweat glistened off her dark brown skin. Her normally perfect swooped hair fell over her forehead as she bent at the waist and sucked in air.

"Thank Jesus! I made it in time," she said between deep breaths. "Your momma is on her way with a look on her face I ain't never seen before. I was at the Blossom Café when

John Wolfe told your momma and dad about the attack. I didn't know a woman nine months pregnant could move that fast. She waddled out of the café, leaving your father behind a trail of knocked-over chairs and an upended table."

"I'm surprised DeAndre didn't spill the beans. He's slacking," Sydney said as she tried to joke.

"Oh no," Aniyah said, standing upright again and putting her hands on her ample, perfectly curved hips. "My Sugarbear knew all about it, but he also knew Piper wouldn't want anyone talking about it. She's shy like that."

Piper felt herself blush, but then the moment was lost when the sound of squealing tires was heard. Aniyah looked out the door as her eyes got wide. "I didn't know a minivan could take a corner on two wheels."

Dread filled Piper as all the cousins began to inch closer to the back door. The cowards! "Your mom is so sweet. You're lucky, your father doesn't put GPS trackers on you," they'd all said growing up. But the second her mom turns into *this* mom that Piper knew very well, they were looking to escape.

"We better get home and check on the puppies. Robyn's been a wonderful mom, but they're up and about now—" Sydney shrugged as she and Deacon darted out the back door.

"Sis, I love you and all, but if Mom . . . Uh-oh. Too late," Jace said as he tried to duck behind Piper.

Tammy didn't so much storm through the door as she waddled, pregnant belly first, with enough force to shake the pictures on the wall. Her mother was barely over five feet tall, but right now, Piper felt all of two feet tall when her mother did that glare thing she did so well. After all, someone so small had to have a powerful glare to keep four kids in line, especially with Dylan as one of those kids.

"How dare you not call me? How can you not tell your own mother you are in danger? Do you know what you're doing to me? You're killing me! Your father is so close to death he was praying to God the whole drive over here." Her mother had been pushed too far. She'd snapped. Her blonde, pixie-cut hair stuck out in all directions, her blue eyes flashed, and her normally porcelain cheeks were bright red as she ranted. "Do you know how it feels to find out from John Wolfe that your daughter was attacked in her lab? What is going on, Piper?" Tammy stomped her foot and a picture fell from the wall.

"Honey," Pierce started, trying to calm his wife, whose hands had stopped flailing in the air to rest on her large stomach. "You need to calm down. At your old age, your blood pressure is already high. And if you have a tizzy, the baby might just fall out. You have to remember, it's been twenty years since you've been pregnant. Things, lots of things, have changed on your body since then. You better sit down. I better sit down. Why don't we all sit down?"

"Take cover, she's going to blow," Jace whispered. Piper agreed as everyone still in the room took a giant step back.

Aniyah made the sign of the cross and lifted her hands up to God. "Dear Lord, please forgive this man as he doesn't know what an idiot he is."

Tammy's lips twitched and some of the anger faded. Piper's father was no longer in danger. Instead, Tammy let out a huff and plopped, with no grace, onto the nearest chair. "Now that we have a smaller crowd," she said as Piper noticed most of her cousins had run away. Only Sophie, Nash, Wyatt, Jace, Aniyah, and Walker were left. Tammy turned to Walker, "Bless your heart, your wife left you."

Walker grinned and Piper would have sworn her mother blushed. “That’s okay. Now I get to spend time with the prettiest woman in Keeneston. You’re glowing, Mrs. D.”

“Damn, he’s good,” Jace whispered and Piper had to nod her agreement. Her mother was preening under the sexy SEAL’s smile.

“Is this about your project?” Pierce asked as her mother’s glow faded and she shot her husband a glare.

“You know what this is about and didn’t tell me?”

Aniyah held up her hands again to the sky. “Dear Lord, please forgive this man. He knows not what a fool he is by keeping things from his wife.”

“He better start praying and fast because I’m going to kill him if he doesn’t start talking,” Tammy ground out between clenched teeth.

“Piper was having some trouble with a project. It was a very delicate situation. In the wrong hands, it could do a lot of harm. She asked me for help, and we set up a lab here in Keeneston to keep it safe while she fixed it. That’s all I know,” Pierce swore to his wife.

“See, the nanoparticles—” Piper began, but her mother’s glare glazed over as she absently nodded. Even her father got a little lost as she realized she was already beyond their understanding.

“And we offered to look out for her, but she doesn’t want someone she knows. She couldn’t live with herself if they got hurt,” Walker filled in after Piper finished.

Tammy let out a long breath and pulled out her phone. “Dylan dear. Your sister is in danger. Can you come home? Is that gunfire?”

Tammy put the phone on speaker. Piper didn’t know if it was gunfire or not, but by the way Sophie, Nash, and Walker looked at one another, it was confirmation it was in fact gunfire. And a lot of it.

"Sorry, Ma. I'm a little tied up right now. Call Abby. She can help or will know someone who can," Piper heard her brother yell out over the sound of yelling in a foreign language. "Love you, sis! I'll call soon." And then the line went dead.

Tammy shook her head. "I don't want to know. I don't want to know."

"A man who answers his momma's call during a gun battle. Could your brother get any hotter?" Aniyah asked Piper as she fanned herself. Piper supposed Dylan *was* hot with his tall, dark, and dangerous vibe, but she'd never thought about it. According to the Keeneston Belles, the young women in town who were supposed to be a charitable organization but really were a group of husband hunters, they certainly thought Dylan was a catch. They were all over him when he showed up in town. And now that Jace, the soon-to-be-doctor, was in town, he was getting his fair share of casseroles, pies, and late night visits to his house closer to Lexington.

Tammy ignored Aniyah as she called Abby on speakerphone. Abby was the daughter of Ahmed and Bridget Mueez, and proof that two badasses who marry have equally badass children.

"Hey, Mrs. Davies. What's up?" Abby asked as she answered the phone.

"Piper needs a bodyguard. She invented something that can kill tons of people and now someone wants it."

"Mom!"

"Cool," Abby said at the same time. "Hold on a sec."

Piper wanted to cry. This was why she didn't want people to know what happened. As if she weren't under enough stress, adding in her mother telling everyone that Piper could be responsible for the next global pandemic made things peachy.

"Okay," Abby said, coming back online. "A friend of my dad does security and they can meet you tomorrow morning at eight at the Blossom Café."

"Thank you, Abby. When are you coming home again?" Tammy asked as if she'd called Abby for a recipe instead of a bodyguard.

"I'll be home at the end of the month for Thanksgiving."

"Oh, good. I'm sure your parents will be thrilled to have you back."

Piper rolled her eyes as her mother continued the necessary chitchat of asking about family and sharing the latest gossip. Apparently Piper's failure wasn't as newsworthy as Nikki trying to date Jace.

Piper dropped onto the couch and placed her elbows on her knees and buried her face in her hands. A hand squeezed her shoulder and she felt the couch dip as her father sat next to her.

"It's okay to mess up, you know. Every time you mess up, you learn something new. What did Edison say about failing?"

Piper sat up as she remembered all the lessons her father had taught her about Franklin, Edison, Tesla, and so many of the other great inventors. "Many of life's failures are people who did not realize how close they were to success when they gave up."

"That's right," her father said, patting her knee. "You know this project better than anyone. One manipulation, one change to the equation, and bam! It works. Just keep trying. I'm always here to talk it out if you want."

"Thanks, Dad," Piper said as her mother finished her phone call with Abby.

"Won't that be nice?" Tammy said, smiling. "Ahmed and Bridget will have their whole family in town for Thanksgiving. Even Kale is coming home. I'd better warn the town so they can watch out for him on the roads." Kale drove like a bat out of hell but was ridiculously smart with computers. Enough so that it made up for the terror of encountering him on the road. Especially since the people of Keeneston had a multitude of reasons to hack secure networks.

"Walker, be a dear and help me up," Tammy said, holding out her hand. Walker bent and helped her to her feet. "Thank you. Now, we'll all meet at the café tomorrow morning before whoever takes you to the police station."

Wyatt and Jace looked at each other and silently communicated. "We'll stay here tonight with Piper," Wyatt said.

"No—" Piper began to argue, but her mother began to glare at her and Piper closed her mouth.

"Thank you, you two." Tammy patted Wyatt's cheek and then kissed Jace before glaring at Piper again. "Don't make me call one of your uncles to put a tracker and listening device on you, and whatever else they do. I want to know where you are at all times."

"Mom, I'm almost thirty—" Her mother glared again. "Yes, ma'am."

Her mother and father kissed her cheek and her father helped Tammy from the house. Piper turned to find her cousin and her brother already raiding the kitchen. Ugh. It was going to be a very long night. How much more embarrassing could this get?

4

Piper didn't have any trouble finding the person she was supposed to be meeting at the Blossom Café. A tall blonde knockout in a tight, scarlet-red sweater and black skinny jeans sat at a table with Ahmed, Bridget, and Piper's parents.

"Ah, here she is now," Bridget said, motioning for Piper to join them. "Piper, this is Mallory Westin-Simpson; she's the owner of Westin Security out of Atlanta."

The woman stood and Piper had to look up at her. Piper was average height but wore fuzzy Uggs instead of four-inch spiked leather boots like Mallory was wearing. "Mallory, this is Dr. Piper Davies."

"It's such a pleasure to meet you," Mallory said in her deep Southern accent. It was slow and sweet all at once.

"You too," Piper said as she took a seat. Mallory tossed her long, perfectly wavy blonde hair over one shoulder and smiled at Piper. Piper's cousin Sydney had been a model and Piper had never felt self-conscious, but she did now as the deadly beauty began to talk.

"As I was saying before you arrived, I'm not able to help

you myself. But after talking to your parents, Ahmed, and Bridget, I think I know the perfect person to help you."

Piper raised an eyebrow questioningly. "And why aren't you able to help me?"

"All my people are booked, and my husband, Reid, and I are only in town to look at an old historic farm that is being sold. We want to keep the horses and the grounds and turn it into a small, elite, luxury resort. He's in some meetings right now, but I had to come see my friends. It's been too long." Mallory reached out a hand to grasp Bridget's hand and smiled at Ahmed. "But, this is what I do, and when my firm is full, I find clients the perfect fit. I know everyone in the security business and I have the perfect man for you. I'll call Aiden as soon as we have breakfast to see if he'll take you on."

"He might not take me on as a client?" Piper shook her head. "This is getting too complicated. I'm fine. I'll have Nash teach me some self-defense."

"Oh, no," Mallory said, her sweet Southern demeanor dropped as she turned into a steel magnolia in a heartbeat. "That's the worse thing you can do. You need to focus on your project, not worry about someone attacking you at every second. That's where close protection work comes in."

"And you're a bodyguard?"

Mallory smiled, her red lips widening to show perfect white teeth. "Yes. I've guarded some of the most powerful people in the world. All the way up until I had my children, that is. Now I run the security firm and delegate the close protection work."

"How are your girls?" Bridget asked.

"They're great. Ten and eight years old already."

"They grow so fast," Tammy said, looking over at Piper. When had Piper lost control of this conversation?

"And your firm handles people like me?" Piper asked, bringing them back to the topic at hand: her safety.

"Some. We do a little bit of everything. Celebrities when they're in Georgia shooting movies or putting on concerts. We handle a lot of politicians and CEOs. But for what you need, I think Aiden would be perfect. He owns his own company, too. However, he usually doesn't take on many clients himself. But I think he'll make an exception for you." Mallory smiled again as she picked up her sweet tea and took a sip.

"And why would he do that?" Piper asked. She was starting to feel like the kid no one wanted to babysit.

"Because you're fascinating."

Piper didn't know what to say to that. When Poppy came to take her order, Piper let the table do the talking while she thought about the idea of having a bodyguard. Growing up in a large family, she liked her space and her alone time. How would she be able to focus on her work with a big hulking guy standing right behind her constantly?

As Mallory talked about her sisters-in-law and their children, Piper silently ate her food until Sydney's name came up. Of course Mallory would know Sydney. They probably modeled together though Mallory did seem to be in her mid-forties, which was about fifteen years older than Syd.

"The whole Simpson family will be at Sydney and Deacon's Daughters of Elizabeth Ball for New Year's Eve. Are y'all going to make it this year? Marshall and Katelyn are always there for their daughter, and sometimes their son makes it. What's his name?"

"Wyatt," Piper told her. Sydney and Deacon owned Sydney's great-grandmother's estate in Georgia, even though they lived in Keeneston. Every year, they held a charity ball at the large old estate to raise money to fight against sex trafficking and to help those affected by it.

"Of course!" Mallory said with a roll of her eyes for forgetting. "You all should come. It's such a wonderful cause and Sydney and Deacon really go all out. And then you can meet my family."

"We'll be there this year," Ahmed told her.

"I doubt I'll be up for travel. I'm due later this month and traveling with a newborn isn't my idea of fun," Tammy said as she looked at her belly and gave it an affectionate rub.

Mallory pushed back her chair, "Well, I hope you'll be able to make it next year then. If you'll excuse me, I'll step outside and call Aiden. I'll be right back with more information for you."

Mallory strode from the restaurant and Piper noticed the slight bulge at her hip. She was carrying a gun under her sweater and who knew what else. If she was a friend of Ahmed's, she could have a whole arsenal on her.

Ahmed and Bridget launched into stories of their dealings with Mallory as Piper watched the woman pace back and forth outside the café. She nodded some, then turned and looked back at Piper and gave her the thumbs up sign. Well, it looked like she had a bodyguard whether she wanted one or not.

~

AIDEN CREED WAS in his office in London when his secretary paged him. "Mrs. Mallory Westin-Simpson is on line three for you. Do you want to take it?"

Mallory? She must have some work for him here in London. "Yes, I'll take it." Aiden picked up the phone and hit line three. "Mallory, how are you?"

"I'm well, thank you. How are you doing?" Mallory was Miss Southern Manners. That is, until things got cocked-up. Then there was no one he'd rather have by his side.

"I'm doing great. Are you coming to London for a visit?" Aiden asked. They'd have dinner whenever she and her husband came to town to check on one of his hotels or to check in on a client.

"No, I have a client for you," she said, and Aiden could hear her smile over the phone.

Aiden pulled up his firm's schedule on the computer. "Eddie is available. Who's the client?"

"Not Eddie. You," Mallory said it nicely, but there was no room to question her in her tone either.

"You know I don't take on many clients. And no offense, but most of your clients would drive me to kill them instead of protect them," Aiden reminded her.

"Not this one. Dr. Piper Davies. Look her up," Mallory ordered, but there was amusement in her voice that told Aiden she already knew he'd take her as a client.

Aiden typed her name into his state-of-the-art intelligence database and had results instantly. He clicked on her résumé and read. Impressive. He then clicked on the link to a newspaper article detailing her role in the creation and start-up of the Rahmi International Nanotechnology Laboratory. Again, very impressive. As was the picture of her standing next to Prince Zain of Rahmi, who was apparently a childhood friend from Keeneston. Where the bloody hell was Keeneston, Kentucky? Aiden searched out the city and then sat back in his chair with an amused smile on his lips. Mallory was right. This was intriguing enough to consider taking.

"There are plenty of people from Keeneston she can

have help her. Why does she want me?" Aiden asked, his curiosity piqued.

"Well, she wanted me, but I'm booked." Mallory's voice laughed melodically. "But I knew she'd be perfect for you. She doesn't want anyone hurt, and she's afraid her family will be if they help her. She's already been assaulted once."

Aiden's secure email showed Mallory just sent an email. He clicked it and saw cell phone pictures Dr. Davies probably didn't know Mallory had taken. His gut clenched as he took in the bruises on her face.

"From what I'm told, she's banged up on her body as well."

"Why is someone after her?" Aiden asked, already knowing he'd take the case.

"She's working on something that could be very dangerous in the wrong hands. And the wrong hands know it. She needs time to finish it. When she does, it'll save millions of people. They don't know who is behind the threats or assault, but you can bet that since she was attacked, her family and friends, including close family friend Ahmed Mueez, will look into it."

Aiden was already staring at Ahmed's name in the research he was looking at as he explored the citizens of Keeneston. Everyone in the military knew of the famous soldier. They studied his techniques in training. "So, I'll have professional backup if I need it?"

"You'll have a whole freaking army if you need it. And I'm afraid you might."

Mallory knew this was the exact type of client he would take on. And right when he was trying to expand into the United States, too. But he was supposed to be making proposals and talking to lawyers and realtors, not guarding someone twenty-four hours a day, seven days a week.

"How long?" Aiden asked even as he pulled up his email to tell his secretary to postpone his meetings and to book him a ticket to Kentucky.

"Until the threat is neutralized."

"Is she going to be a problem?" Aiden hoped not. He'd done his time guarding princesses and divas of all kinds and really didn't want to have to get back into that.

"I don't believe so. But, she does seem to like her privacy and isn't completely comfortable with the idea of having a bodyguard around all the time. She wanted to take some self-defense and do it herself," Mallory told him. He could envision her rolling her eyes just like he wanted to. Self-defense was something he'd teach her, but it wouldn't help her in this situation. Not when she'd already been attacked once. It would only escalate from here.

His secretary emailed him back. He could be in Keeneston in twelve hours. "Tell her I accept. I'll be at her house tonight at eight. Until then, she's to remain with Ahmed—or—I see a Miles Davies and his brothers are there as well. I'm reading they are military. Relatives?"

"Her father is Pierce Davies, the youngest son of the Davies family. Miles is her uncle. Her cousin Ryan Parker is also an FBI agent. Her cousin-in-law Walker Greene is a retired SEAL. Then there's the whole Rahmi security force here, too."

"All of those are good options. Have someone with her at all times until I get there and send me the FBI cousin's contact."

Aiden hung up with Mallory and stared at the two pictures of Piper Davies side by side. One showed a smiling young woman and the other a haunted and damaged one. Mallory knew him well. He was interested. What was an intelligent woman like Piper Davies working on? It had to be in the field of viral nanotech and that interested him even more. Add onto it who her family and friends were and this became a job he'd kill for. And kill to protect. England didn't like him carrying weapons, but by the articles he was reading about Keeneston, he knew he'd have no issues there. He had agreements with multiple countries to carry concealed and the United States was one of them.

Aiden closed his laptop and put it in his carry case. He quickly gathered his papers, his passport, and all necessary licenses he might need and walked out of his office ten minutes later. His flat was a short walk from the office and within the hour he was boarding a plane for the United States. As soon as he able, he was on the computer working. He emailed Piper's cousin Ryan Parker who turned out to be head of the Lexington FBI office, and Matt Walz, the local sheriff, to inform them of his imminent arrival, his intent to carry concealed, his licenses, and requested their assistance if so needed.

Sometimes local law enforcement could be hard to work with. They saw him coming into their territory and often perceived personal security operators as demanding and overbearing, which could be true when dealing with high-profile principals. But in cases such as Dr. Davies, he'd try to fly under the radar as much as possible. It turned out he needn't have worried. The sheriff was her cousin-in-law as well. One thing was for sure—he'd never had such a networked principal before.

Aiden closed his computer once he'd finished reading everything he could find on the town and his principal. He leaned back in his seat and closed his eyes. Surely not everything he read was true. First, there was no evidence of a boyfriend and from what he could see, Dr. Piper Davies was a catch. She was brilliant, beautiful, and there were many articles in the *Keeneston Journal* that talked about her compassion and volunteer work. Second, he had read about the military training center that was being built and would love to hear more about it. Third, and maybe the most intriguing, the archived photo of a Miss Violet Rose holding a crepe pan alongside her sister, Miss Lily Rose, holding a broom and their other sister, Miss Daisy Rose, holding a wooden spoon grabbed his attention. The caption read *The Rose Sisters Deliver a Beatdown on Drug Dealers*. Keeneston was sounding more and more like his kind of town.

When Aiden closed his eyes, images of the smiling Dr. Piper Davies filled his dreams, but they slowly turned into nightmares of her beaten and bloodied body. His eyes popped open as the wheels touched down in New York City. One more flight and he'd be in Lexington. An email from his secretary told him a black SUV was waiting for him in Kentucky along with a gun. Three more hours and he'd be in Keeneston and he'd do whatever it took to keep his nightmare from becoming a reality.

5

Everything went downhill after Mallory had informed Piper that a Mr. Aiden Creed would be arriving. Ahmed had called Nabi, the head of security for the Rahmi royal family who lived in Keeneston, to get a report on Mr. Creed. He had seemed pleased with his "extensive experience," but Piper didn't care about some old guy's work record. She just wanted to get to work. However, Mr. Creed was already interfering with her life. He'd *ordered* her to have protection at all times until his arrival that evening.

Piper supposed she should have asked Ahmed about this man who would be protecting her, but instead her mind was on FAVOR. She needed to get to her lab, the hidden one only a few people know about. And she wanted to keep it that way. She'd agreed to let Ahmed stay with her that day, but the fates had something else in mind. Ahmed, now retired from the Rahmi Security Forces, was a partner with Mo Ali Rahman, Prince of Rahmi, at his horse farm. Mo and Ahmed had a special meeting they couldn't get out of, and her family took it upon themselves to arrange a babysitter. Walker Greene, her cousin-in-law, had been picked since he wasn't really required to be at the building site today.

So off they went to the police station to meet with Officer Edsel. It had taken an hour to get Walker to swear not to tell Layne or anyone else where her facility was. She knew her family, and she knew they'd start showing up there whenever they felt like it. In the end, she'd blindfolded Walker when she neared the property and had to slow-walk him through the field and down the hidden entrance. Then she spent an hour telling him to stop touching things.

Finally she was able to get to work. Walker had scoped out the building, finding the ventilation and the door to be the only entry points. He got up from his stool every fifteen minutes to make sure each entry point was secure. However, work was not easy. She stared at her recent notes trying to find where she went wrong. And that was the problem—she had no idea.

"You look stuck," Walker said from his position at the back of the lab. The seat gave him a full view of everything, including her frustration.

"I am," Piper finally admitted as she slumped her hip against her stool. "The window at the Lexington lab is being fixed, and I should be there, not my dad. When I can finally focus on this, I have no idea where to start."

"At the beginning," Walker said with a shrug.

"What?" Piper asked as she tried to keep her emotions in check. She wasn't one to throw fits, but right now she was so frustrated she felt like crying.

"Start at the beginning. Do you have your original notes? Your original ideas? Start on page one and slowly work your way through it."

Hmm, Walker might have a point. She was operating off

her lab notes, not her development notes. That notebook was hidden at her house. "It's worth a shot. The notebook is at home."

"Then let's go," Walker said, standing up and reaching for his blindfold. "You know this is only to make you feel better, right?"

"What is?" Piper asked as she blindfolded Walker.

"The blindfold. I already know where we are. We're in the field about five miles from town. Out on Keeneston Pike. It has cows on it. I heard and smelled them before you brought me through the hidden entrance and down below ground. Now, I know the security is tight and the place is hidden, but I could find it."

Piper's stomach plummeted. He knew exactly where they were. "I'll give you salmonella if you tell Layne."

"I swear," Walker said, crossing his heart. "You do know being in DEVGRU meant everything I did was classified, right? I think I can keep a secret. Plus it's good for a couple people to know where you are in case you need help."

"Fine," Piper grumbled as she tore off his blindfold. "Let's go get my notes."

"Then maybe dinner at the café?"

Piper looked down at her watch. How had it become dinnertime already? They hadn't eaten lunch and Walker hadn't complained once. But now that he'd mentioned it, her stomach rumbled. "Maybe dinner first? Are you sure you don't mind spending the day with me? I'm sure you want to get home to Layne."

"Piper, I'm good. This was my job, you know? And I loved my job. Plus Layne is working late tonight with some charity patients. I have all the time in the world to make sure you're safe. Plus, I kind of want to meet Aiden Creed. Ahmed told me he was in the British SAS."

"SAS?" Piper asked as she locked the lab and walked into the dark field.

"It's their version of Delta Force. I want to see if he's ever worked with my father-in-law." Walker grinned, his teeth flashing in the moonlight as Piper laughed.

"You want dirt on Miles, don't you?"

"Of course I do."

Piper shook her head and smiled. Layne was a very lucky woman. Walker was handsome, strong, brave, and had a wicked sense of humor. Plus he loved Layne's father, Miles, as if he were his own. "How's Edie doing?" Piper asked of Walker's recently widowed sister.

"She's doing well. She's finished redecorating her new home and is hanging out with Gavin and the rest of your cousins in Shadows Landing. She has a job at the school and works weekends at your cousin Harper's bar." Walker's smile dropped a little. "I don't think she's able to move on from her husband's death. I know I haven't gotten over it either," he said of the mission that had taken the lives of his entire team, including his best friend who had been married to Edie.

"So she's filling all her time," Piper said with understanding. Piper had begun to email with her cousins in South Carolina over the months. They were her grandmother Marcy's side of the family, and there had been an estrangement long ago that was recently mended with the current generation of Faulkners. She'd enjoyed getting to know them and hoped to visit Shadows Landing in the near future. But her cousin Tinsley, who was best friends with Edie, had mentioned Edie was just getting by with life instead of living it.

"Edie's coming up for Thanksgiving, and then Layne and I plan to visit after Christmas," Walker told her as Piper slid behind the steering wheel of her car. She asked him to tell her more about Shadows Landing since he'd grown up there and was best friends with her cousin Gavin. She was lost in the story about a bar brawl over who had better barbeque as they approached downtown Keeneston.

"So, barbeque is a really big deal in South Carolina?"

"Very. It's all about the sauce," Walker began to explain. "Watch out!"

Walker's arm slammed against her chest, pinning her to the seat, as an SUV slammed into her door. Piper had hit the brake as soon as Walker yelled, and the car shuddered as the SUV tried to shove it off the road. Her airbags deployed, but Walker's had already been torn away as he pulled a gun from his waistband, ripped her airbag away, and shot across her into the SUV.

The sound of an engine revving was heard, and suddenly a minivan careened into the side of the SUV currently T-boning Piper. "Come on," Walker ordered. He had already unbuckled her and was dragging Piper across the center console and over the passenger seat. Walker had his hand fisted in the collar of her shirt, shoving her out of the car as he pushed her to run from the scene. When Piper looked up, she could see smoke from the spinning back tires of the minivan as they pushed the SUV to roll over.

Walker shoved Piper behind the nearest building, which happened to be the Keeneston Feed Store. "Stay here."

Piper peered around the corner of the old red brick store and Walker took off running as a man climbed from the SUV. The minivan backed up and revved the engine as both Walker and the minivan shot off after the man running down the middle of Main Street.

"Stop!" Walker yelled a moment before firing off a shot. The man turned and returned fire, causing Walker to dive behind Piper's car for cover. The minivan accelerated as the tires squealed across the asphalt. Piper gasped as the minivan hit the man, bouncing him onto the hood, rolling him over the roof, and dropping him on the pavement in a heap.

The minivan slammed to a stop and went into reverse as the man staggered to his feet. Walker ran toward the man, but the man had seen the minivan reversing to run him over again and began to hobble off.

Piper watched with horror as the man fired off another round at Walker, sending him diving to the ground. A second SUV appeared, racing up the street and coming to a screeching halt in front of the man. Piper couldn't see because the SUV blocked the man, but she was sure the man leapt inside as Walker emptied his clip into the SUV. The minivan didn't give up either. Tires spun as the vehicle rocketed forward, slamming into the front of the SUV. But the SUV was able to reverse into a fast turn and shoot off down the road away from town.

"Piper?" Walker called as he jogged toward her. "Are you hurt?"

Piper looked at herself. Small pieces of glass were stuck to her hair and possibly in her face. Her body shook with fear, but she didn't think there was anything more besides the burn from the airbag and the seatbelt. "I think I'm okay."

The door of the minivan opened and Pam Gilbert jumped out. The former head of the school's PTA stopped with her hands on her khaki-clad hips and tapped her penny loafer. "Dang, I thought for sure I was going to get that guy. Did you see how high he bounced?"

Walker bent down and put his arm around Piper's waist and helped her onto the street where Pam surveyed the damage to her minivan. Patrons of the Blossom Café were spilling onto the street a couple blocks away.

"Thank you," Piper said to Walker as a sheriff's car with lights on drove the three blocks to the site of the overturned SUV. The sheriff's deputy, Cody Gray, got out and placed his hands on his hips as he stared at the overturned SUV, the banged-up minivan, and Piper's wrecked car.

"So, just another night in Keeneston," he said with a smile that had Pam laughing. But then Cody's smile slipped as he took in Piper's appearance. In a few long strides, Cody was by her side, his spring-blue eyes filled with worry. "I'll call you an ambulance."

Piper shook her head. "These are from yesterday. I think I'm okay. Thanks, Cody."

Cody rested his hand at the small of her back as he looked her over for injuries. Cody was sweet, full of gentlemanly manners, but he was also a couple years younger than her. He also had a tendency to go to bed with a woman and not be there in the morning. He'd offered her that deal at Reagan and Carter's wedding. As tempted as Piper was to accept it, she was too focused on work to even think about her lack of a sex life.

"You let me know if you need anything, okay? Should I stay with you tonight?" Cody asked, and Piper was pretty sure he meant to keep her safe.

"Piper's family has hired a bodyguard. He's arriving soon," Walker told Cody. "I'm sure he'll be in touch with your office."

"Want to tell us all what happened?" Cody asked, stepping slightly off to the side so Piper could see the huge crowd of people looking worriedly on.

Piper felt like crying. She hated the attention. She never wanted to be the focus of so many pairs of eyes. She was boring. Sophie inventing a new weapon, Layne protecting Walker, people trying to hurt Zain and the royal family . . . Sure. But her? Oh, how many times had she sat in the café feeling superior because everyone else was under the town's gossiping microscope? But now it was her turn.

Walker looked at her and shrugged. That summed it up nicely. What other choice did she have? If she didn't tell them, the gossip would race through town like an out of control wildfire.

"Something I created can be the next global pandemic and I'm trying to fix it, but someone wants to steal it before I can get it right."

Piper held her breath and waited. They looked at each other and then to Pam.

"Did you hit another one?" Miss Violet asked.

"I did," Pam beamed. "Bounced like a ball right up and over."

"Wish I could have seen that. Remember that one you took out that was trying to get to your sister? That was a good bounce that time, too," Miss Lily remembered fondly.

"You have a real talent for hitting people," Miss Daisy told her as Pam beamed.

"I'm just excited I get a new vehicle now. Since the kids are grown, I might switch to an SUV."

Piper looked with wonder between everyone. No one was calling her a failure. No one was asking her any questions at all. "Is that all?" Piper asked to no one in particular.

"Oh, sweetie," Nora, the owner of the Fluff and Buff hair and nail salon, said. "We wouldn't be able to understand anything more with all that nanotech stuff. You made something and someone will kill you to get it. We're good."

Piper felt Walker's body shaking with laughter next to

her as all talk turned back to the man Pam bounced off her minivan and if she should maybe consider getting a Hummer next.

"Why don't you go ahead and tell me what happened while they're preoccupied," Cody said, pulling out a notepad.

Piper started to give her statement as Pam regaled the crowd with stories of black SUVs and bouncing men.

6

Aiden was almost there. His plane had landed, his SUV had been waiting for him, and within twenty minutes of landing at the Lexington airport he was on his way to Keeneston. The November darkness had already fallen, slowing him as he learned the winding country roads on top of getting back in the habit of driving on the right side of the road.

He had spent the entire flight studying his principal and the town she lived in. It had seemed strange to him that Dr. Davies wouldn't have wanted someone she knew to protect her, however, it made sense in a way too. She wanted separation. She wanted privacy. All things someone who knew her wouldn't give her. Aiden's job wasn't to chat with her. It wasn't to be her best mate. It was to guard her, and he'd do it with no emotional attachment and no previous history. He would be invisible around her, and *that* he could understand Dr. Davies wanting.

Aiden took a sharp curve and saw the lights of a very small downtown. He slowed down as he entered Keeneston. Looking around, he got his bearings from the maps he'd studied on the plane. He looked up to the left and knew the town's only bed and breakfast was up that street along with numerous residential houses. He looked to the right at the small businesses with big front windows before the courthouse loomed large on the left. Which meant . . . he looked to his right at the Blossom Café. The café had been featured in many of the articles he'd read online. However, this was not the café Aiden was expecting. From the news, he was expecting to find it full of patrons and life. Instead, what he found was an empty shell of a place. He stopped as he looked in through the large windows. Cars lined the road in front of the café, but the booths were empty and chairs were overturned or shoved away from the tables. Food sat on the tables forgotten. The place was completely abandoned.

Lifting his foot from the brake, Aiden began to creep forward. Something was going on, and he didn't like it. He looked ahead and found the missing people of the café. They were all in the road a couple blocks ahead of him and police lights were flashing. His principal. Aiden knew it had to be her. Something had happened, and he hadn't been there to protect her. Aiden sped up as he rushed toward the gathered crowd. He expected them to part, but instead they turned as one and lifted their weapons.

Aiden slammed on his brakes as he was met with a wall of citizens armed to the teeth. Various pistols were pointed right at him as he put the SUV in park and lifted his hands for them to see. Emerging from the crowd was a sheriff's deputy and someone who strongly resembled his own mum, right down to the penny loafers. The deputy had his gun drawn and the mum look-alike was ready to swing a bat at him.

Aiden scanned the crowd for Piper. People were three rows deep, but beyond them he saw a wrecked minivan, a smashed car, and an SUV identical to the one he was driving, flipped on its side. The mum look-alike reached for his door with one hand and slowly opened it as the deputy and the rest of the townsfolk kept their guns trained on Aiden.

"My name is Aiden Creed. I'm a security specialist and am carrying a licensed firearm." Aiden kept his hands up as he slowly got out of the SUV.

"Pam, get his wallet," the deputy ordered. The woman stepped forward with her bat pulled back.

"My husband and I sponsor the Little League team here, so don't you be thinking I don't know how to knock your head off with one good swing," look-alike mum, whom he now knew as Pam, said as she reached behind him and dipped her hand into his back pocket.

"Oh my," Aiden heard her say under her breath a moment before she pulled out his wallet and flipped it open. She turned to show it to the sheriff's deputy who nodded.

The deputy turned to the crowd, "He's the bodyguard. You can put down your weapons."

A little old lady bustled forward with a spatula in her hand and two similar old ladies trailing behind her. She looked him up and down and then reached so quickly for Aiden's shoulders that he was pulled down into her bosom in a blink of an eye. Aiden would have thought he was under attack if it hadn't been for the muffled, "Aren't you a handsome one? And that accent!"

"Violet!" someone snapped.

"What? You know I have a thing for accents."

Aiden braced his hands on his knees and tried to breathe as she continued to hold him tight. Luckily, he had learned torture survival in the British Army, or he may not have made it out alive.

"Miss Violet, let my bodyguard go," Aiden heard a woman call out from what sounded like very far away.

Aiden was released and when he stood up, the old lady named Miss Violet winked at him. He winked back and she blushed. As he looked around for his principal, a woman in a tight-knit, gray, mini sweater-dress with a very low scoop neck and thigh-high black-heeled boots strode toward him, wiggling her ass. Aiden wasn't expecting a slag to approach him so boldly in the middle of this crowd to procure a john for the night.

"Hi, handsome," the woman cooed through overinjected lips that resembled a pair of wax candy lips from when he was a child. "I'm Nikki, and I'll happily show you around our little town."

She leaned forward and her oversized tits teetered out. The sweater's yarn strained under the weight and eventually lost out to gravity. One thing was clear. This woman was all fur coat and no knickers.

"Oopsie," Nikki laughed, taking her time to stuff herself back into her sweater. "As I was saying, I can show you a whole new world. I'll stop by tonight."

"Bad!" a young woman dressed in a suit called out a second before she squirted Nikki with a water bottle. The young woman turned to Aiden as Nikki fumbled to reattach a gigantic false eyelash. "I'm sorry about that. I'm Addison Rooney, the town prosecutor. You must be looking for Piper. We've had a little bit of excitement here tonight when someone tried to kill her, but we're all good now. Here she is."

Addison gestured to the woman walking toward him with a slightly surprised expression on her face. She would have looked like the woman he'd seen pictures of, except for the bruises and cuts on her face. Her mostly light-brown hair, streaked with natural blonde highlights, was pulled back from her face into some kind of messy bun. There was no pretentiousness surrounding her. Dressed in scrubs and worn sneakers, Dr. Piper Davies was still the most beautiful woman Aiden had ever seen. It wasn't the kind of beauty that left a man speechless. It was more of an everyday beauty that was sincere and unassuming. And by the way Piper was now standing in front of him nervously holding her breath as her hazel eyes took him in, she had no idea what a beauty she was.

"Aiden Creed," he said, holding out his hand for her. A man with military written all over him stepped up behind Piper and protectively put his hand on her shoulder. Aiden didn't frown as he wanted to, but in that split second, both men acknowledged that they'd sized each other up.

"I'm Piper Davies," she said as she placed her small hand in his larger, rougher one. "You're my bodyguard? I thought you would be older." Aiden nodded as he squeezed her hand gently while he shook it and felt like cursing. The number one rule of close protection work was to keep your emotional distance from the principal. Emotions and feelings did nothing to keep your principal safe, but emotions and other things were growing with every second he touched her.

"A pleasure to make your acquaintance," Aiden said, reluctantly dropping her hand. "Would you like to tell me what happened here?" He directed the question to the man similar in height and build to himself.

Aiden was 185 centimeters and was able to look this man in the eyes, which made him slightly over six American feet tall. However, the man looked to have a couple pounds on

Aiden's 14-stone body, but not much. They were both near two hundred American pounds.

"Walker Greene, SEAL," he said as way of introduction. Ah, yes, the man who was betrayed by his own team leader. Aiden remembered reading about him.

"Aiden Creed, SAS," he replied, shaking the man's hand.

"If y'all wouldn't mind, could we move this somewhere else?" Piper asked as she lowered her voice.

"Is she still in danger?" Aiden asked Walker. Piper rolled her eyes and crossed her arms over her chest, which jutted her lovely breasts up at him.

"You think this is bad?" Piper asked, gesturing to the crowd. "That's *nothing* compared to what will happen when my mother, aunts, and uncles show up." She paused, and in that moment Aiden saw exactly who Piper Davies was. She was someone very uncomfortable being the center of attention, which was so different from his other clientele who loved the spotlight.

Aiden held out his hand, wrapping it around her shoulder and gently pushing her toward the SUV. "Then let's go." Aiden didn't miss the release of breath Piper was holding when he told her he'd take her home. He also didn't miss the uneasiness she had when he opened the back door to the SUV instead of the front.

Piper slowly slid in the back while Walker stopped at the front door. "Why don't I come with you and fill you in on the drive? My wife can pick me up at Piper's house."

"That's fine with me, but make sure your wife knows Piper is likely unavailable to guests."

Walker snickered. "The Davies family, hell, the whole town of Keeneston has no understanding of what the word *unavailable* means. If you thought keeping Piper safe from the people after her was the hardest part of the job, you have a surprise coming. A five-foot, very pregnant surprise."

"Welcome to Keeneston, young man," Miss Violet called out. "We'll pop by with a basket soon."

Walker chuckled as he shook his head and walked around to the passenger door. Maybe this assignment wasn't exactly what Aiden had anticipated, but pivoting at a moment's notice was something he excelled at.

Aiden closed his door and drove while Walker recounted the day's events. By the time they arrived at Piper's house, he was completely caught up. "Do you have any idea who is behind the threats?" Aiden asked when he opened the door for Piper.

She shook her head and a piece of her hair fell into her face. She shoved it behind her ear and looked up at Aiden. "None. I don't even know how they found out about my project, but more importantly, the dangerous state that it's in."

"Nash is working on it," Walker told her before looking to Aiden. "Want me to do it or you?"

"I will," Aiden said, pulling his gun from his hip. "Stay here with her."

"I have a name, you know," Piper called out as Aiden walked up the sidewalk with the key to her house in hand. He grinned to himself as he unlocked the door and swept the house for intruders. He took in the small living room leading to an open kitchen, the short hallway with the bathroom, guest room, and master bedroom with attached bath. The house fit Piper's personality perfectly. It was well cared for, pretty, and cute. All of which described his principal.

"I like that painting in the living room," Aiden said as a way of letting them know it was safe to come inside.

"Thanks. My cousin Tinsley Faulkner from South Carolina painted it for me," Piper said as she walked up the stairs toward him. She kept her eyes focused on the door and not on her bodyguard, who was so hot she could fry an egg on him.

She hadn't known what to expect, but it wasn't the smooth, toned, and sophisticated Aiden Creed. His accent only made it worse. It was like it upped his sexiness whenever he spoke.

Piper had expected someone militarily or law enforcement trained, but not someone trained as an elite SAS and appeared to be only five years older than her twenty-nine years. Someone who wore a suit cut perfectly to his body and not fatigues. Nope and nope. And not someone with the sexiest hazel eyes she'd ever seen. Emerald and gold glittered back at her whenever he looked at her, which was why she was currently keeping her eyes on the floor.

"Pack a bag." Aiden's English voice washed over her, sending her blood pumping—until she realized what he'd just said.

"Excuse me?"

"Pack a bag. We're leaving." He didn't ask her what she thought. He didn't tell her where they were going. He simply ordered her as if she were one of his soldiers.

"Where are we going?" Piper asked as she stood rooted to her porch. Walker closed the distance, and she could feel him frowning behind her.

"My job is to keep you alive. I can't do that here. As Walker confirmed, even if we tell people not to visit, they will. The old lady with the saggy breasts, the slag with the breasts that didn't bounce, and Walker's wife—"

"You better not mention Layne's breasts," Walker warned.

Aiden ignored him and kept his eyes locked with Piper's. "As they've all said, they will be stopping by, along with your family, to a house we know is no longer secure. Is that a correct statement?"

"Why does everything come down to breasts?" Piper asked. Even as she told herself not to look down at her average ones, she did anyway.

"The perfect pair of breasts can take a man down. I'm sure you know that." Piper looked up at Aiden and when his eyes dropped to her chest, she had no problem realizing he approved of her breasts. Wow, so that's what it felt like to be seen. Normally she didn't like it, but if it was Aiden seeing her, she was afraid she might become addicted to it.

"Hey," Walker said, interrupting them. "You are not here to get laid."

"No, I'm not. I'm here to keep her alive and to do that we are getting out of this house—a house that has been broken into, searched, and probably bugged."

Piper saw Walker's jaw tighten before he nodded. "You're right."

Aiden put his hand on the small of Piper's back and gave a little push to move her through the door. "Thank you for your help today. Here's my number. Call if you discover anything."

Piper looked over her shoulder as Aiden gave Walker a card and then closed the door on his face. He flipped the dead bolt, leaving the two of them completely alone. "Pack your bags, Piper."

Piper rolled her eyes at the order but headed to her

room anyway. In minutes she had enough clothes for a week tossed into a gigantic duffle bag. She needed one more thing, but it wouldn't be easy to get to. Her notes.

"Can you help me move the couch?" Piper asked as she dropped her large bag on the living room floor.

"Now isn't the time to redecorate," Aiden lectured even as he moved to help her.

"My concept notes for all my projects are hidden. I keep them in a fireproof box in case any of my patents are challenged," Piper told him as she let Aiden move the large couch as if it weighed nothing. She rolled back the rug, ran her hand over the hardwood until she found what she was looking for, and pressed. The large rectangular piece of hardwood popped up enough for her to put her fingers underneath and then pop off.

"A spring-loaded hidden panel. Smart. No scrape marks from prying it open."

Piper looked up and felt herself heat under his praise. "Thank you. I designed it myself." She reached down and pulled out the fireproof case before closing the hidden compartment and rolling the rug back over it. Without being asked, Aiden pushed the couch back into position and stood.

"One last thing. I need your phone," Aiden said, holding out his hand.

"Why?" Piper asked, holding tight to her cell phone.

"Do you trust I will do everything I can to keep you safe?"

Dear Lord, she hoped so. Right now it was easy to believe someone like Aiden Creed could defeat many of the battles in her life, but even this one might be too big for him. Nash and Ahmed hadn't figured out the source of the threat yet. All they knew was they were well financed and had plenty of manpower.

"Yes, but—"

"No buts. Hand over your phone."

Piper reluctantly handed over her phone. She saw him pull out a new phone, take out her SIM card, and place it in the new phone before dropping the old one in the back of her silverware drawer. "This is a secure phone that won't be able to be traced. You can use it as you normally do."

"Thank you." Piper took the new phone and bit her lower lip as she thought about what was happening to her. "Where are we going?" She asked as he lifted her bag and opened the front door. Walker was still there looking pissed.

Aiden didn't answer her as he opened the back lift gate and set her bag down before opening the back door for her. Piper sighed and climbed in. Through the windshield, she saw Walker and Aiden exchange a short word before Aiden climbed into the SUV.

"We're going someplace I can keep you safe."

7

Some place safe turned out to be a large historic mansion in the countryside of Lexington. Lexington was neat like that. In one mile, you could go from thriving community to farmland. The old brick house was built in the eighteen hundreds and stood overlooking the training track at the attached horse farm.

"I know this farm," Piper said, looking around at oil paintings of horses and large glass chandeliers in the entryway. "This farm has been in the Burnstine family for generations. They had the Horse of the Year two years ago."

"That's right," Aiden said as he carried her bag up the sweeping wooden staircase.

Piper followed close behind as she took in the classic elegance of the house. "How did you get permission to use this house?"

"Mr. Burnstine is a satisfied client. He's in Florida for the winter and gave me permission to use the residence while he and his family are gone." Aiden stopped at a door with its antique bronzed handle and turned it. "This is your room. My room connects, leaving you an exit in case of emergency.

There's also no exit other than this door and the connecting door."

Piper looked around the pale green room at the solid mahogany four-poster bed so tall there was a step stool to get into it, the two large floor-to-ceiling windows that overlooked the farm, a rocking chair by the window, and a chest for clothes.

"There's a bathroom there." Aiden pointed to a closed door. "And my room is right here." He turned to his left and opened the connecting door. The rooms were similar, but his was pale yellow and had a balcony. One she'd kill to sit out on and watch the horses, but Piper understood why it wasn't her room. She was contained in her room. His had an external entry and exit. If she could get in and out, so could someone else.

"I still need to go to work," Piper said, deciding it was time to put her foot down.

Aided nodded his head and ran a hand over his five o'clock shadow. "I know. Do you usually go at a certain time?"

"I usually get to Lexington by eight-thirty. And then my secret lab in Keeneston is anytime I can get there," Piper explained. "And I'll need you to sign a nondisclosure agreement."

"No problem. But we'll leave here tomorrow at ten. You'll be to work in less than twenty minutes. We will never arrive to work at the same time or via the same route." Aiden looked down at his watch. "Would you like to rest or anything while I make dinner?"

Piper felt her eyes widen. "You cook too? Is there anything you can't do?"

"No," Aiden said, his lips spreading into a smile that

turned his face into one Hollywood actors only wished they had. "I'll call when dinner's ready."

Piper watched as Aiden closed the door behind him and held her breath as he walked down the old staircase. She heard every footfall and every creak the old wood made. When he was finally out of earshot, Piper grabbed her phone and made her way into the bathroom. It was obvious it had been renovated. The countertop was marble and there was a solid glass shower with multiple showerheads. But it was the old cast-iron claw-foot tub sitting under a stained-glass window that caught her eye.

Piper was undressed and running the water when her phone rang. She wasn't going to answer, but Abby didn't call very often, so it might be important. "Hello?"

"Aiden Creed? Mallory got Aiden freaking Creed to protect you?"

"Hi, Abby. I'm alive, thanks. And how are you doing?" Piper asked sarcastically.

"I know you're alive. I get the Keeneston text tree in Washington, DC. Aiden Creed hardly ever takes on new clients. I saw him once at a conference, and let me just say it would have been worth whatever to get one night with that man."

"Abby! He's not here to sleep with me. He's here to keep me safe."

"He could watch you even closer if he was in bed with you. Oh, and I'm supposed to ask where you are."

"Ah, that's the reason for the call. Who called you?" Piper asked, feeling the water with her hand and adjusting it.

"Layne. She found Walker on your porch and you were gone."

"I'm not supposed to say."

"That is so hot."

"Abby!" Piper said, the censure no longer in her voice as she laughed.

"Tell me you didn't think about pushing him against the nearest wall and having your wicked way with him," Abby challenged. Well, it wasn't the wall . . . "See," Abby said as she laughed at Piper's silence.

"Okay! I admit it. He is drop dead sexy. But he has zero interest in me, and right now I kinda just want to live long enough to fix my mistake."

"I'm only a phone call away and I want all the details! You wouldn't believe what I heard about his peni—"

"Goodbye, Abby," Piper said hurriedly. She didn't want to hear the details. That was like waving a fresh batch of brownies under a girl's nose and telling her she couldn't have a taste. Piper was not the kind of woman to inspire men to lose control. She was the best friend. The buddy. The girl next door who lived through her friends' lives because no one liked to date a girl who forgot pencils in her hair and worked on things most people couldn't understand. And don't get her started on dating other scientists. Those men couldn't face the fact that she was smarter than most of them. It wasn't like she tried to be. She thought it would be helpful to show them where they were wrong in their work. Right now she'd give anything for someone to show her where she'd gone wrong.

Piper turned off the water and slid into the tub. The hot water enveloped her as tired and sore muscles slowly began to unwind. Piper turned the music from her phone on and closed her eyes. Chemical equations swirled in her mind as she let go of everything else and let her mind go down the rabbit hole.

Aiden opened the pantry door and pulled out a box of pasta. What was wrong with him? His mind was all over the place. Actually, it was in one place—Piper's body. Her pert breasts, her hazel eyes, the sculpted cheekbones, and her perfectly shaped ass. Aiden had protected celebrities, models, and heiresses. Not once had he felt this strong pull to someone before. Maybe it was because Piper Davies was so real while the others had been so fake. He'd broken up with his last girlfriend just last month, and it wasn't like he had a shortage of woman willing to climb into his bed. There was just something about Piper Davies. It was probably because he was fascinated. Piper was so intelligent, quiet, unassuming, and utterly adorable. Whatever it was, he needed to push it deep down. He couldn't let this affect his job. Piper was clear that she wasn't thrilled to have him there. The last thing he needed was to show her what he really thought of her. She'd be running back to Keeneston before he could stop her.

Aiden's phone rang as he poured the Alfredo sauce over the chicken, broccoli, mushrooms, and penne. He didn't recognize the number except to know it was from Kentucky. "Hello?"

"It's Nash Dagher. Is your phone traceable?"

No pleasantries, he definitely liked this town. "No."

"Good."

"What's going on?" Aiden asked as he stirred the ingredients.

"We're trying to track down who is behind this. While we were doing so, someone broke into Piper's house after you left. No casserole or pie was left behind."

"So it wasn't a local," Aiden stated, picking up on what Nash wasn't saying.

"Exactly. We've put up cameras now in case they come back."

"What about the SUV?"

"It was stolen out of Alexandria, Virginia, a week ago. We're running prints now and should have something by tomorrow morning."

"Keep me updated," Aiden told Nash.

"You keep Piper alive, and we'll find out who is behind this."

Nash hung up and Aiden slid his phone into his suit pants pocket. It was good working with a team again. Though Nash was from Rahmi and Walker was from America, it was like he was back in the SAS with his team.

Aiden covered the pasta and headed upstairs to tell Piper dinner was ready. "Dr. Davies?" he asked as he knocked on the door. No answer.

Aiden's heart picked up speed and he honed his ears for sounds of struggle. Nothing. Aiden knocked again. "Dr. Davies?"

Nothing.

Placing one hand on his gun and the other on the doorknob, he slowly turned it. The door swung silently open as he looked into an empty room. The soft strands of Dvořák's "Slavonic Dances" drifted under the bathroom door. "Dr. Davies?" Aiden asked again while knocking on the door. Again, no response. An image of Piper strangled in the bathroom flashed into his head as he pulled his gun and flung the door open.

Aiden scanned the room and paused, gun aimed as movement caught his attention. The tub. The water rippled inside it a second before Piper's head surfaced. Before he could say anything, Piper was standing up. He hadn't seen her under the water, but he swallowed hard as the rivulets of water ran down her body. "Dinner's ready," he said as calmly as he could.

Piper's eyes flashed open as she let out a surprised squeak. One arm covered the loveliest tits he'd ever seen, and the other dropped lower. "What are you doing in here?" she asked frantically as she eyed the gun.

"You didn't answer the door. I was afraid you'd been hurt." Aiden slipped his gun back in its holster as Piper's eyes lowered and froze. Her face was bright red as Aiden reached for the towel on the counter next to him and handed it to her. "I'll have dinner on the table for you after you get dressed," he said as professionally as he could before walking out of the room and closing the door behind him. He took a deep breath, and it was then he noticed why Piper had turned red. It looked as if his prick were saluting her.

Aiden groaned and not because of the raging erection he had. He'd never lost his cool before and here he was only a couple hours into an assignment and practically poking the lass with his prick. "So professional," Aiden muttered as he took off for the kitchen, determined to put aside any feelings he had and focus solely on his job.

WELL, dinner was awkward. After Aiden had closed the door and left Piper to get dressed, she had to stop herself from calling Abby and confirming that the size of Aiden's penis was definitely something to talk about. And it was *her* naked body that had caused it to rise and wave hello. Piper was still in disbelief.

During dinner, Aiden had told her about growing up in the small town of Lynton in Devon. How he went rock climbing, swam in the cold ocean, and hiked constantly with the local goats as he grew up. It had seemed as if the SAS was made for him. And so he left his small town, joined the Army, and quickly knew he wanted to submit for the elite SAS training. Aiden went on to serve four years in the SAS before joining the private sector.

Finally, after the plates where cleared and they had mugs of tea in hand, they headed to the back porch. The night air was chilly and Piper sat on the bench swing, wrapped up in the blanket Aiden had gotten for her from the living room, with her hot tea in hand. Aiden took a seat on a nearby chair, placed his ankle on his knee, and leaned back.

"Nash found out the SUV was stolen from Alexandria, Virginia. Know anyone from that area?"

Piper took a sip of her tea and shook her head. "My friend works in Washington, DC. That's the only connection I have there."

"Who's your friend?" Aiden asked.

"Abigail Mueez."

Aiden chuckled into his tea. "I should have put two and two together. Abby is Ahmed's daughter, isn't she?"

"Yes. You know her?" Piper asked, suddenly defensive about how Abby knew about Aiden's package.

"Met her once at a conference. She's . . . memorable." Piper raised a questioning eyebrow and Aiden continued. "She was there with this man, but she was what everyone was talking about. Apparently there's a story about her taking down this rogue military regime on behalf of the Bermalia government."

Piper's eyes went wide. "King Draven hired Abby to do that?"

"You know the King of Bermalia?" Aiden asked, surprised.

"Yeah, don't you?"

"No, I don't," he answered with amusement.

"What exactly does Abby do? I thought she did what you do."

Aiden shook his head. "Nope. She doesn't do personal security work. I know everyone who's worth knowing in this field, and I can guarantee Abigail Mueez doesn't work for a security company."

"Then who does she work for?" Piper wondered out loud.

"She's your friend, why don't you ask her?"

Piper suddenly smiled. "I don't think I want to know." She laughed and enjoyed the sound of Aiden's laughter joining hers. It was deep and rich and seemed to fill her with warmth. Her eyes drifted down and before she knew it, she was staring at his package again. Her eyes snapped up and Aiden's grin widened. Busted.

Piper took another drink of her tea and stared at the stars as she gently swung. "Dr. Davies," Aiden started before Piper interrupted him.

"Please, call me Piper. I hate being called Dr. Davies. It's so impersonal."

She saw Aiden smile softly, and she looked back at the stars to keep herself from looking at his package again. "Mallory said you wanted someone you didn't know to watch you so you wouldn't worry about them. That's very noble, protecting your friends. I do believe they are more than capable of looking out for you."

"Yes, they are. But what if Walker were killed? I would be the reason my cousin was widowed. I couldn't do that to them. They're all retired, looking forward to children and grandchildren and building their training center." Piper sighed at how cold that sounded. Not to her friends and family, but to Aiden. "I don't mean to imply that your life is worth less than theirs."

"I didn't think you were. Emotions are tricky in close protection work. I'm not your best friend. I'm not your assistant. I'm here for one purpose: to keep you alive."

Piper didn't know for sure, but it sounded as if Aiden were reminding himself of that. But she needed to hear it too. They needed to be professional, and she needed to work. "Will you stay out of the way while I work?"

"Of course. You won't know I'm there," Aiden said before giving her a wink. Yeah, good luck with that. Piper was positive she'd know exactly where Aiden Creed was at all times.

8

Piper stretched in bed while she slowly woke up. She'd slept way better than she thought she would. Maybe because Abby had put thoughts of a naked Aiden in her mind. But anyway, she'd slept. She rolled over and looked at the clock. Seven in the morning. Aiden wasn't going to take her to work until ten. Maybe she could get him to take her to her lab in Keeneston first.

Quickly dressing her in her standard work attire—jeans and a sweater for the cold fall day—Piper hurried downstairs. Aiden was sitting at the kitchen table sipping tea and reading the news on his tablet.

"Good morning," he said, his accent causing Piper to flash back to some of the dream she'd had the night before.

She cleared her throat and gave him a smile as if she hadn't just pictured him naked. "Morning. I thought maybe we could go into Keeneston this morning."

"You're the boss," he said, setting down his tea.

"I am?"

"Yes, you are. I'm to keep you safe, not handcuff you to the bed." Aiden froze the second the words were out of his mouth, as did Piper. Her face felt heated, her heart beat faster, and boy, did her hoohah tingle at his words.

"What do you need to pick up?" Aiden asked after clearing his throat.

"Well, I thought we could grab breakfast at the café and then head out to my lab for a couple hours. I have my old notebooks I want to review, and it would make more sense to have FAVOR with me so I can compare my initial thoughts to the actual steps I took."

"When do you want to leave?"

"Now?"

Aiden cleared his throat again. "Sure. I'll, um, meet you in the garage."

AIDEN WATCHED as Piper walked from the room and groaned. Her ass was perfect. And it didn't help that he'd been picturing it, and other parts of her, all night long. He felt like beating his head against the table. The second he'd said that about her being cuffed to the bed, he turned as hard as a rock and showed no signs of subsiding, which is why he sent Piper to the car.

Standing up, Aiden cleaned up the kitchen as he repeated the SAS Oath of Allegiance. By the time he got through humming "God Save the Queen," he was finally presentable enough to meet Piper in the garage.

Piper looked up from where she sat in the front seat of the SUV and smiled nervously. Could she feel how much he wanted her?

"Is it okay if I sit up here? I hate sitting in the back."

Ah, not the sexual tension he thought. "Sure. So, to the Blossom Café then? Is there anything you'd recommend me getting there?"

"Everything is good," Piper said, launching into all of her favorite foods, an explanation of the Rose sisters, their retirement, and how their distant cousins, Poppy and Zinnia, now ran the café.

In twenty short minutes, Aiden pulled up to the café he'd passed the night before. "They're not going to shoot me, are they?"

Piper laughed and he began to recite *God Save the Queen* in his head again. Piper laughing was the most erotic thing he'd ever heard. She put her whole soul into it. "No. Now they know who you are they'll leave you alone. Well, as much as they leave anyone alone. Walker has mentioned being the new guy in town is a lot like Hell Week during SEAL training. Does that help?"

Aiden raised one brow and glanced at her to see if she was jesting. By the look on her face, he could tell she wasn't. As long as he didn't get shot, he could handle a friendly group of people who shared his love of guns and tits.

Piper was already out the door before Aiden could open it for her. "Next time let me get that."

"I can get my own door. I have hands, you know."

Aiden chuckled. "It's not that you can't open the door, it's so I can make sure the area is safe first and put myself between you and the building in case someone decides to shoot at you."

Aiden almost felt bad for telling her that. Her face fell so fast as she grabbed his arm. "You're wearing a vest, right? Oh my gosh! How could I be so selfish? I've been thinking about how this will affect me, but not you. You need one of my jackets."

"Piper, this is my job. You haven't been selfish. And I have a jacket, thanks," Aiden said, ignoring how good it felt to have her touch him.

"Not my jacket. And you will as soon as we get to my lab," Piper said with such determination Aiden didn't bother to argue. If she wanted him to wear a different jacket, then so be it.

Aiden opened the door to the café and the boisterous room grew quiet. "He's just the bodyguard," Pam called out. Suddenly everyone went back to eating and completely ignored him. Except for the slag.

She sauntered all hips, ass, and tits toward him. Her eyelashes, which resembled fingers reaching out to strangle him, batted. "Good morning," she said seductively as she ran her hand down his chest straight to his prick.

"Sorry. I don't pay to sleep with women, but good luck to you." Aiden grabbed her hand and removed it from his body.

Aiden heard Piper snort behind him as the slag gasped. "You think I'm a hooker?" the woman screeched.

Aiden saw the table of law enforcement and figured she was putting on a show. Tables full of people turned to see what was going on. He lowered his voice, "If the tits fit. But I'm not interested. Go find someone else and leave me alone from now on."

Her long-taloned hand came back as if to slap Aiden when all of a sudden she gave a little squeak and fell to the ground. *Brrrrffft.* Aiden stared down at the woman who just farted as if she were a trumpeter. He looked around and saw that no one was paying attention except for a young man with bright reddish-orange hair. He shoveled in the last bite of his food, set some money on the table, and walked over to them.

"Sorry. Nikki is a little . . . well, a lot. Just a lot. I'll take her home. I'm Andy Dinkler," he said, holding out his hand.

"Aiden Creed."

"Hiya, Piper. How are you doing after last night?" Andy asked as he bent down and scooped Nikki into his arms.

"Good, thank you. How's police academy?"

"I finish up in May, and Matt already said I had a job waiting at the sheriff's station," Andy said proudly.

"That's great. Do you need any help with Nikki?" Piper asked.

Ppppffffttt. Andy ignored the fart coming from Nikki. "Naw. I have a key to her place now since I've carried her home so often. Sophie really loves her stun gun."

Piper nodded and Aiden hurried to hold open the door for him. "Sophie? Taser?" Aiden asked as soon as Andy was out the door.

"My wife," Nash said suddenly by his side. "She's a weapons developer and her little joke project is a fart stun gun. Apparently I married a woman with the sense of humor of a twelve-year-old boy."

"I'm so going to tell my cousin you said that," Piper teased as she headed for a nearby table.

"We need to talk," Nash said to Aiden instead of responding to Piper.

"You found out who's after her," Aiden stated.

"I think so, and it's not good."

"Should we go someplace to talk?"

Nash shook his head. "They find out everything anyway. And my wife is involved, so we might as well do it here."

Aiden followed Nash over to the table that fit four people. Piper was talking to a pretty woman around her age. "Darling, this is Aiden Creed. Aiden, my wife, Sophie."

Aiden shook her hand and took the seat next to Piper. The waitress, Poppy, came over before Nash could talk. "What can I get y'all?"

"Y'all?" Aiden tried out. Piper laughed and Poppy sighed dreamily.

"I just love your accent."

"I'm rather partial to *y'alls'* accent too," Aiden said even as the word felt funny in his mouth. "Piper, why don't you order for us both?"

"Two biscuits and gravy," Piper ordered without hesitation. Aiden's forehead crinkled with confusion, but Nash was already pulling something up on a tablet.

"Have you ever heard of Red Shadow?"

Aiden nodded. He remembered it from his time in the SAS. "Weapons deals and black market trades run by a man who called himself Poseidon. But over a year ago, maybe two, he and his entire organization were taken out. The King of Rahmi claimed responsibility . . . Wait." Aiden looked up at Nash. No? Yes? Maybe? "Were you a part of that?"

"I was that," Nash responded as if taking out a criminal organization of that scale was nothing.

"I think you would be safe with Nash looking after you. You don't need me when you have him here," Aiden said with a shake of his head.

"He can't," Piper said suddenly. "I can't put his life in danger. Not now."

"I think he is the definition of danger," Aiden responded.

"It's because of me," Sophie said quietly as she rested one hand on her flat stomach. "I'm pregnant."

"Did you say *pregnant*?" Miss Lily shouted from across the room. A room that suddenly fell quiet for all of a brief second. Just long enough for Sophie to give a single nod.

"We told our families last night, but Piper was with me when I bought the test," Sophie told the café.

"That means she's probably twelve weeks, which makes it . . . twenty dollars on May 10th!" a woman shouted out.

"Aunt Paige!" Sophie gasped. "You're betting on me?"

"Of course. Momma needs a new rifle."

"I bet she's only eight weeks. Twenty dollars on April 19th!"

"Aunt Morgan," Sophie said, shaking her head at one of the other women at the table.

"How could you not tell us?" one woman accused another.

"That's Aunt Katelyn. And the woman she just yelled at is Sophie's mom, Annie," Piper whispered to him as Aiden watched with wonder as bets began to ring out. Poppy ran around collecting money while others, including Piper, pulled out their cell phones and logged onto some kind of app.

"Cade and I celebrated still being just Mom and Dad instead of grandparents. We were a little busy to call all y'all," Annie grinned.

Sophie groaned. "Ew! Mom!"

"I offer you my felicitations," Aiden said as he held out his hand to Nash who shook it. The man who had single-handedly taken down a massive criminal organization smiled like an idiot and kissed his wife. Aiden had to admit, it was the most beautiful thing he'd ever witnessed.

"Thank you. But now you know the real reason Piper was so against me helping to protect her."

"Piper Davies! And you didn't tell your own mother?" a small sprite of a woman with a massively pregnant belly and spiked blonde hair accused. Mother? The woman looked like Piper's older sister.

"Mother?" Aiden stammered.

"Do you doubt it?" the sprite snapped.

"No, you two have the same smile, but I thought you couldn't be old enough to be her mother. You look like her sister," Aiden said, jumping to his feet and holding out his chair for Mrs. Davies.

"Oh!" she said, suddenly glowing more than she already did. "Did you hear that, Pierce? This sex-on-a-stick of a young man thinks I look like Piper's sister. So take your *too old to get pregnant* and shove it up your—"

"Mom!" Piper groaned, cutting off her mother. The man behind her must be her father. They had the same hazel eyes.

"Mr. Davies, Mrs. Davies, I'm Aiden Creed. It's a pleasure to make your acquaintances," Aiden said, shaking their hands.

"Are you married?"

"Mom!" Piper turned bright red, but Mrs. Davies didn't seem fazed at all.

"No, Mrs. Davies. I am not."

"How do you feel about older women? I plan on killing my husband before this baby is born. It'll be justifiable, won't it, Kenna?"

An auburn-haired woman nodded at a nearby table. "If Pierce makes one more comment about you being too old to have a baby, I think the entire female population of Keeneston will kill him for you."

Tammy turned to her husband. "Just remember that, Pierce. Even the judge won't convict me."

"Congratulations," Pierce said to Nash and Sophie, ignoring his wife's threats. "Do you have any information about who is after our daughter?"

"I do. I was about to fill them in," Nash told them as Tammy took the seat Aiden offered. Pierce and Aiden pulled up chairs, which left him pressed against Piper's side. Her leg rubbed against his, and he felt like a randy teenager again.

"You were saying about Red Shadow," Aiden prompted.

"Poseidon's second-in-command, Ares, broke from the group, deeming them too old school. He was into hacking, trafficking everything from weapons to humans, and wasn't afraid to get down and dirty and take the assignments Poseidon refused to," Nash explained. "He found out about a weapon Sophie had developed and came after her. We took him and his organization down."

"I have a feeling there is a *but* coming," Aiden said, leaning forward and resting his elbows on the table. Thigh-to-calf-pressed against Piper, he felt her shivering. She was scared. He looked around and when he knew no one would see, he lowered his hand and placed it comfortingly on her knee. Her shivering stopped as she turned to stare at him in surprise. Her warmth felt so good under his hand, there was no way he was going to remove it. Slowly, she turned her blush-cheeked face back to Nash.

"But, what?" she asked Nash.

"Ares left behind a computer with the full list of his comrades on it. We tracked them all down and either put them in jail or eliminated them. All but one person we weren't able to find."

"And you think this is who is after me?" Piper asked as Aiden felt her body shake under his touch again. But she didn't show her fear. She sat calmly and listened.

"Yes. The man was Ares's right-hand man. We don't have a real name. He only went by Phobos. In mythology, he's Ares's son, representing fear. And Ares didn't disclose Phobos's real name like he did others. That's why it's been hard to find him. Actually, we thought we had them all and that Phobos was one of the men we took out," Nash told them.

"Why do you think it's him?" Aiden asked.

"The print in the car was from a criminal who had recently been in South Asia, a safe spot for dealers and traffickers and is the rumored homebase for Phobos. Right now it's just a guess, but based on what Ares would have taught Phobos, it fits. They might have knowledge of a viral weapon that could be altered to take out most of the world's population, or limited to take out a certain family with similar mitochondrial DNA. It's priceless. And exactly what the wannabe world's most feared weapons dealer would want to corner the market. It's loose, but the print did take us to that criminal, who is origionally from Belgium, which led us to an outstanding warrant. The warrant is for illegal sales of weapons on the black market," Nash explained. "So, while we don't know for sure it's Phobos, the connection is there, and there's been a lot of chatter about Phobos making an entrance in the criminal world as the new *it* guy. Who else would know about Keeneston but someone who has been here?"

"Does Phobos have a group, like Red Shadow? Or is he on an individual basis like Ares was?" Pierce asked Nash.

Nash shook his head. "We're trying to figure that out. He's new. Ares was captured and his group wiped out not that long ago. Phobos's name is popping up fast. He's making a play to live up to his name, meaning *fear*. He's murdered rivals in very public and gruesome ways."

"And because he was here at some point with Ares, he might have heard about Piper and her project?" Aiden wondered as he tried to figure out the source of the information leak.

"Yes. I don't know how else he could have found out. I've reviewed all the emails and social media accounts of Piper's employees and nothing. But, we know Ares had men in the area beforehand reporting back to him as they tried to locate Sophie," Nash answered.

Aiden turned to Piper. "Who knew exactly what you were working on? We find that person, find who they told, and maybe we can trace it back to the origin of the threats, be it Phobos or someone else."

9

Piper sat stunned. She knew that somehow the guy who had been calling her had to know what she was working on, but she never really thought someone had betrayed her. But that was the only answer. Someone told someone else what she was working on. And there were only a small handful of people who knew.

"Let me see," Piper said, taking a deep breath, "my father." She looked at her dad sitting nervously at the table. He knew the importance of keeping experiments a secret. He didn't even tell her mom, so she knew he wasn't the one, which was also why he was looking rather nervous. Her mom hated being kept in the dark. "My second-in-command at the Lexington lab, Dudley Fieldhouse, and the head of the Rahmi lab, Sada Kourtney."

It still didn't make sense to her. "How would Phobos know to look into me? I wasn't very involved in Sophie's rescue or anything."

"Could it be your jacket?" Sophie asked with a shrug. "It did save Nash's life."

Piper saw Aiden look strangely at her, but she ignored it.

"I guess? I mean, if they were looking into people who are from here, I guess they'd see I work with viruses and nanotech. That's not a secret. But to find out not only what I'm working on, but how it's gone wrong and could be weaponized?"

"I think we'd better talk to the two people who knew what you were working on and see if they told anyone," Aiden suggested. It was a place to start at least. And with Nash sidelined, it looked as if Aiden was back in the intelligence business.

The door to the café flung open and Aiden instinctively placed his body in front of Piper's as a woman in tight jeans, spiked heels, and a sweater that accentuated curves men could play with for hours, stormed in. Her dark skin and brown eyes glowed with anger as she searched the café for someone.

"Sugarbear! How could you not tell me it was Sophie who was pregnant? I had to find out from the text tree!" she yelled as she stomped one foot.

"Now, baby," a state trooper said, standing slowly with his hands held out as if he were being held at gunpoint. "I told you I wasn't going to spill their secret. If it were anyone else I'd tell you, but Sophie and Nash would probably kill me if I spilled their secret."

"Wait, DeAndre. You knew?" Sophie asked the state trooper.

"He's known since before Reagan and Carter were outed as a couple." The woman's bracelets jingled as she put her hands on perfectly curved hips.

"Crap," Morgan Davies said with a frown. "That makes her closer to twelve weeks. I gotta change my bet."

"We'd better talk to Dr. Fieldhouse," Aiden said as the

woman sucked in a breath as her hand fluttered to her heart.

"That is the sexiest thing I have ever heard. Will you say, 'put another snag on the barbie'?"

"Aniyah, this is my bodyguard, Aiden Creed. Aiden, this is Aniyah and her boyfriend, DeAndre," Piper introduced. "DeAndre is amazing at finding out gossip before anyone else and Aniyah, well, if she pulls a gun, find someplace to hide. She has a tendency to shoot off toes."

"I'm up to shins now," Aniyah said defensively before turning back to Aiden. "Oh, oh, I know. Say *crikey* . . . no, no, *dingo*! Oh, oh, call me a *sheila*! And you have to say *G'day ma*te!"

"Baby," DeAndre groaned, shooting Aiden an apologetic look.

AIDEN FELT his smile break into a full grin and saw the moment Aniyah stopped hopping around and noticed. "Lord have mercy. They say it's hotter Down Under, but crikey!"

"That's very kind of you, but I'm from England, not Australia." Aiden tried to keep his smile in check as the smile fell from Aniyah's face.

"Oh. That's not nearly as sexy. Have you seen the actors who come out of Australia?"

"We *do* have James Bond." Aiden had to bite the inside of his cheek to prevent himself from laughing. Piper was shaking next to him and this time it was with silent laughter instead of fear.

Aniyah sighed. "That's true. And that man is fine. I can see you leaping from building top to building top in a suit. Or racing a car through London. But why does he always carry that small gun? Someone like James Bond needs a big sexy gun, like this one." Aniyah reached into her purse and pulled out a Colt 45.

Breakfasts were flung to the ground, tables were turned on their sides, and patrons dove for cover.

"Baby, where did you get another gun?" DeAndre asked as if he were a long-suffering husband. "I thought we'd promised no more guns."

"*You* promised no more guns. I just nodded. This is my baby. A nice man was selling it out of his van in Lexington. I've already named him," Aniyah said, stroking the gun.

Aiden had pulled Piper onto his lap and tucked her there while using his body to shield hers the moment he saw the butt of the gun being pulled from the zebra print purse.

"Admit it. You've never had an assignment like this one, have you?" Aiden heard Piper say from where he had her face shoved against his chest.

"Never. This may be my favorite one yet. No one is going to believe this story."

"You haven't heard the name of the gun yet," Piper reminded him.

"Luv," Aiden said, lifting his head and getting Aniyah's attention. "What did you name the gun?"

Aniyah turned her back sharply on DeAndre who was trying to grab it to show it off to Aiden. "Thor."

"Ah," Aiden said as he smiled. "That makes sense with your love of Australian actors."

"If you're not going to give it to me, at least put it in your purse so these people can finish their breakfast," DeAndre said with resignation.

As Aniyah put her gun away and the patrons climbed out from behind their overturned tables, Aiden found himself still holding tight to Piper. "What would she do if I told her I was Thor's bodyguard when they were filming in London?"

"I don't think you'd want to know. Let's go on the assumption that's a secret you never share with her," Piper whispered as Aiden finally sat up with her, though he didn't set her back in her chair. He held her a moment longer until she looked at him with a question in her eyes. Only then did Aiden lift her from his lap and set her in her chair.

"Sorry about the delay. We had to clear a path to the kitchen after Aniyah's gun wave," Poppy said with two plates of biscuits and gravy on them. She set them in front of Piper and Aiden and hurried away to help with the cleanup.

"Ah, not what I was expecting. I forgot you Americans call these biscuits."

Piper laughed and Aiden was glad he was sitting down. Between having her on his lap and the sound of her laughter, he'd embarrass himself if he stood up right now. "You really thought we'd put sausage gravy over a cookie?"

"Momentary lapse in our minor language differences," Aiden replied before taking a bite. He needed to move here for the biscuits and gravy alone. There were plenty of high-profile clients right here. Or maybe the café could air mail the biscuits to England once a week?

"Like them?" Piper asked with amusement. When Aiden looked down, he noticed he was already on the last bite.

"They're the best breakfast I've ever had," Aiden said as he took his last bite. He listened as conversation around them went back to normal. Tammy and Sophie talked babies while Pierce warned Nash of all the things that could go wrong during pregnancy. Aiden took the time to grow accustomed to the speech, the slang they used, and the people and places everyone was talking about.

Piper set her fork down and looked over at Aiden's profile. He had finished already and was casually leaning back in his chair, but his eyes were anything but casual. He was taking in every person and conversation in the room.

While breakfast and Aniyah had been a nice diversion, it was time to face her work and possibly the people who betrayed her. "I'm ready whenever you are," she said quietly to Aiden. His eyes didn't move to hers, but instead focused on the comings and goings of the kitchen.

"You're the boss. It's never about when I'm ready. Remember, Piper, you're in charge of your life. I'm in charge of protecting it."

Right. She was in charge. Piper looked up at the table and smiled at her family. "We need to get going. Congratulations again," she said to Sophie and Nash before placing a kiss on her parents' cheeks.

Aiden's hand rested on the small of her back as he let her lead them out of the café. People called out their goodbyes as they left. He was already becoming integrated with the town. In one breakfast, everyone had learned his name, he was from England, and probably more since she knew a thing or two about the Keeneston grapevine. MI6 would be envious of their network.

"Do you want to go to your local lab or do you want to head straight to Lexington?" Aiden asked when he realized she was already seated in the SUV.

"Lexington, please. I don't think I can focus on my work until I figure who leaked the information. It has to be one of those two. No, wait!" Piper called out as Aiden slowed to a stop in the middle of Main Street. "Let's go to my local lab. I'll give you directions. I'm suddenly scared if they found out what I'm working on, they can find where I'm hiding it. Can you make sure we're not followed?" Piper asked as horns honked behind them. Aiden didn't seem to care about the noise as he looked her in the eyes.

"I know a thing or two about evasive driving. Tell me where I'm going."

Piper gave him directions, and he shot down Main Street, through an alley, down the other direction of Main Street, behind the feed store, and finally out of downtown.

"That's it!" Piper cried as Aiden flew past the drive she used to go to her lab.

"I know. One, we have a car about a quarter mile behind us. And two, it's an obvious entry and would alert someone that this cow field is important. I'm going to go in through the back."

"Back? There is no back," Piper started to say as Aiden turned left onto a small one-lane road a couple miles past her land.

Aiden kept his eyes glued behind him and when no car came, Piper saw him relax. He smiled when he turned the SUV off-road and began to cut down the side of sleeping soybean fields until he came to the fence that surrounded her property.

"You can park here. It's not too far of a walk. The cows will move." Piper smiled as she thought about a London man in his leather loafers and suit walking through cow patties.

"You're lucky. The Lynton wild goats will sometimes decide you need a good head butt." Aiden didn't seem squeamish in the least about hopping into a cow field. He didn't seem concerned about his shoes or his pants as he straddled a cow patty so he could help her over the fence.

Piper looked down at his outstretched hands. She didn't

need help climbing down. She grew up in the country and could climb trees, walk on top of fences, and dig for worms for fishing. Even still, Piper fell into his arms with a smile. His hands tightened around her as he carried her away from the cow patty and slowly set her down. Goodness, being in Aiden's arms was an experience. The heat, the strength, the way he smelled of sandalwood and cedar with a hint of warm amber that made Piper instantly think about Aiden pressing her up against a tree in the middle of the woods where no one would hear her crying out in pleasure.

"Are you okay? You're all red." As soon as Aiden pointed that out, Piper was sure she turned five shades redder in embarrassment. She needed to focus. Get dangerous sample from lab. Keep it safe. Fix it so the whole world doesn't die. Not focus on a sexy, panty-dropping Brit.

"Good. Just worried about my sample. Let's go."

Aiden looked around the field as the cows lumbered by them. "Where is it?"

"Underground."

"Clever," he said with admiration in his voice. And what that did to her panties was going to be left unsaid.

Piper showed Aiden how to enter the lab. He made her wait in the field while he cleared the lab and hurried back out. "Get what you need. I'll stay out here."

Piper nodded and headed into her lab. She ran for the cooler and pulled out a holding tank that would keep her sample at the right temperature for transport. Piper opened her refrigerator and pulled the samples from inside. She secured them safely in the cooler and looked around for anything else she might need.

Ah, jackets. She had a box of them. She'd get one for

herself and one for Aiden. Piper hurried to the small storage closet and dug through her box of jackets picking out the correct sizes. She was halfway across the room when the earth shook and the cooler bounced dangerously close to the edge of the table. Her breath lodged in her throat as Piper shoved rattling stools aside and leapt forward as the cooler gave up purchase and fell.

With hands outstretched, Piper dove for the small cooler. She hit the cool concrete floor hard with her chest and stomach as her hands closed around the hard shell of the cooler. Air whooshed out of her lungs as the earth shook again. This time the sound of gunfire accompanied it. This was no earthquake. They had found her.

10

Aiden fired on the pickup truck as it tore through the field straight at him. Cows thundered by in panic as a man fired a rocket grenade launcher at Aiden. He dove to the side and took cover behind a thick tree as the grenade exploded far enough away to not harm him.

Aiden reached into his suit and pulled out another magazine and reloaded. He shot at the person holding the launcher. His second shot found its mark and the man fell from the truck into the path of stampeding cattle. Another man riding in the back who had been loading the launcher picked it up and fired at Aiden. Aiden cursed as he was forced to retreat farther from the entrance to the lab. He just hoped Piper would stay put.

Since they were a man down, Aiden charged as soon as the shot exploded. The man would have to reload, and Aiden would be ready for him. He stood his ground, lined up his shot, and waited. The second the man stood with the launcher, Aiden fired. The man went down. Aiden prayed there were no more men riding in the back of the pickup.

"Aiden!"

Ah, bollocks. "Get down!" Aiden yelled as Piper ran toward him.

The passenger window of the pickup rolled down and Aiden was already running toward Piper as the first shot was fired. Aiden's heart stopped when the bullet slammed into Piper's chest, sending her flying backward and falling hard to the ground.

"No!" Aiden yelled as he stopped, aimed, and emptied his clip into the windshield of the pickup. It veered suddenly to the right, the front tire clipping the tree trunk sticking up out of the ground, causing the front tire to lift off the ground. Aiden didn't watch the truck flip. He dropped to the ground, hitting it hard, as his hands were searched for a pulse on Piper's limp body.

"Ow," she groaned. Aiden felt relief wash through him as he almost fell down. And when her eyes fluttered open, he finally let out the breath he'd been holding. "That hurt like a stick in the eye," she gasped as he continued to look for blood.

Aiden ran his hands over her shoulders, down her chest, over two breasts he would remember later how wonderfully they filled his hands, and over her stomach. "Where's the blood? I saw you shot," he asked more to himself than to her as he lifted her clothes up to look at her skin.

"Hey!" Piper yelled as she tried to shove down her clothes, but it was too late. He saw where she was hit. There was an angry bruise forming slightly above her left breast, just inches from her heart.

"Stop," Aiden ordered as he stared. That wasn't possible.

"Listen to me," Piper said in a ticked-off voice as she tried to wriggle out from his grasp, but Aiden put his hand on her exposed stomach, and she instantly stilled.

"I saw you shot," he said with confusion.

"It's my jacket. I told you, I'm into nanotechnology. This jacket and other clothing items will be hitting a small select market soon. They're bullet- and knife-proof."

"I don't believe it," Aiden said with disbelief. The jacket was just a windbreaker.

"Do you see a bullet lodged in my chest?" Piper asked sarcastically. Aiden looked back at her chest. No bullet. But a pair of beautiful breasts encased in the ugliest cotton bra he'd ever seen. It was white, but there were black lines of various spacing across it.

"No. What's on your bra?"

"DNA sequence, now would you let me up?"

Aiden grinned as a whole slew of dirty thoughts ran though his mind. "I kind of like you like this."

"Ugh! Let me up. I have to check my sample."

Aiden rocked onto his heels as she shoved her top and jacket down. She was blushing again, and it was definitely affecting him. Especially when she rolled over and crawled to the cooler with her ass wiggling in his face. This assignment was going to kill him. One way or the other, he was a dead man.

PIPER UNLOCKED the cooler and looked inside. Her heart rate instantly slowed when she saw the sample was safe inside. "It's safe."

"Good, now let's get you that way," Aiden called as he walked toward the truck. He kicked a window in and pulled a man from it. Piper gagged slightly. She'd never really been around a dead guy before, especially one missing part of his head.

"Who is he?" she asked and was slightly embarrassed when her voice cracked.

Aiden took a picture and stood. "I don't know. I just texted Nash. They'll be here soon." Piper watched as Aiden bent down and started going through the man's pockets. He pulled out a phone and Piper inched her way closer as she clung to the cooler.

"What did you find?"

"His cell phone. The last text was GPS coordinates to this location and a picture of you—a picture taken this morning in the café. There's someone who doesn't belong in Keeneston."

"Let me see," Piper said, ignoring the dead guy as she rushed over to grab the phone. "Angle is all wrong. It was taken from outside. We would have noticed someone inside."

"The car that was following us. It had to be them."

Piper nodded as she scrolled through the rest of the texts. "Dudley," she gasped as she turned the phone for Aiden to see. There was no doubt about it now. Dudley Fieldhouse had sold her out. The text instructed the driver to be at the Lexington lab at five tonight, and Dudley would let him in the back door if he knocked twice, paused for three seconds, and knocked twice more. I don't believe this." Piper plopped onto the ground and stared out the now calm cows at the far end of the pasture. "He's been with me for years. I thought he was my friend. Why would he do this?"

"Money, fame, jealousy. I've seen it all," Aiden said, taking the phone from her and scrolling through more of the messages. "But it's clear Dudley's contact isn't this man. He's a lead, and we need to talk to him to find out exactly who he's been talking to."

Piper nodded absently as the sounds of sirens in the distance could be heard. Aiden got up and went person to person taking their cell phones and pressing their fingers to the home buttons so he could access them. He took photos of texts with his phone as Matt rolled up in the sheriff's cruiser and Nash and Nabi pulled up in a Desert Farm SUV.

"Are you all right, dear?" Nabi asked as he rushed toward her. He wasn't quite at uncle status for her, but he was close. He'd always taken care of Ahmed and Mo's kids along with their friends. He'd taken over as head of security for the royal family when Ahmed retired. Similarly, that was what Nash would do when Nabi retired.

"I'm pissed," Piper said, looking at Nabi's worried face. "I was shot. That asshole shot me. But then Aiden shot him, so ha!"

Piper stood so fast, Nabi had to jump back. It was like a delayed adrenaline surge. Her body was shaking and her breathing was heavy. "I'm going to kill him. If Dudley thought he would get away with this, well, he was just delusional. And it won't be fast like a bullet. Oh, no. I have a much better idea." Piper stormed off for her lab as she failed to notice the four men staring slack-jawed at her.

When she returned a few moments later, the men were looking through the phones. They paused when they saw her, and Aiden handed the phone to Nash.

"Luv, what's in your hand?" Aiden asked politely.

"Just a little virus that will make Dudley double over in pain, vomit, and shit himself for forty-eight hours before it slowly eats his organs and causes a horrific death," Piper said cheerfully.

"Um, maybe you should let me take that," Aiden suggested as he held out his hand.

"I'm the expert in this case. If you want to shoot or stab him, he's all yours. But this is my way. Let's go."

Aiden looked to the others who suddenly looked

interested in the grass. "Sorry, I don't have diplomatic immunity," Matt said when he looked up. "I'm out."

Nabi let out sigh. "I'll go with them."

A second police cruiser pulled to a stop as Deputy Cody Gray got out and looked around. "Well, I can say one thing. It's never boring here."

Piper rolled her eyes. This wasn't going to be boring either. She was going to make Dudley pay for this. Trying to kill her was one thing, but turning her project over to make it into a weapon of mass destruction was downright evil.

"Um, you do have an antidote for that, right?" Aiden asked as he caught up with her.

"Of course. I developed it a month ago. I've just been too consumed with this project and haven't sent it off for mass production. That's why I picked it. Dudley doesn't know I have the antidote."

"I always thought you were the nice one," Nabi muttered. Well, she might have been, but that was before being shot and betrayed.

11

Piper muttered the whole drive into Lexington. The anger had built and built as Aiden and Nabi kept giving her side glances as if they were afraid she'd blow at any moment. Of course, she knew she was losing it. She was losing her Southern manners, and she was losing her willingness to always be polite. *Don't cause a fuss*. Well, screw that. She was going to make Dudley pay for this.

"We need to clear the lab," Aiden told her as they pulled to a stop out front. The broken window had already been replaced and Piper looked in at the secretary sitting out front.

"Except for Dudley. He's mine."

Nabi nodded, got out of the SUV, and disappeared inside. A moment later, the lab was empty except for Dudley. Nabi opened the lab door and waved at them before going back inside.

"Now, luv, remember to breathe. Are you sure you don't want me to hold the deadly virus?" Aiden asked without the fear she'd seen in Nabi's eyes. Nabi wasn't used to her freaking out and was scared. Aiden didn't know any better.

"I've got this," Piper said with confidence as she tightened the grip on the syringe. "But y'all might want to put on gloves and a mask."

Aiden grabbed the protective gear next to the door and handed some to Nabi as they entered the lab. Dudley was standing at his table with his eyes in a microscope. He looked up when he heard her stop next to him.

"Oh, yeah. I figured you were coming in when the lab was cleared out. How are you feeling? I can't believe you were robbed here," Dudley said with such concern that Piper almost bought it.

She sneered at the pudgy man with the slightly balding light brown hair, big bushy beard, and dressed in a shirt with a DNA sequence that sadly resembled her bra. Maybe she needed some nicer underwear.

He looked surprised at her reaction and took a small step back. "We need to talk," Piper said between clenched teeth.

"Look, mate," Aiden said calmly as he stared Dudley down, which wasn't hard since Aiden towered over him and was all muscles instead of fluff. "Do you see the crazy scary look Dr. Davies is giving you?"

Dudley nodded.

"So, cut the shit and tell her what you did."

Dudley's eyes were wide as he looked back and forth between them and then over to Nabi, who, he decided, looked the most friendly. "What is he talking about?"

"You almost got me killed. I was shot! And then you dare ask me what this is about?" Piper snarled, her voice so deep and animalistic that it was unrecognizable.

"You were shot?" Dudley asked as his voice rose. "Are you okay?"

"Too bad for you, I lived."

Dudley's face creased in bewilderment. "I don't understand. Of course I'm glad you lived. Why would you think otherwise?"

Piper growled and Aiden stepped back in. "Maybe because you told someone what she was working on. You sold out your boss so someone could weaponize the viral nanotechnology she was working on."

"What?" Dudley sputtered, but his bright pink cheeks gave him away. Piper lunged, Aiden grabbed Dudley, and Nabi grabbed her.

"Let go of me!" Piper yelled as Dudley seemed to seek protection from Aiden.

"Sorry, mate, I'm not here to protect you. I'm here to protect her. Nabi—" Aiden had Dudley in one hand and held out his other to Nabi, who plucked the needle from Piper and handed it over.

"Let me go," Piper growled.

"Let the professional killers handle this, babe," Aiden said with a slow threatening grin for Dudley. "This is . . ." Aiden looked to Piper questioningly.

"C1B3."

Dudley tried to pull away, but Aiden had him tightly in his grasp as he popped off the cover to the syringe. "So, you know what this is?"

Dudley nodded frantically. "I'm sorry! I didn't mean to tell anyone about your project. I was just showing off. I was trying to make myself sound more important than I am. You're beautiful," Dudley cried to Piper. "You wouldn't believe how hard it is for a man like me to get a date. I wanted to impress her. I'm even meeting her tonight for the first time."

Dudley started to whimper and sniffle as if he were seconds away from bursting into tears. Piper felt her body relax and almost laughed out loud at Aiden's face. He looked ready to slap Dudley's sniffles away.

"Tell me more about this date," Aiden ordered.

"She's a model from Asia. Can you believe it? She found my profile on a dating service and contacted me. She said she was coming here in May for the horse races and hoped I'd be her date. Then last night she texted saying she would be in town for tonight only, and she wanted to stop by the lab."

Nabi let go of Piper as Aiden put the cap back on the needle. "Let me see all your electronic devices," Nabi ordered as he held out his hand for Dudley's phone. "Unlock it, genius."

Dudley unlocked his phone and handed it over to Nabi. "Did you talk to her on your computer?"

"Yes," Dudley admitted, hanging his head. "I know I wasn't supposed to use a work computer for it, but my other computer's video camera isn't working, and I really wanted to talk to her in person, you know? And see her on a bigger screen. She's so beautiful." Dudley sighed.

"Unlock it too," Nabi ordered. "Any other electronics you used to talk with her?"

Dudley shook his head. "Am I fired for telling her about your project? I might have made it sound as if I were more involved with it than I was. But I swear, I didn't give many details. I just told her all the good it could do."

"And the bad?" Piper asked. When Dudley cringed, she had her answer.

"I hate to tell you this, but you were played," Aiden said, letting go of the man.

"Played? How?" Dudley asked.

"Is this the woman you talked with?" Nabi asked, turning Dudley's phone for him to see.

"Yes, that's my Kimmie."

"No, this is an actress from Shanghai named Zhang Li," Nabi told him before he picked up his own phone and ordered Nash to find all bank transactions for Zhang Li.

"An actress?" Dudley asked with confusion and hurt written all over his face as the realization began to sit in. He dropped onto his stool with his shoulder slumped forward. "I was played. I should have known a woman as beautiful as that wouldn't want anything to do with a nerd like me."

"Some people find intelligence incredibly sexy," Aiden said even though Piper realized he was looking at her when he said it.

"Not attractive ones," Dudley muttered and Piper's face flushed. Aiden was beyond attractive.

"If it makes a difference," Nabi started as he read through the private conversations between Dudley and the actress, "it appears he didn't mean to sell you out. This actress must have been coached, or more likely, it was Phobos or one of his men doing the chatting, and they just used the actress when Dudley started asking to see her. He was catfished."

Dudley's shoulders shook silently, and Piper could no longer be angry when it was clear his heart was breaking. Well, she was still angry, but she no longer felt like killing him. Now she just felt sorry for him.

"I'll work on tracking this down, but in the meantime, let's use this to our advantage," Nabi said as he set the laptop on the table. "Should we send them on a wild goose chase?"

Nabi didn't have time to type anything when a new message came across. "They're writing," he said seriously. Piper sat up and held her breath as she waited for Nabi to read the message.

"*Good morning, handsome. I just got done with a meeting*

and thought I'd see how you are doing being a superhero to millions. Have you been working on your project today? I'm excited to see you tonight."

Dudley's red-rimmed eyes looked up as he bit his lip to stifle another sniffle. "How could I have been so dumb?"

"*No*," Nabi said as he typed out the response. "*I am working on something new. Piper is solely working on the project now*. Is that what you would say?"

Dudley looked even more deflated as he instructed Nabi to insert a frowny face.

"*That sucks. What a bitch to take away your project when you were so close to figuring it out. Where is she? I'd like to give her a piece of my mind when I see you tonight. She should respect you more."* Nabi read.

"I have to hand it to them, they're excellent at manipulation. The way they're hiding the question in the anger for your loss of the job is perfect," Aiden said as he moved closer to take a look at the messages. "Tell them Piper left town. Let's see how much they know."

"*Piper left town this morning. I don't know when she's going to get back, but when she does, I'm going to talk to her about it."*

"Add an angry face," Dudley told him. "I use a lot of emojis."

"Don't we all?" Aiden deadpanned.

"Maybe she went to Rahmi? Did she take the project with her or can you work on it while she's gone? That way you can solve it and rub it in her face when she gets back," Nabi read before looking to Aiden. "How do you want to handle this?"

"Vagueness is good. And we don't want them coming after Dudley here. So tell them you don't know where it is. She cleaned out her office here," Aiden told Nabi who started to type.

"Have to go. Just got a text that I have to fly to Paris tonight. I'm sorry I won't get to meet you tonight. Talk soon, handsome."

"I'm thinking you're not going to hear from her again. Sorry, mate," Aiden said as he clasped Dudley on the shoulder.

Piper drew a deep breath. "I'm sorry, Dudley, but for now you're suspended. I'll reevaluate when this all gets resolved and someone isn't trying to kill me. Until then, I need you to get your things and leave." Piper had never felt so awful as she did watching Dudley pack up his things and leave the lab.

"I'll turn off access for his keycard. He won't be able to log on to the website or enter the building. I'm sorry, Piper," Nabi said, grabbing Dudley's electronics. "What do you want to do now?"

Piper wanted this over, that's what she wanted done. She didn't want to wait until who knows when. And there was one way she knew to hurry this along. "They know I'm not here. I could go to the Rahmi lab, safely away from all those I care about, and ambush them when they come after me."

"I don't like that idea," Aiden said, his voice low and stern.

"I don't either," Nabi added. "It's bad enough they would be able to get to you, but also the virus? That's too dangerous."

Piper grinned as the idea came to her. As much as she wanted to keep the virus in her grasp, she had a better idea —one that would keep her alive if she ever got caught. "Anyone have a refrigerator I can borrow?"

12

"You want to hide the virus that could kill millions, if not billions of people, in someone's fridge?" Aiden asked with disbelief.

"Yes, preferably someone with zero connection to me or Keeneston."

"A bargaining chip in case something happens to you," Nabi said, putting the pieces together as they drove back to Keeneston.

Aiden let out a sigh as he drove the car to Desert Sun Farm. Nash was going to meet them there so they could formulate a plan. But Piper had a good point. They needed to get the virus someplace safe. Damn, and he knew exactly where to go. "I know where we can store the virus. It's even on our way, kind of, to Rahmi."

"So, it's a go then?" Piper asked as she tried to sound brave.

"It's a go. But I don't like it. I want to keep you safe, not make you a target," Aiden said, hoping she'd change her mind, but it was to no avail. Soon they had dropped off Nabi, talked to Nash, gotten permission to use Prince Mo and Princess Dani's private plane that night, and were already back at Piper's packing in no time.

He made her pack with the bedroom door open so he could hear her as Aiden placed his phone call. "Hello, mate."

"Aiden? What a bloody surprise," Byron Wickens, or Wick to all his friends, said. "I haven't heard from you in a month. But your mum said business is going well."

"It is, and that's why I need your help."

"Anything," Wick said without even asking. After all, that's what childhood chums did.

"I'm flying into Chivenor tomorrow and need a ride into town," he said about the Royal Marines' base that also allowed private planes just a short distance from Lynton.

"Is that all? Flying fancy in a private plane and you just need a lift?" Wick asked as he teased Aiden. They'd grown up together and gone into the military together, except Wick had gone into the navy and was now back in Lynton, stationed at Chivenor, the British military airfield on the north coast of Devon.

"There might be a little more to it than that. Does the base happen to have a spare fridge?"

AIDEN HUNG up with Wick as he went off to talk to the base command about storing something for the Americans. Either way, in two hours, they would be in the air, bound for England. Aiden set the phone down and stood up. He stretched as he looked out the front windows and was instantly on alert when he saw a car pulling into the driveway. Aiden grabbed his gun, flicked off the safety, and stood beside the door. He waited, hearing the car doors open and shut. He heard feet on the steps and when they stopped at the door, Aiden flung the door open and leveled the gun.

In seconds he had two guns pointed at him as he eyed the two men. "Miles and Cy Davies," Aiden said, recognizing them from their pictures online. "I'm Aiden Creed."

"We know," Miles said as all three lowered their guns. "We're here to have a little chat with you."

Aiden stepped back from the door, and they walked inside. He loved hanging out in the bars back home and listening to retired soldiers tell their war stories. He bet these two had some he had never heard. The fact that Cy had been a spy and not a soldier meant his stories would be even more interesting.

"What can I do for you, sir?" Aiden asked, standing at attention. It was a hard habit to break when talking to a man like Miles. It was clear he had been a high-ranking officer by the way he comported himself.

Miles and Cy looked around and then stepped closer so as to not be overheard. "My brother Pierce has been way too slack with his parental obligation toward his daughters," Miles said as Cy nodded and held out his hand.

Aiden looked at what Cy was showing him and then back at the two brothers. "Spot GPS trackers?"

"Put them on all of Piper's clothing, shoes, phones, and whatever you can get your hands on. Then we'll know where she is all the time. And I have this great app to hack into her phone so you can see where she is and listen in," Miles said in a whispered voice.

"I used them with both my girls," Cy added.

"Didn't one of your daughters secretly date a man for a year?" Aiden asked Cy.

Instead of anger, Cy smiled. "I also taught them well."

"Pierce has never done this. He's never read their messages, hacked their email, or followed them on dates . . . not that I would do that," Miles said sheepishly.

"I did and I'm not ashamed. My daughters are happily married now. I chased off all the pansies who were too scared to face me," Cy said with pride. "But, the point is Piper wouldn't be looking out for these things, which would make it easier for you to keep tabs on her."

Okay, so they did have a point. Maybe it wouldn't hurt to cover all his bases. Aiden reached out and took the handful of tiny spot GPS trackers and shoved them in his pocket. "Thank you," he told them.

"Let us know if you need anything," Miles said, handing over his card. "We are very good in situations like these, and we have connections you can only dream of."

Aiden added Miles's phone number to his phone right then and gave the card back. "I'll take you up on that. I do need something stored in a fridge at Chivenor."

"Consider it done."

"It's good to know there's someone out there who has your back," Aiden said to them.

"I know several older SAS men. Good guys and I'm sure you are too."

"You're just saying that since Layne is married, and you don't have to worry about her anymore," Piper said teasingly from her doorway.

Miles shrugged. "True. Never thought I'd like a froggie, but Walker's a good guy."

"What are you two doing here?" Piper asked as she walked down the small hall and into the living room. Aiden couldn't keep his eyes off her. She was in black stretchy pants and had on a pale green, long-sleeved T-shirt that hugged her breasts perfectly. She was beautiful. Her hair was down around her shoulders, her eyes lined with a little makeup and her lips seemed to shine. Aiden would give anything to taste them.

"I know that look," Cy whispered to Miles as he pulled out his phone. Aiden looked down and saw it was the Keeneston Betting App.

"Yup," Miles agreed, pulling out his phone and placing a bet before looking back up at Piper. "We're here to offer our help if you need it."

"Thank you, Uncle Miles, but I'll feel better when we get away from Keeneston for a little bit. I don't want to put any of you in harm's way."

"Sweetie," Cy said as he put away his phone, "harm's way is like a fun night out for us. Never worry about that. We're here if you need us. Always."

"Thank you, Uncle Cy," Piper said with a fond smile. As she hugged Cy, he motioned for Aiden to go into the bedroom.

Aiden had to fight the grin he wanted to show as he told Piper he'd get her bags while she talked to her uncles. When she protested, Miles smoothly drew her into conversation, letting Aiden slip into the bedroom. He looked at all her stuff and pulled out the dots. He tagged shirts, jackets, jeans, shoes, and bras that sent his mind down a different path from what he should be doing. After a very vivid image of what he'd like to do if he ever got to see Piper's breasts up close again, he managed to tag all of her electronics before putting them back and carrying out the bags.

"All ready," he said, more to Miles and Cy than to Piper.

Piper took a deep breath and nodded. "Let's go. I already said goodbye to my parents. Make sure my mom doesn't kill my dad, okay?" she asked her uncles as they walked out of the house. Aiden locked the door behind them and used the remote fob to activate the alarm.

"We'll be watching out for you both," Miles promised as Aiden rolled his eyes at them. Son of a bitch, they put a GPS tracker on him, too.

The two older men chuckled as they got into their truck and drove off. "The plane should be ready. Is there anything else you need?" Aiden asked Piper as he put her luggage with his in the back of the SUV.

"I don't think so," Piper said sadly, looking at her house before getting into the SUV. "What if this is the last time I see my house or my family?"

"It won't be. I'll make sure you get home," Aiden swore.

"But what if they get me?"

"Then I'll come after you. I'll always come for you, Piper."

~

I'll always come for you, Piper. Piper sighed as the private jet cruised across the Atlantic toward England. If only it wasn't because she was paying him to do so. After all this, paying a man would probably be the only way she could have a man in her life. No one in Keeneston, even Cody Gray who had shown interest in a one-night stand, would touch her after all this trouble.

It wasn't as if Aiden would either. He was gorgeous. And sexy. And if her Internet search taught her anything, it was that he dated incredibly sexy and sophisticated women who had tea with royalty and wore those beautiful little thousand-dollar hats one time before they stored them away forever.

And that was not Piper. In fact, that was the farthest

thing from her there was. She might rub shoulders with royalty, but it's not like her friends were the Queen of England. Okay, so they were princes. And princesses. But they didn't act like it. They were just her friends. And they didn't invite her to official state business. Aiden was the strong man every mother dreamed her daughter would bring home and only a select few with the right name and political connections had been able to.

Lady Anne, an equestrian, was the latest girlfriend. Her father was an advisor to the queen. She never had a hair out of place. She raised money for charities. She was the perfect girlfriend. Piper let out a sigh and cast a side-eye glance at Aiden. He was sitting on the couch with his legs stretched out and crossed at the ankles while his head was back and eyes were closed. She found talking to him to be so easy. He seemed to understand her, or maybe that was because she was paying him.

Aiden Creed, gigolo bodyguard. Piper felt her cheeks flush at the thought of Aiden sitting up and stripping out of his prim button-up shirt. It was hard to believe the put-together man who regularly wore a suit was once a part of the deadly SAS. He seemed more at home on Wall Street than with a gun. Piper had read Jane Austen. Maybe Aiden was the second son of a wealthy family who had chosen to work for a living. In the world of Austen, they were either clergy or military. It would be a damn shame to have Aiden lost to the cloth.

"If you continue staring at me like that, I'll start to think you want me."

Piper didn't blush. She turned redder than a dog's nose after sniffing a porcupine. "I don't want you," Piper said as she hoped God didn't strike her dead with a lightning bolt for lying.

"The lady doth protest too much," Aiden said, quoting Hamlet. And okay, an Englishman quoting Shakespeare was sexy enough to cause the embarrassing blush to spread down her neck and heat her insides. "Oh, if I knew I'd get that reaction, I'd have quoted Shakespeare earlier. Or Byron? Had to learn both in school as a lad."

Get it together. He's just a man. A drop-dead sexy man. And she knew exactly how to get him to stop teasing her. "Did you know that researchers at the University of Washington Health Sciences found the immune system generated a molecule, nitric oxide, inhibits Staphylococcus aureus' transformation from its benign quiescent colonizing state to virulent form? I just read that in *Science Daily* and found it fascinating."

"No, I didn't know that. Of course, if my science teacher looked like you, I might have paid attention more. Why do you find it fascinating?"

Piper's mouth fell open before she snapped it closed as Aiden leaned forward and focused his eyes on hers. They didn't appear to be glazed over from boredom like all the other men she dated. "I'm sure you don't want a girl to explain it all to you. Most men hate when I talk about things they don't understand."

"I'm not most men. I think it's incredibly sexy how smart you are." Aiden sat back and patted the couch next to him. "Come. Tell me all about staph infections. You know, they're actually a real problem in the military since we're all in close quarters together. Especially when someone gets one that is resistant to antibiotics. It can ruin his career."

Piper stared at the man. He knew what she was talking about. Sure, staph was in the name of the virus, but most men would have zoned-out to even pick up on it, nevertheless ask her to talk about it.

"Really?" she asked.

"Really." Aiden patted the couch again and she stood, took a few steps, and then sat next to him. Aiden put his arm across the back of the couch and Piper leaned back, resting her head against his arm as she talked about staph and the results from the research the article had told about.

Aiden asked questions, listened, and by the end of the explanation, his hand was cupping her shoulder as his thumb drew lazy circles on her arm while she rested her head against his shoulder. "You're doing this because you're being paid, right?" Piper asked suddenly.

"Doing what?" Aiden asked as his body stayed completely relaxed next to hers. And oh God, the smell. His smell. It was intoxicating. Maybe he was doused in pheromones.

"*This*," she said, pointing to his hand on her shoulder. "Talking to me, feigning interest in viruses and my work, feigning interest in me. Because you don't have to do that. I can just as easily work on FAVOR without you making me feel all . . . well, just all. Which I should probably be doing anyway, working on my project, that is. I know you're not my friend. And I know you're not my boyfriend." Piper almost stopped, but while she was the quiet one with a bad track record in dating, it didn't mean she'd fall for the first man to show her any interest.

"I can't be," Aiden said tightly even though he didn't remove his hand from her shoulder.

"So then, why all the pretending? You're a good guy, Aiden. You don't have to flirt with the lab nerd to make me feel better."

Aiden grabbed her shoulder as he sat up straight, bringing her with him as he turned her to face him. Piper was shocked at how angry he was. She guessed he didn't like being called out for it. It wasn't as if he depended on a tip at the end of this like a bartender who flirted with the single women. She didn't understand why he was so upset.

"Listen to me. I'm only going to say this once, so pay attention. You are bloody amazing. You're smart, beautiful, and any man should roll over and thank his lucky stars to have you with him. But it can't be me, even if I want it to be me. And I do. But not while you're my client. Emotions cloud my judgment and reaction time. I'm already attached more than I should be. If we did all the things I have been thinking about, I wouldn't be doing my job. Instead, you'd be too exhausted to make it out of bed, much less work on fixing your project. So, until you no longer need me to protect you, we will have to suffice with dreaming. But *never* think I'm not interested."

Piper blinked as Aiden leaned back against the couch and pulled her back to his chest. He wrapped his arm around her shoulder again as his thumb started rubbing absently, sending her nerves to tingle. "Now that we have that settled. Tell me all about FAVOR. Think back to when you first thought of the idea. Start there and tell me everything."

"Even the big words?" Piper tried to tease as her heart was currently having a hissy fit in her chest. She imagined it as a bunch of girls jumping up and down screaming with excitement. At least that's what it felt like inside after hearing Aiden say he wanted more, only his job couldn't let him. And she understood that. Layne had suffered the same situation, but then when Walker had been discharged . . . Damn, Piper really needed to fix her project and fast, because if Aiden wasn't lying and he was interested, only fixing the project would allow them a chance together.

"I was in the bathtub," Piper started. She giggled when Aiden groaned.

"Details. Every detail is important. Were there bubbles?"

Piper laughed and felt her body relax into his. She closed her eyes and began to talk. She didn't know how long she talked, but it had to have been hours. And then it hit her. It was like a moment of clarity. Somewhere during her retelling, she'd grabbed her old notebooks to show him and explain her line of thinking. And now she was frantically making notes. Talking through it had shown her where she'd made at least two errors in her process—errors that could be the key to fixing FAVOR.

13

He was a bloody idiot. Aiden checked in on his phone as the plane descended. Five hours ago, after confessing to a client he wanted to pin her to his bed and shag her until she couldn't walk, he'd reined in his lust and listened to her talk about her work. When she finished, she didn't say anything. She got up, moved to the table, and started frantically writing. She'd been doing that ever since.

"We're almost there, babe," Aiden said before squeezing his jaw shut. He'd just realized he'd been calling her *babe*. Everyone in England called women *luv*, but *babe* was usually reserved for someone special. He'd have to watch himself now. In America it didn't seem to have been noticed, but at home it would be.

"Okay. I have some ideas, but I'll need some things from the Rahmi lab before I can test them out." Piper's long hair was pulled back into what had been a sloppy bun a couple hours ago. Now half of it was falling out and she was constantly pushing it back from her face. She was adorable.

"So, who are we meeting here?" Piper asked as she began packing up her notebooks.

"A childhood friend of mine," Aiden told her as the plane came to a stop.

"And he'll keep FAVOR safe?" Piper asked, grabbing the container from the mini-fridge and stuffing the cooler with the ice packs.

"It'll be very safe. Especially since your uncle Miles called in a favor." The door opened, the stairs were lowered, and Aiden found Wick grinning up at him, flanked by five armed guards. "That favor."

"Who are they?" she asked.

"Her Majesty's finest. They'll provide around-the-clock protection of FAVOR at the base. Almost nobody will know what it is or what it's doing there. These six men and the base commander only know it is something valuable. The commander is the only one with actual knowledge of what it is."

Piper seemed to relax as she followed him down the stairs. Wick stepped forward with a grin on his face as he thumped Aiden on his shoulder. "Remind me to go into private service," Wick said with a grin as he looked Piper over.

"Don't even think about it," Aiden warned, which made Wick grin even larger.

"Welcome to England, my lady," Wick said gallantly as he bowed over Piper's hand. The cold air whipped around them and Piper, though she grinned, was shivering. Protective instincts raced through him as he pulled her close to him to block the wind.

"Let's get inside," Aiden said, cutting off whatever shenanigans Wick still had up his sleeve.

"Where will they keep my project?" Piper asked once inside.

"In the commander's personal office," Wick answered as

an older gentleman began to walk toward them. "Armed officers will be outside the door at all times until you retrieve it."

"Thank you," Piper said, completely ignoring all the charm Wick was pouring on.

"Dr. Davies"—the older man held out his hand—"I'm Commander Suffolk. I've been briefed by your uncle and am ready to take possession of your work. No one will touch it. I swear to it."

"Thank you, commander," Piper said as she reluctantly handed over the cooler. A guard took it, and Aiden could tell she didn't want it out of her sight.

"Why don't you go with him to make sure everything is properly set up," Aiden suggested. He was rewarded with a smile before Piper trailed after the guard.

"You lucky bastard," Wick said as he watched Piper head toward the office. The commander shook his head.

"It's an interesting family your client comes from. I take it her uncle was a higher-up in Special Forces. When you're given the number for the head of the Rahmi Security Forces, an untraceable number to someone named Dylan, and another number I'm pretty sure belongs to the White House, you pay attention."

Aiden smiled, not surprised at all. "Nothing about that surprises me. You wouldn't believe the residents of that town. Ahmed lives there. A DEVGRU man. FBI. And three old women who threatened me with kitchenware. And that's not counting the woman who reminds me of my mum who ran over a man in a minivan."

"We were asking questions, and you're teasing us," Wick said with an eye roll.

"Ahmed, as in the Rahmi soldier?" the commander asked with wide eyes.

"That's right. His mentees are looking into who we think is behind the attacks on my client."

"Who's he?" Wick asked, suddenly interested.

The commander let out a low whistle. "Ahmed is the deadliest soldier ever known. I can't even begin to know how many people he's killed. They say he single-handedly overthrew King Nassar some thirty years ago."

"So, why isn't he looking after the hot scientist?" Wick asked.

"She didn't want anyone from town to do it. She was afraid something might happen to them. And it's a good thing too. She's been attacked three times already. Once when she was alone, once when I was in transit when the minivan-mowing mum saved her, and even once when I was with her."

"And you're going to be staying in Lynton? At your mum's house?" Wick asked with surprise.

"No. I'm just picking up some supplies. We're on our way to Rahmi to set a trap."

"I thought you retired from the SAS," the commander said wryly.

"I did too, but I can't trust anyone else with this," Aiden admitted.

"I'm ready."

Aiden was cut off from having to say anything else when Piper arrived.

"Then let me escort you to your chariot, luv," Wick said as he held out his arm. Piper shook her head in amusement but took his arm. Soon they were on their way home.

"There's my boy!" Aiden's mum cried as she burst from the house.

Aiden opened his arms and wrapped his mum in a tight hug, lifting her penny-loafered feet from the ground. "Hello, Mum." Aiden set her down and turned to Piper. "This is Piper Davies. Piper, this is my mum."

"Mrs. Creed," Piper said, holding out her hand. "It's nice to meet you."

His mum shot him an approving look, and Aiden didn't know whether to feel embarrassed or proud. Frustrated. That's what he ended up feeling because Piper wasn't his woman. She was his client.

"Come in, come in. Aiden said you had something you wanted me to keep safe."

Piper looked confused so Aiden stepped in. "Piper, I think you should write down whatever you need from Rahmi, but nothing more. Then leave the notebooks with my mum. That way everything is separate and safe."

He saw her think about it as she nibbled a lip—a lip he wanted to suck into his mouth and run his tongue over. Bugger. Aiden took a deep breath to control himself before his mind ran away from him and his prick followed.

"Won't that put her in danger?" Piper asked quietly, but his mum answered for him.

"Oh, no worries about that, luv. I'll keep it at the pub. No one will bother me there."

"Will someone find it?"

"Not a chance. I'll keep it behind the light hoppy beer imported from the States. That stuff has been in the pub for years. Fancy a cuppa while Aiden gets his stuff? It'll give us a chance to get to know each other."

Aiden watched as his mum dragged Piper into their small cottage house to serve her tea as Wick laughed. "You are so screwed."

"Don't I wish," Aiden said dryly.

"Can you give me a couple hours to get everything together?"

"Sure. I'll pop down to the pub. We'll meet you there. Thanks, Wick."

"Hey, what are mates for?"

Aiden waited for Wick to drive off before heading back to the locked shed in the small garden that backed up to the wilds of Lynton. Mountains, rocky cliffs, valleys, streams, and even the ocean all made up Lynton's views. And right now the cold air and the darkening clouds gave Lynton a very gothic appearance.

Aiden pulled a key from his pocket and unlocked the door. Inside, he turned on the single light bulb to reveal his past. All his SAS gear was packed away in trunks. Unlocking them, he pulled a bulletproof vest to add under Piper's jacket, night vision goggles, guns, knives, and everything else he'd need to keep Piper safe and put them in his old rucksack.

When Aiden made it back to the house, his mum and Piper were laughing. He stood in the doorway and watched the way Piper made his mum feel at ease. She talked, asked questions, and complimented her on the tea. "Oh, luv, I'm so glad my Aiden found a nice girl. I've been worried about him, you know. Going around with women who were all wrong for him."

"Okay, Mum," Aiden said, hurrying into the room. He noticed Piper didn't correct his mum's assumption that they were a couple. "I thought we could walk to the pub where we're meeting Wick so you could see a little of the town."

"I'd like that. Would you join us, Mrs. Creed?"

"Yes, luv. I believe I will."

Aiden walked shoulder to shoulder with Piper and it seemed only natural to turn his hand so he could hold hers. His mum smiled when she caught sight of it while Piper didn't pull away. Instead, she squeezed his hand and sent his heart racing. His heart had been so closed off since he'd lost his father before enlisting it didn't seem possible to break through the walls he'd built up. But sweet, unassuming, smart-as-a-whip Piper was doing just that.

Women at pubs could catch his eye when he was in the SAS. And after, as he became a professional, he found himself fancied by the women of the aristocracy who loved being with someone dangerous. It had been all fun and games, but nothing more. He'd seen his mother's heart break when his father died. And knowing he was going off to battle, he didn't want to do that to someone else. Or himself. He knew the likelihood of cheating while on deployment, so why put him or a woman in that position? Then when he got back he wasn't ready to open himself up to that kind of pain.

But now, his heart was slowly stretching after being asleep for so long. And he felt it—the flutters, the inability to stop himself from reaching out and touching Piper in some way, the dreams he had when he closed his eyes. If he didn't stop this soon, he'd be in love in no time with the one woman who was off limits.

"What a cute town! You weren't kidding when you said you knew how small towns worked. This place is even smaller than Keeneston, but it's so beautiful," Piper said, interrupting his thoughts as she looked all around.

"This is the pub I work at." His mum pointed out the nearest building painted white with brown trim.

Piper looked at the bag she was carrying, and with a

deep breath handed it over to his mum. "Take good care of it. Don't let anyone see it or take it."

"I promise. No one will think anything of it. But to be sure, why don't I send Wick out here so it appears you're here to see him instead of me. Even though there will already be some gossip," she said, staring pointedly to a curtain at a nearby house that was drawn back.

"Just like home," Piper said with a laugh. "Thank you, Mrs. Creed. I really appreciate it."

"Of course, luv. Take good care of my lad. He may not show it, but he has a big heart."

"Mum," Aiden groaned as Piper slipped her hand back into his. Okay, so maybe his mum needed to embarrass him some more if it got Piper touching him.

His mum kissed his cheek and headed into the pub.

"Your mom is sweet." Piper paused as she looked down at their intertwined hands. "This is harder than I thought it would be."

"What do you mean?" Aiden asked, his heart stopping as he feared she'd pull away.

PIPER STARED at their hands clasped together. She'd been around men like Aiden her whole life and never thought she'd fall for a man like him. She'd always seen herself with someone who was quiet—a homebody like her. Someone who worked in a lab or an office. Never someone who spent his youth rock climbing and swimming in a cold ocean just to try to outswim his friends. But here she was, holding hands with Aiden Creed. The man she shouldn't like, but was drawn to nonetheless.

"We shouldn't like each other. We're nothing alike, and you're my bodyguard. I shouldn't cross that line. But I find myself wanting to blow that line to smithereens. It's harder than I thought to stay detached," Piper admitted. She may be the quiet one. She may be the one who never stood toe to toe with a criminal and fought, but she wasn't a coward. She wasn't ashamed of her feelings. Feelings that had turned from lust to something much more during the plane ride. Aiden seemed to complete her in a way. Not as opposites, but rather it was more complementary.

"I know," he said so softly the wind almost stole his words.

Aiden leaned closer to her, pushing her back against Wick's car. She felt the cold metal, but it did nothing to cool her heated body as Aiden stepped so close his feet bracketed hers. His hands came up to capture her face, and she stopped breathing as his thumbs gently brushed her cheeks before he lowered his head toward hers. Piper's eyes closed as she lifted her lips.

"Oi! You ready to go or do I need to give you some privacy?"

"Piss off, you tosser," Aiden growled to Wick who was smirking as he walked toward them with two to-go boxes.

Piper saw Aiden struggle to compose himself, but he finally stood up straight and took a step back from her. Her heartbeat dropped back to normal, and she didn't know if she were disappointed or relieved that the moment had been interrupted. Piper had a feeling a kiss from Aiden would somehow change her and she wasn't sure she was ready for that.

Wick handed Aiden the boxes with a wink and got into the car. "Let's go."

Piper felt herself shaking with unused adrenaline. Her body was pumping with longing, but she knew she couldn't act on it, no matter how badly she wanted to. She could wait.

Just like Layne, she was going to use the time to get to know Aiden and see if they had a shot at something more. How someone based out of London could date her, she didn't know. Piper sighed as she climbed into the car. See, there were problems already popping up and that wasn't even counting the people coming after her for FAVOR.

14

During the long flight to Rahmi, she'd talked to her friends and family who had assured her that her mother was not in labor and no new people had shown up in Keeneston. She was about to close her eyes and take a nap when Aiden knocked on the bedroom door.

"Come in," she called out as she sat up.

Aiden's eyes instantly darkened when he saw her lying on the bed. His hand tightened on the door and Piper would have given anything to be one of those women who threw caution to the wind by ripping off her shirt and telling Aiden to take her now.

"I just got off the phone with Nash. There's been a development," Aiden said tightly.

That got Piper's attention. "Is anyone hurt?" she asked as she scrambled toward the end of the bed and sat up on her knees.

"No. They traced the IP address for the dating site messages used to communicate with Dudley. It didn't belong to the actress, but to a man they suspect works for Phobos."

"Oh," Piper said, sitting back down. "Didn't we expect that?"

"Yes. But what they didn't expect was to find that same IP address communicating with someone at the Rahmi lab."

"Who?" Piper asked, sitting back up onto her knees.

"Don't know yet. Nash ran a diagnostics and found the incoming address on the network. But we need to be careful. There's an inside person at the lab." Aiden cleared his throat. "I'll, um, let you get back to bed."

"Wait," Piper said suddenly. She didn't know what had come over her except she didn't want him to leave. Aiden paused, his knuckles turning white as he gripped the door.

"Yes?"

"Stay with me. We don't have to sleep." Piper heard a low groan come from Aiden. "I don't mean *that*. I mean, sit and talk with me. I want to know more about you."

Aiden didn't move and Piper thought he was going to say *no*, but he stepped into the small bedroom and closed the door behind him before taking a seat at the small desk in the corner of the room. "Did you like growing up an only child? I can't imagine it. There's certainly times I would have loved it. I never had privacy with two little brothers. I was nine before Cassidy came along. And now I'm about to have another brother or sister and I'm almost thirty. However, I can't imagine my life without them."

Piper lay down on the bed and pulled the pillow under her head as she watched Aiden lean back and stretch his legs. "I loved it. Wick was like a brother to me, but one I could leave to go home if he irritated me. He and I used to go climbing together. My parents were so mad when they found out we had climbed without ropes or adults watching us."

"Tell me more about you and Wick," Piper said, settling

into the pillow. She found herself drifting off to sleep as Aiden talked.

AIDEN LOOKED down at Piper as she slept. She looked so relaxed. So peaceful. He reached down and brushed a stray strand of hair from her face. "I'll protect you with my life," he swore before bending down and placing a long soft kiss to her temple.

He quietly left the room and closed the door behind him. He picked up his computer and phone and got to work calling the Rahmi guard he was going to be working with. He studied blueprints and photos of the lab along with the town. They were staying at the palace while they were in Rahmi. Mo had called his brother, King Dirar, and explained the situation. Apparently very thankful to Piper for starting the lab, Aiden was told Piper regularly stayed at the palace and was welcome to this time as well. Further, Ahmed had sent over a drawing of the palace, with exits and safe rooms marked. By the time they landed, Aiden had a mental map of the entire area.

The door to the bedroom opened and Piper stepped out in a wrinkled shirt, hair sticking out, and sleep still in her eyes. "Are we there?"

"Yes, babe. We are. We'll head to the palace and get settled in. I can meet with Nash's contact while you freshen up. He'll be supplying the soldiers to assist with the ambush."

Aiden picked up the bags and waited for Piper to slip her shoes on as he chastised himself. He couldn't stop staring at her as she tied her shoes. He had to push his feelings aside for her and move on. He had a job to do, and he was going to do it. So what if he couldn't get enough of her stories about Keeneston and growing up? So what if he respected the hell out of her accomplishments? So what if he found her delightfully funny? So what if the idea of dating someone longer than a couple weeks at a time sounded good only if that someone was Piper? He had a job to do, and he was going to do it. Bloody hell, as long as she stopped bending over like that, that is.

Piper stood and Aiden's body brushed against hers as he passed her so he could exit first. "Stay on the plane until I have everything cleared."

"Is that why the engines are still running?" Piper asked as she looked out the window.

"Yes. If anything happens, the pilot will take off immediately."

"But what about you?"

"Never stay behind for me," Aiden said sternly before taking off down the stairs.

PIPER NERVOUSLY WATCHED Aiden descend the stairs and look around. He shook hands with a soldier who took the bags and put them in the back of the car as Aiden climbed back into the plane.

"It's all clear. Let's go. And stay right behind me."

Piper stood behind him and looked at the country that had become a second home for her. Now she regarded it with suspicion. Who was there to kill her? Was it someone she knew? Piper stayed tucked in behind Aiden as they quickly made their way to the car. She recognized the driver and felt herself relax when she slid onto the leather seats. Aiden moved to sit up front and sat quietly while they drove to the palace. Aiden watched every building and car while

Piper watched Aiden. He took in everything as his eyes constantly roved from side to side.

Soon they were through the gates and pulling to a stop at the main entrance to the palace. Piper moved to open the door, but Aiden glared at her. Piper let out a huff and waited for him to open her door. Aiden looked so different when he was protecting her compared to when they were safely tucked away talking. All softness was gone. His posture was rigid. His eyes were constantly moving. His hand was hard when he took her hand in his to help her from the car. And when an elegant woman moved from the door to stand atop the steps, Aiden shoved Piper behind him.

"It's okay. That's Princess Nailah. Her husband is Prince Jamal, the heir to the Rahmi throne," Piper whispered as she put a gentle hand on his arm. His muscles were tense under her touch, but he gave her a small nod, showing he understood. Aiden reached behind her and placed his hand on the small of her back and practically propelled her up the steps.

"Piper!" Nailah greeted with a smile as she held out her hands. Piper grasped them as they kissed each other's cheeks in welcome. During Piper's time in Rahmi, she had become friends with the often-neglected princess. Hers had been an arranged marriage, one that neither wanted. And Jamal was definitely difficult to live with. Or at least he was until Mo sat him down and ripped into him a couple years before. Since then, the marriage had improved. It was far from perfect, but the positive changes were noticeable. Jamal was spending more time in Kentucky, learning things from his uncle and cousins that his father, King Dirar, wouldn't or couldn't teach him. They were simple things like working with your hands mucking out stalls for the satisfaction of a job well done.

"Nailah," Piper smiled as she looked closely at her friend. "I feel like it's been ages since I saw you last when it was only a couple months since you were in Keeneston."

"I know. So much has changed, my friend." Nailah paused to look at Aiden and then back to Piper. "Come, let me show you to your rooms, then we shall talk. You're right on time. We're having a large party tonight, and you're invited."

"Nailah, this is Aiden Creed. He's my bodyguard and will need to attend as well."

Nailah nodded without a single hair escaping her beautiful braid. "Of course. Jamal told me everything. I am so sorry to hear of your troubles. You know the whole guard is at your disposal."

"Thank you, Your Highness," Aiden told her as he followed behind the two women.

Piper loved the open-air palace. There were balconies everywhere and large windows with brightly colored drapes that seemed to warm every room. It took a moment to walk to the guest quarters, but Nailah had put Piper in her favorite room overlooking the gardens.

"Sir, your room is right next door. There is a hidden connecting door here." Nailah showed them a Moroccan-inspired wood screen that was really a door. "My husband, Jamal, will call for you shortly. You will be working with his personal security team while you are here."

Piper saw Aiden's surprised reaction, but he bowed his head politely and thanked her. "I'll unpack and await his call. Thank you, ma'am." Aiden turned to Piper and when he looked at her, she felt as if she were the only person in the whole world. "Just call out if you need me. I'll have my phone with me too. I will make sure there is a guard outside your door before I go anywhere."

Piper smiled at him and nodded. "Thanks, Aiden." She waited until Aiden disappeared behind the secret door that Nailah quickly closed behind him.

"Okay, what's going on?" Piper asked with a sly smile as Nailah hurried back across the room.

"Well, you know we've been spending more time in Keeneston, and it appears being around Mo and Dani and our cousins has really made an impact on Jamal. About six months ago he asked me on a date."

Piper grinned as she grabbed her friend's hands and squeezed them happily. "That's wonderful!"

"Yes. And it continued when we got back to Rahmi. We've taken boat rides together. We even snuck out of the palace to walk among the people as a happy couple like Zain and Mila do when they are here. And then, the last night we were in Keeneston a couple months ago, he took me into the gardens at night and told me he loved me!" Nailah could barely contain her excitement.

"Oh, Nailah! I'm so happy for you." Piper flung her arms around her friend and hugged her. When she had first met Nailah, she'd never imagined they would become friends. Nailah was timid and isolated. Now she seemed free and confident.

"There's more." Nailah was practically bouncing off the bright blue couch they were sitting on. "That night Jamal told me he loved me, well, our passions could not be contained. The doctor examined me this morning, and I'm pregnant!"

Piper gasped. They'd been trying to get pregnant for years. The king was so worried he wouldn't have a spare heir that Zain had been appointed next in line for the throne after Jamal. And unfortunately in a very similar way, Mila and Zain were also having problems getting pregnant, though they had been married for a much shorter time.

"I don't know how to tell you how excited I am for you!" Piper almost shouted as she hugged her friend again.

"We are making the announcement tonight. There will be a grand feast. The king also said he has a gift he will present to us, and then dancing. Please say you'll sit with me at the head table. I know I have friends here now, but you'll always be my first true friend."

"Of course. I'd be honored to." Piper froze as she looked wide-eyed at Nailah. "Have you told Zain and Mila yet?"

Nailah nodded with a large smile on her face. "Jamal and I video-called them a couple hours ago. I imagine the look of relief on Mila's face mirrored my own when the doctor told me I was pregnant. Now I must pray it's a boy so we can have an heir."

There was a knock on the door, and Piper called for them to come in. Jamal strutted in, but instead of looking like his cocky self, he looked happy and relaxed. "Have you told her our news?"

"Yes, dear. And she agreed to sit with us at dinner."

"Oh, Jamal. I'm so happy for you both," Piper said sincerely as she gave him a tentative hug. It wasn't so long ago he would have tried to feel her up, but he'd grown a lot under Mo's tutelage.

"Thank you. My cousins were very happy as well." He laughed. "And be prepared to have my father talk your ear off. He's on the phone with Mo now, talking everything from baby names to nursery gifts." Jamal's smile fell then. "But I hear not all is well with you."

"Have you been filled in?" Piper asked.

"Yes. I talked to Nabi and Nash a little while ago. I am on my way to meet with your security. Let me know if you need anything." Jamal reached out and took Nailah's hand in his. "We consider you family, Piper. For what you've done for Rahmi with the lab and for the friendship you've given my wife. I will do all I can to help."

"Thank you, Jamal." Piper felt emotions rushing forward as her voice tightened.

"Now, I will leave you to your chat while I meet with Mr. Creed. I will see you shortly. The festivities begin in two hours."

Jamal left and closed the door behind him. Nailah grabbed her hand and dragged her to the closet. "I figured you wouldn't have anything formal to wear, so I had some of my clothes brought in."

She opened the door and Piper took in the beautiful dresses in bright cheerful colors and for a moment she forgot about the cloud following her. It had been banished, at least temporarily, with happiness and love. "Now, let's get ready while you tell me all about that sexy man you came with."

15

Aiden tightened the knot of his tie in the mirror as he listened to the giggling coming from Piper's room. Apparently the princess was a good friend of Piper's, and they were getting ready for tonight's celebration together. Aiden had been invited, but it was clear he was to be in the background while he was told Piper would be at the head table.

That was better for Aiden. He could easily keep an eye on things from the background. He could move, check out people, and react quicker. Jamal had set him up with his best guards and had given him permission to carry his weapons, which was much appreciated since Aiden didn't have a standing agreement with Rahmi.

Aiden looked at his watch and then knocked on the connecting door. "Come on in, Aiden," he heard Piper call out.

Aiden opened the door and saw Jamal and his wife holding hands. When they stepped out of the room, he saw Piper standing behind them in an emerald green dress that matched the green in her eyes, the gold beading along the bodice also matched the streaks of gold in her hazel eyes. The dress was fitted through the top and consisted of layers of wispy green fabric flowing to the ground. Her normally pulled-back hair was down in loose curls and pulled back from her face with a gold-beaded band that matched the top of her dress.

Aiden couldn't form words. She was breathtaking. But the longer he stood staring, he could see she grew more nervous. She broke her eye contact from him and looked at the floor. "It's a bit much," she said quietly. She didn't think she was beautiful. Aiden couldn't believe it.

"You're the most beautiful woman I have ever seen." Aiden crossed the room as Piper looked up. He cupped her face with his hands as he stared into her eyes. He saw hers looking into his, searching for answers he wasn't prepared to give.

"If you weren't my client I would kiss you right now. As it is, I'm going to have a very hard night. In more ways than one." Aiden looked down and grinned with amusement as Piper's eyes followed. She sucked in her breath at his very obvious arousal. It seemed to be an ongoing problem around her.

But in that moment, Piper seemed to change. She grinned mischievously and when she looked at him, her eyes were heated with desire. Gone was the girl worried about her looks. She'd been replaced by a vixen. And when Piper took a step closer to him and brushed his erection with her body, he groaned and tightened his fingers on the nape of her neck. "For this one moment, I am safe in your arms."

Aiden swallowed hard. "Fuck it," he said under his breath a moment before he dropped one hand to Piper's waist and used the other at the nape of her neck to angle her lips to his.

He didn't try to coax her with his kiss. Instead, he claimed her with it. All the frustration of having her off limits was unleashed. The forbidden element added heat to his kiss as he deepened it, his tongue thrust suggestively against hers as she melded her body to his. She fit perfectly in his arms. He had also thought Piper might be timid, and for a brief moment he thought about pulling back, but she responded with such pure passion he found himself almost frantic with need as she ran her hands down his chest.

"Oh, so sorry," Nailah gasped. "I was just seeing if Piper was ready, but I'll just meet you down there."

Aiden pulled back, expecting Piper to become bashful, and he was again pleasantly surprised when she didn't drop her hands from his chest or step away from him. "I'll meet you in the hall. Just need one minute."

"Sure," Nailah said with a big grin as she closed the door behind her. His Piper—and she *was* his—had just asked a princess to wait so she could be with him.

"I like being safe with you," Piper said in a voice that was so seductive he felt it in his bollocks. "I think it's stopped being a matter of *if* and turned into a matter of *when*," she said as she tilted her lips up to his one more time. Only this time there was a princess waiting for her, so Aiden placed a soft, sweet, and, unfortunately, short kiss on her lips and let her go.

"We'll find Phobos, then you're mine."

"I'll be yours for a night. Then we'll see," Piper said with a smirk that had Aiden wanting to prove himself to her so badly he ached. She winked at him and headed for the door as Aiden took some calming breaths. "Let's go, Nailah. Thanks for waiting."

The party was a surprise to everyone there. Aiden watched from behind and slightly off to the side of the dais where Piper sat at the end as the guests talked excitedly. He couldn't hear everything they were saying, but he could read the curiosity on their faces.

"The bodyguard?" Nailah whispered to Piper. Piper looked quickly over at him, but he was too busy scanning the crowd to care about a little kiss-and-tell. In fact, he was rather proud of himself. He liked being linked to Piper.

"Shh. He'll hear you."

"No, he won't. He's not paying attention. I guess I picked the right dress."

"We're not doing anything," Piper protested. "He's protecting me. That's it."

"Protecting you with his body," Nailah said with a giggle. It was hard for Aiden not to smile at that comment, but he kept to his job as he scanned the crowd.

"We haven't done that yet. And I don't know if we will," Piper confessed. Well, now she had his attention. He was pretty sure they'd just talked about being together after she was safe. Was she regretting their kiss?

"Why ever not? Don't you want to?"

"Of course I want to. Have you seen him? But it's more than that. I like him. Like, I *like* him."

Aiden chanced a glance toward them and saw Nailah shaking her head. "That doesn't make sense."

"I'm afraid I might like him too much and then end up like all his other girlfriends. Dumped two weeks later. I'm afraid I'll want more than that. I'm nothing like his past girlfriends. They're more like you—aristocratic, classy, and perfect. I'm the messy girl next door."

The music began signaling King Dirar's entrance and prevented Aiden from hearing more. But he didn't want to hear more. Piper had already given him enough to think about. It was true. He wanted her underneath him, on top of him, and every other way, but did he want her in his life for more than that? The answer came surprisingly easy for him —*yes*. He did. For the first time in a very long time he wanted more. And he wanted it with only Piper.

PIPER LOOKED at King Dirar as he stood with his wife and motioned for Jamal and Nailah to join him. Jamal was smitten with his wife, and Piper couldn't be more thrilled as she watched Jamal hold Nailah's hand in his as they stood next to his father.

"Ladies and gentlemen. Thank you for coming on such short notice, but much has changed since this morning. My son and his wife have been blessed with wonderful news. My first grandchild will be born in April," the king announced.

Nailah and Jamal beamed with happiness as the crowd went absolutely nuts. The king quieted the crowd and turned to Nailah and Jamal. "And for this special occasion, I have a gift. With the blessing of my council and family, I present this proclamation."

King Dirar turned to the crowd, opened a folded piece of paper and began to read. "I, King Dirar Ali Rahman, with the blessing and approval of the council, hereby enter into law absolute primogeniture for those born in the line of succession from this date forward."

Piper sucked in a breath as Nailah's mouth dropped open a moment before the king turned to her and handed her the paper. "I, on behalf of the people of Rahmi, celebrate you and wish all our blessings on our future king *or* queen."

Tears rolled down Nailah's face as the king and queen hugged her and Jamal. The crowd gathered at the palace was cheering and Piper heard fireworks and shouts coming from the town outside the palace walls. For the first time in history, the people of Rahmi could have a queen ruling them.

Piper looked to Aiden and found him scanning the crowd, but then his eyes landed on hers. She could only describe them as hungry as he looked at her. Would she have this someday? Not the crown, but the celebration of love that created a new life? An image of Aiden standing next to her with his hand on her swollen belly flashed through her mind. And just as fast it was replaced with the gossip columns she read about Aiden having new semi-famous society girlfriends every month.

Her smile slipped and Aiden strode toward her. "What's wrong?"

"Nothing," she said as she turned to look at Jamal and Nailah waving to the crowd. Music started up and the royal couples took to the floor to open the dancing.

"I know enough about women to know when they say *nothing*, it is absolutely something." Her smile fell more and she knew the second Aiden put it together. "We need to talk."

"No, we don't. It was a silly feeling brought on by our circumstances," Piper said, suddenly feeling as if her heart were breaking.

"I won't let you do this," Aiden said sternly.

"Do what?"

"End us before we even begin." Aiden looked at the dance floor now filling with couples. "Dance with me."

He didn't give her a chance to argue. He took her hand and pulled her from her seat. "Aiden!"

"I'll have you crying my name in pleasure, not disappointment." Piper's heart and body tingled at his proclamation. "I'm not the best with relationships. It was hard to want one when I was always being shipped out at a moment's notice, and after, I was too busy building my company. But I know enough to know the real thing when she's dancing in my arms. Give us time, Piper. I can't commit right this second to a future together, but give me time. I need to end the threat against you. Then I want you to get to know me. Give us time to make something together. Something real. Something lasting. Will you give me that?" he asked as he stopped their dancing.

Piper's breath had caught the second he started talking. And now, standing together in the middle of the dance floor, Piper felt like a queen when he focused all his feelings on her. "Yes. I'll give you that. But, Aiden, I'm not a one-night stand. If I wanted that, I would have been with Cody."

"Cody? The deputy?" Aiden asked between clenched teeth. "I never liked him."

"So, where does that leave us now?" Piper asked, ignoring his posturing.

"It leaves me with a job to do and one hell of a first date to plan the second Phobos is dealt with."

Aiden pulled her close to him as she rested her hand against his chest and they began to sway to the music again. Piper felt his heartbeat under her hand. She felt every breath and the way it quickened as the hand holding her waist began to dip lower. And she felt the way her body heated as his eyes communicated everything they weren't able to say since the future was so unsure.

They could have been the only couple on the dance

floor for all Piper knew. She heard the music weaving a cocoon around them as Aiden masterfully led her around the floor. Their bodies brushed against each other, and his eyes never left hers. Piper could feel the heat from them as her breathing quickened in response. By the time Aiden brought her to a stop at the end of the song, Piper was heated, flushed, and her heart pounding as if Aiden had just made love to her.

"Promise me you'll give us a chance, Piper."

Piper didn't know what they had, but even a scientist like her could feel the chemistry. And it was off the charts. "Yes. I promise." Aiden lifted her hand to his lips and pressed a kiss on her knuckles before holding out his arm to escort her back to her table.

The party went well into the night, but Piper couldn't remember any of it after her dance with Aiden. Her heart was already thinking about love, while her brain was reminding her she'd only known him a couple days. Her heart and mind battled as her mind reminded her he lived an ocean away while her heart reminded her how she felt in his arms. By the end of the night, Piper was hopelessly confused as to what she should do. But one thing she was not confused about. She could easily fall in love with Aiden Creed.

16

Aiden scanned the area one last time before opening the door to the SUV. Rahmi guards were stationed all around the nanotech laboratory as he walked with Piper toward the front door. He hadn't slept much, and it made him jumpy. Deep down he knew it was the revelation that Piper had the possibility of being someone very special to him, and that led to the second reason he was jumpy. Someone in this lab was working with Phobos.

Piper showed no nerves as she walked into the facility she'd helped build. She knew everyone from the janitor to the receptionist and every scientist she passed. This visit had been announced, and Aiden was on high alert. They had an ambush planned, and Piper was the bait.

A young woman around Piper's age smiled as the two women hurried to hug each other. She looked similar to Piper with dark tanned skin, black hair pulled back into a messy ponytail, and a pink set of scrubs.

"Sada!" Piper said happily as she hugged the woman.

"Oh, Piper! I am so pleased to see you again. There's so much I can't wait to show you."

Piper turned with a smile on her face to introduce Aiden to her friend, but her smile fell when she took in his hard features as he scanned the lab. She'd momentarily forgot why she was there. Bait. With Dudley telling Phobos about FAVOR, they had to know she was here by now. Plus, in the back of her mind was the fact that Phobos had been in contact with someone in this lab.

"And I can't wait to see it." Piper felt as if everyone could see her smile turn fake as Sada took her around the lab and caught her up on what everyone was working on.

"It's so great you're here. I've missed our talks. I was just telling my boyfriend—" Sada was saying before Piper cut her off.

"Boyfriend? When did that happen?" Piper asked, excited for her friend. Like Piper, Sada spent way too much time in the lab. The two friends had frequently commiserated over their lack of love lives as they ate lunch while waiting for experiments to finish running.

"It's only been a couple of months. I met him on that dating site for scientists I told you about," Sada whispered as she eyed Aiden standing nearby.

Piper looked to Aiden and smiled. "Sada, this is my friend, Aiden. He's very good at keeping secrets. Go on, tell me more."

"Well, he just got to town yesterday, and we already had our first date. He's amazing," Sada sighed. "In fact, I was hoping you would join us tonight for dinner. I've told him all about this totally cool chick I work with," Sada winked, and Piper quickly agreed to dinner with her friend.

"He has a friend with him he could hook you up with," Sada said as she wiggled her eyebrows, which made Piper laugh.

"No, I'm good. But thank you."

"I'll let him know and make sure he's free. Tonight at seven at our usual place?"

"It's a date." Piper hugged Sada before heading to her office with Aiden hot on her heels.

"There's a dating site for scientists?" he asked as he closed the door to her office.

"Yup. Sada told me about it, but I was too busy to check it out."

"You won't be needing to anymore either," Aiden said, and Piper realized he was jealous of a site she hadn't even joined. It made her feel good in a slightly wicked way. "Anyway, as you were touring, we ran diagnostics on the network. No ingoing or outgoing communication from that IP address in the last couple of days. We also didn't catch anyone trying to use their cell phone or their computers while you were there."

"What does that mean?"

"I don't know," Aiden said truthfully. "So, what do you need to get here? I want to get you back to the palace. I don't like having you out in the open."

"I have some paperwork here, and I need to grab some equipment from the lab. That's all I need and then we can go back to the palace until dinner."

"Where is your regular spot? I need to check it out after I drop you off."

Piper told him about the small restaurant she and Sada always went to near the lab before enlisting some of the Rahmi guards to help her carry her lab equipment. She got some questioning looks from the other scientists, but no one asked why she was taking the equipment. One of the benefits of being the head scientist, she guessed. Either way, she was back in the palace in short order with the equipment she needed to take back to England so she could work on fixing FAVOR. At least now she felt as if she had a place to start.

~

AIDEN WALKED from the palace to the restaurant. He wore jeans, a T-shirt featuring Rahmi's professional cricket team, and a baseball cap down low over his eyes. He took a seat on the outdoor patio and ordered a drink as he watched people come and go. There were three exits, although more likely four: a front and back door, and a window in the men's restroom, which he guessed matched a window in the women's room.

Aiden smiled at the pretty waitress who brought him a refill. "I'm visiting the science lab and they recommended I come here. The drink is excellent."

"Thank you," the woman, who was probably twenty, blushed as she leaned forward across the table to put an extra napkin down for him, giving him a good view of her pert tits.

"How long have you worked here?" Aiden asked as he let approval show in his eyes. The woman preened and Aiden sat back waiting for her to talk.

"Forever. My parents own it and all of the family works here. I've been here since I was six, I think." She laughed as she bit her lower lip and batted her eyelashes at him.

"Must be hard working with your family all the time."

She shrugged a shoulder. "But I get to meet many fascinating people. Like you scientists from the lab. They come from all over the world to work here and most stop by to eat so I get to know them."

"I'm coming back tonight with some people from the lab. Sada set me up on a blind date with the head of the lab .

. ." Aiden pretended to forget Piper's name and the waitress quickly jumped in.

"Piper? Is she back in town?"

"I guess. We'll be here tonight. Is she nice?"

"So nice! Sada was talking to her new boyfriend last night about Piper hopefully coming back soon. I can't wait to see her."

Aiden nodded along as she continued to tell him all about Piper. "So, I don't have to worry about finding an emergency exit in the back?"

The woman laughed. "Oh no. You won't need the back door or the kitchen for Piper. She's very lucky to have a date with you."

"It sounds like I'm the lucky one." Aiden stood up and put extra money on the table. "Thanks for calming my nerves before my date. I'll see you soon."

Aiden walked around the back of the building and took in the area. City alleys filled with large trash cans and employee parking filled the space behind the restaurant. A small marina was a couple blocks away. Then around the side of the restaurant was the main strip of the city lined with shops, clubs, and places to eat. Across the street were businesses, including the lab, and a large park. He'd post men at every exit, in the park, and in the nearby alleys just in case.

Aiden walked back to the palace, flashed his credentials at the gate, and found Piper sitting in the gardens talking with Nailah. Not wanting to interrupt, he took position behind them and began to scan the area, but he was in trouble. His eyes kept going back to his principal. He might not have officially crossed the line and started a relationship with her, but he'd be lying to himself if his feelings for Piper hadn't begun to affect his work.

Aiden stepped into the shadows and pulled out his phone. “Eddie, it’s Aiden. How fast can you be in Rahmi?” Aiden asked his trusted employee.

“Let me see. You need backup?” the older man, who had done four tours of duty, asked. He was in his mid-forties now, ten years older than Aiden’s thirty-four years, and had been happy to leave his training job in the British Army to take the protection jobs he wanted when he wanted. And it paid a hell of a lot more.

“Not exactly,” Aiden hedged. “It’s personal.”

“The scientist turned out to be too high maintenance for you, huh?” Eddie chuckled.

“No. Like I said, it’s personal.”

“Oh. I see. That’s a first for you. I can be there in ten hours.”

“Thank you,” Aiden said before hanging up. He wasn’t one to ask for help, but he also cared too much for Piper to put her at risk because of his feelings for her.

Aiden put away his phone and stood quietly in the shadow of the breezeway watching Piper. His mother had said she’d fallen in love with his father in the blink of an eye. Aiden had never believed it possible, but despite trying to keep his feelings professional, the quirky, smart, and sometimes disheveled Piper was slowly making a home for herself in his heart. Now he just needed to keep her safe so he could finally ask her out.

“I CAN’T SAY I blame you. That is one handsome man. And Jamal couldn’t stop talking about him last night. He impressed Jamal very much,” Nailah said as she cast a quick glance over Piper’s shoulder. “And by the way he’s looking at you. Goodness. Is it hot out here?”

Piper fought the urge to look behind her. Aiden had occupied her thoughts more than she wanted him to. After dancing with her the night before, he'd gone back to being a professional bodyguard. Even while she was trying to work this afternoon, her thoughts kept turning to Aiden. She wanted to bounce some ideas off him. He didn't even know about her work, but she found that talking to him about her project opened her mind to new ideas. He saw things differently than she did and asked questions she wouldn't think of. Because of that, she found herself putting down her work this afternoon and going in search of him. Instead, she found Nailah who wanted to spend a little time together. And they had, until Nailah had pointed out Aiden was behind her. Ever since, Piper only heard every fifth word Nailah had said.

The clock chimed and Nailah said something. Piper smiled, wondering what it was she'd said. Then when Nailah got up and kissed her cheek, Piper figured it out.

"I'll see you after your dinner. I want all the details," Nailah whispered before heading into the family's private wing. Piper didn't need to turn around to know Aiden was there.

"How did scouting go?" Piper asked, closing her eyes and lifting her face to the warm sun. The smell of flowers, fresh-cut grass, and fruit trees mingled with Aiden's masculine smell. For one moment, Piper let herself soak it in.

Aiden sat next to her, his body brushing against hers. "Good. I got to know the waitress. She gave me information on the exits. I have guards posted just in case. I talked to Nash, who said everything from that IP address has been quiet. There doesn't appear to be any communications with anyone outside of the normal from the lab. We may have to do something big to draw them out."

"I trust you. Just tell me what to do." Piper felt Aiden's muscles tighten. Something was wrong. "What is it?"

"I've become compromised. In ten hours I'm going to resign as your security detail and my second in charge, Eddie, will take over. While I have some ideas, I need to wait for Eddie's arrival and discuss them with him." Aiden turned to her. His eyes pinned her to the spot as his jaw clenched and unclenched as if he were battling some inner demons. "Do you understand what I'm saying?"

Piper felt as if she'd been punched in the gut. "You're leaving me?" In such a short time, she had begun to think of Aiden as part of her team. For some reason when they were together it felt as if they would always be together. But now, her body was ravaged at the idea of him leaving, and she felt oddly alone. And she didn't feel like being alone anymore. Aiden's hand came up and cupped her cheek. Piper instinctively leaned into his hand and let out a shaky breath. "It's okay. I understand. I'm a strong, independent woman, and I will get this done with or without you. Besides, we don't know for sure if Phobos is even behind this, and he certainly isn't here. I'm good if you need to leave now."

"Babe, I'm not going anywhere."

Piper's heart did a double take. "What? You said you are resigning."

"As your detail, not as your friend, and not as what I hope to be as more than your friend. My emotions are compromised. They're fully occupied with you, and as such, I can't protect you to the best of my ability. That's why Eddie is coming."

Aiden took all questioning from Piper's mind as his fingers slid from her cheek to the back of her neck, and he pulled her forward and took her lips with his. The kiss was slow, deliberate, and dreamy. His gentleness had her collapsing into him as his strong hands trailed lightly down her spine. He didn't push her or hurry the kiss. Instead, it was a slow burn that left Piper breathless. Aiden groaned when he pulled away.

"Ten hours. Right around midnight tonight. Then I'm all yours," Aiden said as his thumb caressed her cheek. Suddenly, Phobos was the least of her worries. In ten hours she'd open her door and her heart to Aiden.

17

"We've got nothing. I'm sorry," Nash said as Aiden dressed. Nash and Nabi were on speakerphone and sounded as frustrated as Aiden felt.

"It's as if everyone went quiet. Ahmed has threatened black market sources and I've hacked everything I can think of. Still no word on who owns that IP address and no word on if Phobos is real," Nabi told him as Aiden tied his tie.

"How is Piper doing? Tammy has been calling me every three hours," Nash asked.

"She's hanging in there. We have dinner tonight with Sada Kourtney."

"I've known her for years," Nash said. "She's a good person."

"Thanks for the update, but I need to go. I'm having one of my men taking over point starting tonight at midnight," Aiden tried to throw in casually.

"Excuse me?"

"I told you that you weren't there to get laid," Walker yelled.

"Look, mate, it's not like I meant to develop feelings for

her. And you should talk. Piper told me all about you and Layne."

"I waited until she was no longer my . . . oh. I get it. Smart man. I should have just hired another physical therapist, but Aaron's a prick, and he was the only other one there."

"Check in tomorrow. I'll bring Eddie into the briefing. We may have to plan an announced public appearance to bring these guys out of the shadows," Aiden said, grabbing his gun and sliding it into the holster hidden in the small of his back.

"We'll get to work on that," Nabi said before they ended the call.

Aiden slipped his phone into the inside pocket of his gray suit and knocked on the door. When it opened, he smiled. She was so Piper, casual and sexy all at once. She wore a sundress and flip-flops with something strange hanging from them. Her hair was down, and he wanted to wrap it around his fingers as he kissed her. Five more hours. He could hold out for five more hours.

"You look beautiful. What is that on your shoes?"

"A nanoparticle. Aren't they fun? My dad got me them for my birthday."

It made Aiden smile. His Piper was so good, sweet, and original. Who else would have nanoparticle flip-flops, the ugliest DNA bra, and still be absolutely adorable in them?

"Then shall we?" Aiden held out his arm for her to take and together they walked out of the palace and into the waiting car. Guards were already in place and when they pulled up to the restaurant, Aiden spotted two of them in civilian clothes sitting on the patio near the front door.

As they made their way inside, Aiden winked at the waitress and took in the patrons. Everyone was eating and talking. No one was wearing an earpiece and very few people even glanced at them as they made their way to their table.

Sada and her date stood up as they approached the table. They were smiling as Sada made her way around the table to hug Piper. "This is your date? You've been keeping secrets."

Aiden held out his hand to a man a couple inches shorter than he was, but also a couple years younger. He was built and looked as if he hung out in a gym a lot. "Hi. I'm Aiden."

"Royce. Nice to meet you. Are you Piper's boyfriend?"

"Not yet," Aiden said, but the implication was clear: he would be.

"Royce, this is Piper Davies." Sada introduced as Piper held out her hand. "Piper, this is my boyfriend, Royce. He's from Germany and flew in to visit me."

"It's wonderful to meet you," Piper said cheerfully as she took a seat across from Sada and Royce. Aiden pushed her chair in and took the seat next to her as the waitress from that afternoon stopped by to chat and take their drink orders.

"So, how long have you guys been talking?" Piper asked as Aiden casually scanned the room.

"A couple months now. We clicked instantly when he sent me a message request. We messaged for a week before talking on the phone for the first time," Sada said excitedly as Aiden and Royce shared a look as the women talked about how they met. Aiden was relieved to see Royce was of the same frame of mind as he was about talking about all the emotional moments of a new relationship. How'd you meet? Online. Discussion done.

"Sada tells me you're the head of the lab. That's a big accomplishment," Royce said when Sada took a breath.

"That's right. And I feel so bad. Where are my manners? Tell me about yourself, Royce."

Aiden listened with half an ear as Royce talked about Germany and that he was a scientist for a lab that handles some kind of chemicals. Aiden scanned the area one more time and then brought his attention back to the conversation when he heard Royce say his name.

"Sorry, what was that?"

"I asked what kind of scientist you are," Royce repeated.

"Well, recently I've found myself fascinated with DNA and nanoparticles." Aiden saw Piper's lips quirk as she tried to stop herself from laughing out loud in reference to her unique clothing habits.

"What interests you about them?" Sada asked, leaning forward.

"Stripping them from the host."

This time Piper choked on her water as she coughed, distracting Sada from asking him any more questions. "Are you okay, Piper?"

"Fine, just swallowed wrong," Piper said as Aiden grinned. She kicked him under the table.

Aiden was stopped from teasing her more when the food arrived. Royce began asking questions about which football club Aiden cheered for. When Aiden looked up, the smiling waitress he'd talked to earlier wasn't smiling. Royce kept talking, and Aiden wasn't able to ask her what was wrong. Instead, he scanned the room. He didn't see anything out of place. Again, no one watching them, no one else scanning the room, no one with visible earpieces.

"This is so good," Piper said, taking a bite of her dinner

made up of rice, slow-cooked meat, raisins, and spices she had dreams about. "I have missed this so much."

Aiden turned his attention back to the table and jumped into the conversation about football while Sada and Piper talked about some friend they had in common from Italy who was due to arrive in a few weeks.

"Do you think O'Neill will get a contract exten—"

Aiden blinked as Royce's words drifted off. His vision blurred, his hearing tunneled, and his body went numb. He tried to reach for Piper, but everything went black.

ONE SECOND, Piper had been chatting excitedly with Sada and the next it felt as if she'd stepped away from her own body. She blinked at her food and over toward Aiden. She had to warn him. But her mouth didn't work. In her vision, Aiden slipped farther and farther away as voices floated to silence. And then nothingness.

IT FELT as if she blinked and was awake again. Piper's eyes snapped open, "Aiden!"

It didn't take but a snap second later to realize she'd been out for a lot more than a blink of an eye. She was on a fishing boat, a man sat across from her, and her hands were bound as she sat on a bench on the deck.

"I'm sorry, he's not here right now," the man said casually in his slight accent. It sounded similar to Royce's and Mila's, so she thought he must be German.

"Where is he? Who are you? Where am I?" Piper let loose with all her questions as she looked around. It was night, but in the distance she saw lights and the vague outline of a coastline. "Is that Rahmi?"

The man laughed and crossed one leg over the other as the old fishing boat slowly chugged through the dark waters.

"Which do you want to know first?"

"Aiden?" Piper asked, having a sinking feeling she had figured out what was happening.

"Is that the boring scientist you were with? Royce also said he had no taste in football clubs. He's fine. Or will be when he wakes up."

"Sada?" Piper asked, almost not wanting to know the answer. Had her friend turned on her too?

"Same. She'll wake up uninjured except for knowing it was her desperation for love that resulted in her friend's capture."

"Is that Rahmi? Where are we going?" Piper tried to take in every detail and file it away in case it was important.

"No, that's not Rahmi. Rahmi is way back there," he said with a nod of his head. "We're heading to a special place. A new lab for you to continue your work in." If Rahmi was back there, they were in the Rahmi Strait. Wait, that meant the shoreline she was seeing a mile off was . . . hope.

"Don't you want to know who I am?" the man asked with amusement as he uncrossed his legs and leaned forward with his elbows on his knees. His serious face came into view.

"I don't need to ask. I already know who you are. We've met before, Agent Rand of the Department of Homeland Security. Or should I call you Phobos?"

18

Aiden's eyes shot open, and at the same time he sat up he reached for his gun. He wasn't in the restaurant anymore. Instead, he was in a well-appointed room with an IV in his arm and an old man who looked like a doctor standing next to him. In a heartbeat, Aiden had the gun pointed at the man.

"Mr. Creed, please. You are safe now." Aiden turned to the soft woman's voice behind him and found Princess Nailah wringing her hands.

"Where's Piper?"

"She's been taken," Nailah said, her voice catching with emotion.

Aiden's heart plummeted and it felt as if someone was squeezing it until it burst.

"It was her coworker's date. The coworker is—" Aiden shot off the table, cutting Nailah off.

"Where is Sada?"

"In custody. They don't think she was an accessory, but we need to be sure."

"And the guards who were on duty?"

"Piper was taken out the back door. The guards reported that the waitress brought them a snack, and the next thing they remember is waking up here. The waitress is also in custody, as is the entire kitchen staff."

"Sir," the doctor said, drawing Aiden's attention, "I understand the urgency, but I need to check you out."

"No time, doc." Aiden peeled the tape from his elbow and pulled the IV needle from his arm. "Thank you," he said, handing it to him before jumping from the table. "Can you get me to where they're being held?"

Nailah nodded and hurried to the door. Aiden was right behind her. They didn't talk as he followed her into tunnels underneath the palace and into a secret holding center underneath the security building. She knocked on the door and a guard opened it. "Give Mr. Creed full access to the detainees." The guard nodded and opened the door. "Mr. Creed," Nailah said, gripping his arm, "do whatever it takes to find Piper."

"I promise. I'll find her or die trying."

Aiden's body was tightly coiled as he followed the guard. He wanted to spring, he wanted to attack, and he wanted to kill. But right now he needed to keep calm. He had to gather more information.

"Right in here, sir," the guard said, opening a door. Aiden walked into the dimly lit room and found Prince Jamal standing with his arms crossed, looking into a two-way mirror.

"Aiden," Jamal said tightly, "they're interrogating the coworker now."

"Have you called Keeneston yet?" Aiden asked.

"Not yet. I want to be able to have some answers to the questions I know will follow. I failed them. I won't fail them again."

"We all failed. But I for one refuse to fail again." Aiden's determination to find Piper overpowered his fear of what could be happening to her.

Jamal nodded his understanding, and Aiden turned to watch the man yell at Sada, who was crying hysterically. "Do you mind if I talk to her?"

"Do whatever it takes to get answers."

Aiden left the room and opened the interrogation room door. "Aiden!" Sada sobbed. Aiden motioned for the guard to step outside. Aiden and Sada were now alone. "Where's Piper? Where's Royce? What happened?"

Aiden took a seat across from her and reached out for her hands. They were damp with sweat and shaking as he grasped them. "Sada," Aiden said in such a tone that Sada instantly stopped sobbing, "listen to me. Piper is missing. I need to find her. She's your friend, right?"

"Yes," Sada said as she tried to calm herself.

"Tell me everything about Royce you can remember. Every time he asked about Piper or the work you did at the lab. Every time he asked about FAVOR."

Sada's eyes snapped up, "How do you know about FAVOR?"

"Because I'm the man hired to protect Piper because someone wants to steal FAVOR and turn it into a weapon. Now they have Piper, and I need to find them."

Sada was quiet for a moment as her eyes drifted off. Then she gasped and fresh tears poured from her eyes. "It's all my fault! Oh my God, he told me he loved me. He . . . he . . . he," Sada gasped for air as she sobbed.

"Sada," Aiden snapped. "You'll have time for tears later. I need answers. Now."

Sada swallowed hard and took a deep breath. "He didn't ask about Piper or what we were working on for a month. It wasn't until he video-messaged me while I was at the lab that he got into specifics. I knew I wasn't supposed to say anything, and I thought I was vague enough. I didn't tell him exactly about FAVOR. But if he were smart enough, he could have figured it out. And then he didn't ask me again until a week ago. Again, it was real casual. He asked what Piper left behind when she went back to Kentucky and how hard it must be to maintain two labs."

"Go on," Aiden ordered.

"Then out of the blue, he called and said he was coming to visit and hoped he could meet my friends. He specifically mentioned Piper. I told him that was funny since I had just gotten word she was coming here." Aiden saw her struggle to keep her composure as reality set in. She'd been played, just like Dudley. "I slept with him," Sada cried, ripping her hands from Aiden as she hugged herself. "I slept with the man who took my friend. I led him right to her."

"Sada, where would he go? Did he mention any cities, towns, friends, anything?"

Sada thought for a minute as she tried to scrub his touch from her body. "No. He didn't talk about himself much. I'm so sorry. I'm so stupid."

He wasn't going to get any more from her, so Aiden stood and headed for the door as Sada sobbed. The guard opened the door and Aiden whispered to him, "Collect any evidence from her person and let her shower. She's not an accessory. She's just a victim. Got it?"

"Yes, sir," he said as Jamal opened the door to the observation room and nodded his approval of the plan to the guard.

"City services called. They found video from cameras at the marina. She's on a boat."

"And the restaurant staff?" Aiden asked.

"Held at gunpoint."

"You need to call Nabi. I'm going after her," Aiden told him as he strode for the exit.

"Wait," Jamal ordered.

Aiden stopped in his tracks and slowly turned. "Don't try to stop me."

"I'm not. Come with me." Jamal walked away, expecting Aiden to follow. Aiden looked at the door—Piper was somewhere beyond it—but he followed Jamal instead.

They went up three flights of stairs and into the main control room. There were desks, television screens, and offices. People were hurrying around as everyone was on high alert. "You," Jamal ordered a guard rushing by them. "Take Mr. Creed to the armory and give him everything he needs. Meet me back here in ten minutes."

TEN MINUTES LATER, Aiden had a vest, wetsuit, and a duffle bag of various weapons. Jamal was waiting for him with an envelope in hand. "I've talked to my Uncle Mo. He'll fill in his security. He suggested I give you this."

Aiden opened the envelope to find diplomatic papers. "What's this?"

"The ability to do whatever it takes to get Piper back."

"These are Rahmi papers. I'm British," he said, shoving the papers back to Jamal.

Jamal looked around and grabbed a letter opener from a nearby desk. "Kneel."

"What? I don't have time—"

"KNEEL!"

Aiden knelt. "By the power invested in me as the Prince of Rahmi, I hereby pronounce you a citizen of Rahmi, where you will henceforth hold dual citizenship with the United

Kingdom. You are granted a post in our foreign office to act as a diplomat for and on behalf of Rahmi and to do whatever necessary to protect our interests in the Rahmi International Nanotech Laboratory and its founder." Jamal tapped the letter opener on each shoulder. "Rise, citizen of Rahmi."

Aiden stood and Jamal shoved the papers back to him. "There will be a legal notice regarding your citizenship and a new post up in ten minutes to make it public. Just don't kill anyone until then."

Aiden shoved the papers into his suit coat. "Got it." He grabbed the duffle bag and strode from the building. As soon as he was outside, he pulled out his cell phone and called the one person he knew could help.

"I figured you'd be calling. Mo told us what happened."

"I need your help, Miles."

"Help is already on the way."

"Don't send help here. Pull up your account. I had a GPS dot in her bra."

"I knew I liked you. Hold on."

Aiden tossed his bag into the car he'd been borrowing and sped from the palace grounds.

"All GPS dots are in the palace except one. It's in the Strait of Rahmi, a mile from the Surman coast."

"Watch that signal and text me every five minutes with the new coordinates."

"You got it."

Aiden hung up the phone and sped through the city. Someone had taken the woman he loved. No man, mountain, ocean, or army was going to prevent him from getting her back.

19

Phobos smiled as he sat back on the bench across from her. "You remember me? I'm impressed. I thought I was rather undercover."

"You were trying to take a missile from Sophie and were pissed no one would let you talk to her alone or get inside the barn. I thought it was government posturing, but now I see what it was. You were part of Ares's group and wanted to complete the mission," Piper said as she slowly tested her bindings. They were tight, and there were also four guards spread out on the deck of the boat.

Piper jumped when thunder suddenly rumbled and a flash of lightning lit the sky. Phobos laughed in delight at her fear. "My mentor's failure was the best thing to happen to me. It led me to you."

"What do you mean?" Piper asked as rain began to fall. Phobos stood and stepped to where she was sitting.

"Because it allowed me to hear all about Sophie Davies's brilliant cousin who was currently working on something involving viruses and nanotech—something to save the world. And as we both know, anything that can be used to save the world can be manipulated to hurt the world. After that, it was easy to get Dudley to talk. The poor boy would say anything to get laid. That's when I learned of your project and all the potential it held. I could make a larger name for myself than Ares or Poseidon. And all with something so small you'd have to have a microscope to see it."

The clouds opened up and rain fell in sheets as the ship began to rock. It might have been hot in Rahmi, but the rain chilled her to the bone as it soaked her thin dress. "I'll never give it to you."

"We'll see about that," Phobos said tauntingly. He turned and walked toward the cabin. "Get her inside," he ordered the guards as the ship dipped and a wave crashed over the bow, completely soaking her and sending her sprawling to the deck. Piper felt the roughness of the boards on her hands and knees as she fought the rocking ship to try to sit up.

Phobos disappeared inside the cabin as two guards stumbled forward. Each grabbed an arm and hauled her to her feet. Piper looked over at the dim lights of Surman flashing through the heavy sheets of rain and then back at the cabin. The ship rocked and Piper flung her body toward one of the guards. The one guard lost his hold on her rain-slicked arm and she took the other guard down when she stumbled. He was under her but already had one of her arms grasped in a tight grip.

Well, she might not be Abby, Sophie, or Layne, but you didn't have to be a world-class badass to know kneeing a man in the balls would take him down for a second. And that second was all she needed. Piper slammed her knee into the guard's balls, causing him to scream in pain and release her as he grabbed his bruised boys. Piper rolled off him and struggled to her feet as the other guards raced toward her. The boat pitched again, lightning filled the sky, and Piper jumped.

It felt as if she were falling forever. Her legs flailed as they tried to feel something solid under them. But then she was under and encased in dark water. Piper kicked hard and clawed at the water with her tied hands as she fought the current and the waves to find the surface. Her face broke free as her body was thrown about the crashing waves. She gasped for air, her dress clinging to her legs and getting in the way of her kicks. Piper had grown up swimming in the rivers and lakes of Kentucky, but nothing could prepare her for the waves roaring down on her.

She heard the men's shouts from over the thunder and rain. She looked back at the deck of the boat as she kicked with all she had toward the shore. "If you make it to Surman alive, we will find you, Dr. Davies!" she heard Phobos yell. "We already have men there. You'll never make it off the beach."

She looked over her shoulder and the moment before a wave crashed on her, sending her back into the water's depths, she saw the boat turning toward Surman. Piper kicked hard and pushed her way back up to the surface, losing a flip-flop in the process. Her flip-flop! Piper took a deep breath and dove underwater so she could reach her other flip-flop. Gripping it for dear life and nabbing the other one floating its way to the surface, she kicked her way upward.

Treading water and riding the waves the best she could, Piper shoved one flip-flop into the neckline of her dress and angled the metal nanoparticle of the second against the rope and began to saw at the knot hoping to weaken it enough for her to slip her hands free. She sputtered as another wave took her underwater, but she never gave up. Her lungs burned. She could barely see with the rain and spray from the waves hitting her in the face, but she fought on. And then she felt it. The rope loosened. She moved the metal frantically across the rope and twisted her wrists. With a hard yank, her hand slid free. Piper practically drowned in relief, but a wave beat her to it.

She was now able to use both arms to swim and made it back to the surface faster. She looked around and saw that the boat was beating her to Surman. That was fine because she had a plan. Piper put the flip-flop between her teeth, and pulled off her dress so she could swim without her legs becoming tangled. She shoved her shoes into her bra for safekeeping. She had some serious swimming to do.

"I NEED THIS BOAT!" Aiden yelled at the man who was standing with the keys to a speedboat. Piper was well over two hours away and he needed that speedboat right then.

"Twenty thousand pounds," the man grinned as he crossed his arms over his chest. The weasel.

"By order of Prince Jamal, you will hand over that boat. You'll get it back." *Most likely.* The man laughed and Aiden had enough. He slammed his fist upward, hitting the man's chin and sending him crashing to the docks. Aiden reached down and plucked the keys from his hand and leapt into the speedboat. A text came through.

Miles Davies: *She's slowing down and changing direction. Heading to Surman. Here are the last coordinates.*

Aiden revved the engine to life and entered the coordinates into the boat's navigation. He pushed the throttle and aimed the boat straight for the thunderstorm.

He'd go through hell for Piper. A thunderstorm wasn't about to stop him for rescuing her.

~

PIPER LET her body sink into the water. She wasn't worried about trying to swim as if she were in a pool. She let the tides, waves, and buoyancy of the water keep her afloat as she reached with her arms and battled her way toward the shore at an angle away from Phobos and toward the buoys that outlined the shipping lane. They were hard to see, but when she rode a wave she saw the lights of the buoys just a hundred yards away.

Piper coughed as water surged down her mouth, but she didn't stop reaching for every inch to get closer to those buoys. As she fought the water, the waves, and the cold, she heard what she'd been waiting for. The sound of an engine.

"Help!" Piper yelled and then screamed it in Rahmian. Adrenaline surged her forward as she kicked with all her might toward the sound of the fishing boat. "Help!" she screamed again when she finally saw the lights of the small trawler. Judging the speed of the boat and the angle of its light off the front of the ship, Piper adjusted her direction and pushed herself until she was sure she was going to drown.

"Help!" she yelled in every language she knew, which was really only English, Rahmian, and a little German she'd picked up from Mila. She treaded water as she frantically waved her arms. "Help!"

The boat was going to run her over. Piper pushed herself slightly to the side. Maybe she could grab onto the net and pray it didn't drag her under. But then the boat slowed and men were running to the deck. Piper cried out, "Here! I'm here."

Tears streamed down her face mixing with the rain and the ocean water as a life preserver attached to a rope was thrown toward her. Piper tried to remember to breathe as she battled the last ten yards to the ring and blissfully slid her arms through it. The men were shouting a language that seemed to be close to Rahmi's language as she cried, "Thank you," over and over again in Rahmian.

Then she was being pulled up out of the water and rough hands gripped her, pulling her until she thought her arms would rip from their sockets. More hands gripped her side and she was painfully hauled over the side of the boat and landed hard on the deck.

Piper rolled over and vomited up a gallon of ocean water as a rain jacket was thrown over her mostly nude body and she was hauled up to stand. Her legs wouldn't hold her and a man scooped her into his arms.

"What happened to you?" one of them asked in something close to Rahmian.

"Kidnapped. I need to get to safety. Do you have a cell phone?"

He shook his head *no*. "Radio. Are you from Rahmi?"

"America. Can you get a message to Queen Suri?"

The men looked at each other and laughed. "Are you serious?" the man who must be the captain asked. He was in his sixties and looked as if he'd lived every rough second of it—leathered skin, callused hands, deep wrinkles, and numerous missing teeth. But his eyes were wise with experience.

"I can't have anyone know I'm here. The men who took me, they're waiting at the shore for me. I've met Queen Suri. She'll help me," Piper pleaded.

"Look, lady, we can't just radio the queen." The captain turned to his men and they began to talk. Piper felt her anger rise. She was heaving up half the ocean, she was weak, and she was desperate, but she wasn't going to back down.

"I'm right here. You will talk to me and not about me," Piper ordered, sounding surprisingly like her mother did when she was breaking up a fight between Dylan and Jace.

The men all spun around and looked at her. For good measure, she crossed her arms and tapped her toe, now very thankful for the raincoat that fell to her knees.

"Who are you?" the captain asked.

"Dr. Piper Davies, the head scientist at the Rahmi International Nanotechnology Laboratory. And who are you?"

"Captain Msamaki." The captain looked thoughtfully at her for a minute. "Why do these men want you?"

"They want to take something I made and use it to hurt people."

The men all looked at each other. "And you know the queen?"

"And the king of Rahmi, all the princes and princess of Rahmi, and the king of Bermalia."

"You know King Draven?" one of the men asked skeptically.

"Yes. From his time in Kentucky. It's in the United States."

"We know it. We're from Bermalia. Because of the Treaty of Keeneston, we are allowed to fish. We have passage now from Bermalia through Surman where we can fish and bring our catch back to our country to sell," the captain said, nodding as if he had come to a conclusion. "We'll help you."

"You can get me into Surman?"

"Better. We can get you to King Draven. We deliver a portion of our catch directly to the palace. From there you are on your own. They probably won't kill you if you can really prove you know the king or if you take off the raincoat."

"Deal," Piper said, holding out her hand. The man shook it.

"Good. Now take this," he said, reaching for a snorkeling mask and handing it to her.

"Why?"

"Because we'll have to get through customs and to do that they search the ship."

"So I'm going back in the water?" Piper dreaded the idea of getting back into the rough sea.

"No," he said with a gap-toothed smile. "You're getting in with the fish."

20

Aiden turned the boat and headed to the new coordinates. Piper was moving faster, and according to Miles, she was heading into the port of Surman. Aiden had the motorboat at full speed and was gaining ground. Now he was only forty-five minutes behind her. "Hang on, Piper," he kept repeating.

Rain pelted his face, which was now as numb as his heart was. He didn't think it had beaten since he'd woken up and heard Piper had been kidnapped. Bloodlust fueled him now. With the rage and fear that filled him, Aiden had no doubt that he loved Piper. It was a desperation he'd never felt before. It was hard to control, but control it he must. Tapping into his SAS training, he kept a cool head as he raced toward the new coordinates.

~

WELL, this was only slightly better than being back in the ocean. Piper shivered and struggled to breathe with the weight of the iced fish on her. The men had dressed her, wrapped her in an emergency wet suit, and slapped the mask and snorkel on her before burying her in cold fish as they pulled into the harbor.

"Don't worry. You'll be fine. Just stay still and don't make a sound," the captain told her before he closed the lid on the large cooler.

Sounds of boots hitting the deck reached her and suddenly the cooler was opened. Through the fish covering her, she saw a flashlight beam and then the cooler was closed again. If Piper hadn't vomited everything in her stomach because of the seawater, she would have at the smell of the fish and the jerky movements of the crane lifting the cooler into the air to unload it.

The cooler swayed and then slammed onto the bed of the truck. Every five minutes of so, another cooler was slammed down. After what seemed to be an eternity, the truck roared to life and began to rumble off down the pier. Five minutes later, the truck stopped and the cooler lid was opened. One of the men pushed the fish from her face and smiled down at her.

"Want to ride up front for a while or stay with the fish?"

Piper's roll of her eyes answered the question as the man laughingly helped her out of the cooler and helped steady her as she peeled the wetsuit from her body. The man shoved the wetsuit into the corner of the flatbed before jumping down and holding his arms out toward her. Piper put her hands on his wide shoulders as he wrapped his large hands around her waist and easily lifted her from truck bed.

"Come on, fish princess, let's get you to the king."

Aiden navigated into the Surman harbor as his phone rang. He was looking everywhere for Royce as he grabbed the phone. "Hello?" he shouted over the rain.

"It's Nash. I'm with Miles, and I think I know where they are heading."

"Where?"

"Bermalia."

"What?" Aiden yelled as thunder rocked the air.

"Bermalia. The border is only three hours from the harbor. I've been mapping out her location, and she's on the main road to Bermalia. Has been ever since she got off the boat. Main roads all the way. They must have a way to sneak her across the borders because she should have been stopped in the harbor," Nash told him.

"I'll need to get through customs," Aiden said more to himself than to Nash.

"Zain has already taken care of that," Nash informed him. "I'll call with any updates. I'm sending you directions now for your car's GPS."

"What car?" Aiden asked as he turned off the boat's engine and tied it to the dock. But Nash had already hung up.

"Mr. Aiden Creed?"

Aiden looked up to find a Surman soldier standing there. "Yes?"

"Queen Suri has instructed me to assist you. Your car is right this way. It is loaded with everything you might need. Further, you will be provided a military escort to the border. Upon reaching Bermalia, you will be on your own."

Apparently that was what Nash meant when he said Zain had taken care of it. Aiden followed the soldier to a large Hummer surrounded by two military vehicles in the front and the back of it. "Just honk if you can't keep up," the guard told him as he slipped into the lead vehicle.

Aiden hurriedly got into his vehicle. It was filled with water, a change of clothes, and food. He tore into the food as he followed the guards from the harbor. As soon as they hit the open road, they sped up to well over 150 kilometers per hour. It seemed that time slowed to a crawl as they made their way through the early-dawn light. Everywhere he looked was wide-open desert. Towns surrounded water sources as they raced toward Bermalia.

Aiden was growing frantic. It had been almost ten hours since Piper had been taken. At least he had hope she was still alive. His phone rang and the Bluetooth picked it up.

"She's at the border. Their vehicle is stopped. It's being searched," Nash told him.

Aiden's heart pounded so hard he was afraid it might explode. "Do they have her? Is she safe?"

"The head of the border patrol is live-streaming it. They can't find her."

"That's not possible!" Aiden yelled as he slammed his hand on the steering wheel. They were thirty minutes away and Aiden revved the engine, riding the Hummer right up the escort's ass. They got the hint and sped forward.

"Hold on. I'm sending you the picture." Aiden heard Nash speak in Rahmi and a minute later a photo came through of a rough-and-tumble fishing crew. "Any of these guys Royce?"

"No. Never seen them before." Aiden felt his hope fade. "Wait, those big coolers, please tell me there's no body in them."

"No. Just fish. The GPS is good within a half mile. She could be in another car or sneaking across the border just a little ways away. Since the treaty, the borders are more open."

"The men are all verified. They're Bermalian fishermen. No criminal history. They don't even own cell phones. They're not Phobos or part of his crew. Cut them loose," Aiden heard Nabi order.

"We'll find her," Nash promised, but for the first time Aiden was starting to have his doubts. "You are cleared into Bermalia, but King Draven isn't answering his phone. You'll be on your own once inside their country."

Aiden disconnected as they sped closer to Piper's coordinates. He didn't mind being on his own. In fact, right now he'd prefer to use his new get-out-of-jail-free card by killing Phobos without worrying about laws and the soldiers who followed them.

~

PIPER COULDN'T BREATHE. They'd buried her under hundreds of pounds of frozen fish. But even she knew it was worth it when they had been pulled over. It had taken twenty minutes before they were back on the road again. And another twenty until they pulled over to help her out of the cooler.

Piper couldn't stop shaking as the captain took his jacket off and wrapped her in it. "They had your picture and were looking for you."

Piper nodded or, more accurately, she shook with the coldness of being in an ice cooler. Plus the cold desert night air had yet to warm up with the new day's rising sun. "H-h-how l-l-l-ong?" she sputtered out through shivers.

"We'll reach the palace in an hour. Now, get in here and we'll get you warm."

Piper sat in the middle of the bench seat surrounded by fishermen and with the heat on full blast.

"You know, you smell," the captain said with a smile.

Piper narrowed her eyes and shot him the middle finger. It was a gesture they all understood. The guys laughed, and Piper finally felt herself start to relax. Phobos and his men would be searching Surman. They wouldn't think to look for her at the palace of the king of Bermalia. Piper felt as if there were weights attached to her eyelids as the heat began to thaw her. Slowly, her lids closed. As she slept, she dreamed of Aiden. In her dreams, he was coming for her. But when the noise from the capital woke her, it was with the stark revelation that she didn't even know if Aiden was alive.

"I'm going to be sick," Piper cried as the captain slammed on the brakes. Men fled the truck as Piper rushed out and fell to her knees. She sucked in air, but the image of Aiden dead and lying on the dinner table had her vomiting what little was left in her stomach.

"And I thought you couldn't smell worse. Come on, fish princess. We're almost there," the captain called out the door from behind the steering wheel. With a shaking, battered, and exhausted body, Piper pulled herself up. She could do this. She had to do this. For herself. For Aiden. For her family. For the people Phobos wouldn't think twice of killing.

"Up we go, princess," one of the men said, shoving her by the butt into the cab. Piper scooted to her seat, and they were off once again. She looked around the capital with curiosity as they drove. Street vendors were opening. Their carts lined the river walk that ran through the middle of downtown. It was certainly a poor town, but one now prospering under King Draven's more mature approach to governing. He'd learned from Zain and Mo, and then Suri had also taken him under her wing.

"Here we are," the captain said as he pulled up to a guard's gate. Piper looked out the window at the giant palace with a massive painting of Draven dressed in full military uniform, brandishing a sword, and sitting astride a rearing warhorse. Okay, maybe he wasn't fully mature yet.

"Papers," the guard ordered as everyone but Piper passed theirs over. "Yours too."

"Who, me?" Piper said in Rahmi.

"Yeah, the smelly one."

Piper smiled and batted her eyelashes. "I don't have papers. See, I was shipwrecked and these nice men rescued me and brought me here to see King Draven. I'm a friend of his."

"Sure you are. Out of the truck," he ordered.

"No, really. I'm a friend of his from Keeneston, Kentucky," Piper said in Rahmi and then in English.

"And I'm the next king of Bermalia. Out of the truck, now."

"You know me," the captain said to the guard. "I believe she really does know the king. Maybe check first. You know he loves women. He might get mad if he doesn't get his chance to sleep with her again."

Piper inhaled sharply to argue she'd never slept with the king when the guard shrugged. "Good point." He held out his cell and snapped a picture of Piper in full righteous indignation.

"I did not sleep with him," she whispered harshly to the captain.

"You can go through. A guard will meet you at the unloading dock," the guard said with some surprise.

Piper crossed her arms over her chest and fumed.

Draven better not be getting any ideas. She needed his help as king, not as a horndog of the top order.

Five guards were lined up when the truck pulled to a stop. "Out!" the leader ordered as the fishermen climbed from the vehicle and showed them their papers. "You all get to unloading. You, the smelly one," he said, grabbing her arm, "come with me."

"I will do no such thing," Piper said, digging in her heels. "I demand to see King Draven. I am a friend of his and—"

"We've heard it before, lady. But never from someone like you," he said with disgust as he and another guard began to drag her toward an outbuilding that was likely a jail.

"Halt," the command came sharply from behind where they were dragging her.

"Draven!" Piper yelled over her shoulder as the guards' eyes widened at her informality.

"Piper Davies? I thought surely the disgusting woman in the photo wasn't someone actually from Keeneston," King Draven said with shock.

"Yes! It's me," Piper almost wept with relief, ignoring the comments on her current looks.

"Let her go."

Piper turned and quickly covered her eyes with her hand. "Um, you might want to close your robe."

When Piper opened her eyes again, he was standing proudly with his royal member dangling for the whole world to appreciate. "I remember everyone from Keeneston admiring the royal member."

"Look, I'm not interested in your royal member," Piper said, trying to keep her eyes on his face. Because of that eye contact, she saw the moment he smelled her. His nose wrinkled, and his eyes began to water.

"You have killed the royal member with that smell," he said, looking at his retreating penis. "You don't have to worry. It won't touch you with a three-meter pole. Now, what are you doing here, smelling and looking like that?"

"I was kidnapped," Piper said, but before she could explain more there was the sound of an engine revving and yelling at the front gate.

King Draven was shoved toward the palace, but he shook off his guards and grabbed the nearest gun. "Who dares to attack me at my home?" he shouted as he reached for Piper and flung her behind his back.

"It could be Phobos and his gang. They want me."

"Who is this Phobos? It doesn't matter. I will kill him for you and then you will bathe many, many times before you show me gratitude for rescuing you," Draven said as he spread his legs, his royal member rising with excitement. He aimed his gun toward the Hummer barreling toward them.

The large Hummer skidded to a stop, the door was thrown open, and guards shouted, but Piper didn't hear them as the man emerged in full military gear armed to the teeth.

"Aiden!" Piper shoved past Draven and raced toward him. She saw the second he found her with his eyes.

"Piper!" Aiden let the guns he was holding in both hands drop. They were caught by the straps he had attached to his military vest and hung loose as he ran from the cover he'd taken behind his door toward her.

Tears poured from Piper's eyes as they collided. Her arms wrapped around his waist while his arms wrapped around her back. He pulled her tightly against him for a hug before placing both hands on her cheeks and crushing his lips to hers. Piper felt the urgency, the relief, and the fear in the wild kiss. "Are you okay, babe? Oh, luv,

I was so scared. Are you hurt? I'll kill them. I'll kill them all."

"I'm assuming you're not talking about killing the king," Draven said drolly as he ordered his guards to lower their weapons. "And you must be in love with her, otherwise you wouldn't risk your nose to kiss her. I'll give it to you, you must have balls of steel for getting close to her right now."

"You do know your bollocks are just hanging out there, flapping in the breeze, right, mate?"

The guards shifted uncomfortably and Piper laughed. "Um, Aiden Creed, meet King Draven of Bermalia. King Draven, this is Aiden Creed of England. King Draven is about to offer us shelter and a bath," Piper said, catching a whiff of her fish smell as the breeze blew.

"He'd better not be in the bath with you," Aiden muttered.

Draven raised an eyebrow and laughed as his balls bounced. "Draven, put that away. I saw enough of the royal member when you were in Keeneston," Piper demanded.

Draven tied his robe as he chuckled. "I have missed my Kentucky friends. I believe I will accompany you back to Keeneston to guarantee your safety. I recall one woman there who I think would appreciate my royal member very much."

"He's talking about the slag, isn't he?" Aiden whispered, and Piper was laughing too hard to tell him Nikki wasn't a prostitute.

"King Draven rescues internationally famous doctor." King Draven smiled. "Has a nice ring to it, doesn't it?"

"I'm pretty sure I rescued myself," Piper mumbled before her head shot up. "I have to call home! I'm sure they know I'm missing. And Sada? Was she—?" Piper couldn't bring herself to ask if her friend was behind her kidnapping.

"No, she was duped just like Dudley. She's inconsolable."

"Come, come, we'll all call Zain together. Is that little hellion there?" Draven asked as he led them into the palace.

"Which one?" Piper asked. *Little hellion* described half the town.

"Abigail. Talk about a woman to get a man's motor running. You wouldn't know if you were going to get the best sex of your life or end up dead." Draven stopped in an office and typed away at the computer. A second later, Zain flashed onto the screen. Nash, Nabi, Ahmed, and Zain's twin brother, Gabe, were behind him.

"Draven?" Zain answered with surprise.

"I have a surprise for you. Now, where is my friend?"

"Sloane," Gabe called to his wife. "Draven wants to talk to you. Look, this really isn't the best time."

"Hi, Draven. Lord, can you cover up your junk?" Sloane said with a roll of her eyes. "That is not the surprise I was hoping for."

"Maybe this is," Draven said, turning the computer's camera around.

"Piper!" they all yelled. Piper smiled as fresh tears started.

"I'm so glad to see y'all," she said as she sniffled. But that only made her gag. She really did smell bad. "Will you please let everyone know I'm okay?"

"Of course," Miles said as he pushed his way onto the screen. "Your backup is en route. ETA two hours." Then Miles disappeared from the screen, and she could hear him calling her parents.

"We're exhausted and need to clean up. Can someone inform Jamal and have my man, Eddie, flown here?" Aiden requested.

"On it," Nash said before walking away with his phone to his ear.

"I met Phobos," Piper informed them. That quieted the whole room and stopped Nash in his tracks. "And we know him."

"What?" Nabi asked with surprise.

"Agent Rand from Homeland Security. Remember him from Sophie's incident?"

"That asshole who wanted to get to the missile?" Nash asked, putting whoever he was talking to on hold.

"That's right. He's Phobos."

"We're on it," Nash said before rapidly talking into the phone as he hurried to the nearest computer.

"Get cleaned up and we'll touch base in three hours," Zain said with a nod before calling out his thanks to Draven.

"Now, I get you for a little bit all to myself," Aiden whispered in her ear as Piper clung to his hand. She was never going to let him go.

21

"Tomato juice?" Piper asked the stern maid Draven had assigned to her.

"Yes, you stink. It works on dogs. Maybe it'll work on you. Strip. We're going to burn your clothes," she ordered in a tone that evoked no argument from Piper. She was five-foot-nothing, perfectly rounded, around sixty years of age, and Piper had a feeling she was the force behind keeping the palace and Draven running.

"This wasn't exactly what I had in mind when I said I wanted to get you naked," Aiden said with a smirk as he leaned against the vanity in the bathroom with his arms crossed over his chest. His eyes danced with amusement at the five-gallon bucket of tomato juice sitting in the shower and the rough scrub brush in the hands of the woman who had introduced herself as Mrs. Tuma.

Before he could make another smartass comment, a hand thwacked him up against the back of his head. "Naughty. Out!"

"Don't leave me," Piper pleaded.

"Is he your husband? I don't think so. Out!" she said,

thwacking Aiden against the head again. "You help Mrs. T by taking clothes and burn them."

Piper looked with a combination of fear and laughter as the little woman shoved Aiden out the door and slammed the door on his face. "Strip. Now!"

"Yes, ma'am," Piper said on instinct. In the South, you always reverted to manners when faced with an angry woman and a five-gallon bucket of tomato juice.

Piper stripped off her clothes and Mrs. T put them in a bag and shoved them out the door as Piper stepped under the hot spray of water and promptly gagged. The hot water made the smell of the fish even worse.

"Now, we get down to business," Mrs. T said, her voice suddenly sounding strange. When Piper looked over at her, she had a clothespin on her nose and yellow kitchen gloves up to her elbow as she advanced on Piper with the brush.

"Swear to me you won't tell another soul about this," Piper pleaded as tomato juice poured over her.

"Mrs. T swears. We must get you pretty for that man out there. That must be love. He still around when you smell like this," she said with her restricted voice from the clothespin as she began to scrub.

"You think so?" Piper asked as Mrs. T poured more tomato juice over her and went back to scrubbing.

"Mrs. T knows. You two can't stop looking at each other. And Mrs. T saw when you arrived. He storms a palace for you. You two crazy love."

"Crazy in love, you mean?" Piper asked before she was pushed back under the water to rinse off.

"No. Crazy love. Love make you two crazy stupid. Who takes on a whole armed palace? And who hides in tub of fish? See? Crazy love."

Okay, maybe Mrs. T had a point. But love? As Mrs. T

poured more juice over her hair, Piper was lost in thought. Thoughts of her, thoughts of Aiden, thoughts of how he was everything she thought she didn't want in a man but turned out to be perfect for her. As the last of the juice was rinsed from her hair, Piper suffered a major revelation. Aiden Creed had found a place in her heart. How much of a place she didn't know yet, but the thought of letting him go brought a pain to her heart. She had two more hours until they would talk to the group in Keeneston to develop a plan. For two hours, she was safe, clean, and wanted to explore what she was feeling. No more over-thinking. No more analyzing. She was going to follow her heart.

AIDEN SAT on the bed in the room they'd been given. King Draven had winked when he'd shown it to him and whispered to Aiden to check out the nightstand. After dropping off the clothes with a maid who was going to burn them, Aiden arranged for a set of clothes to be sent to Piper's room and headed back to wait for her to finish her skunk scrubbing.

Aiden had been to war, behind enemy lines, rescued hostages, and killed enough people that it unfortunately had become second nature. But never, not once, had he felt the kind of panic he'd felt when he'd woken up and Piper was gone. Aiden was ruthless and emotionally detached. It was why he excelled as a member of the SAS. But now, he felt anything but detached. Every move Piper made, every facial expression, every little breath—he felt them all. Mrs. T and Draven were right. He was in love. And not just a little. The kind that brought him to his knees and begged to be good enough for her.

The knock on the door had Aiden answering and

finding a woman holding a beautiful bright pink tunic embroidered with silver and white, wide-legged linen pants. Aiden thanked the woman and set the clothes on the back of a chair before his eye caught the nightstand. What was Draven talking about? There was a lamp on it, but nothing else.

He listened and heard the shower running and decided to take a look at whatever Draven had left for him. Aiden crossed the brightly colored carpet over the tiled floor and went to the massive four-poster bed. He sat on the side and opened the dark wood drawer. He felt his eyes go wide and then a smile broke out across his face.

"What are you smiling about?"

Aiden looked up to find Piper wrapped in a towel, water dripping from her still wet body. Mrs. T sent him a wink as she carried the empty bucket from the room and closed the door behind her.

"Draven left us a gift."

"What is it?" Piper asked as she padded over in her bare feet. "Oh my God," she gasped as she looked into the drawer filled with condoms, lube, some toys that perplexed them both, and a giant, detailed, penis-shaped dildo. "You don't think . . ."

"Oh, I do. It's a mold of his royal member. At least that's what I'm guessing since HIS ROYAL MEMBER is engraved in the silicone up the shaft."

Piper broke out in deep belly laughs. Her head was tossed back and the sound was pure heaven to Aiden. This is how he liked her. Aiden closed the drawer and reached for Piper. His hands circled her hips as he pulled her between his legs. Her laughter stopped as she put her hands on his shoulders and looked down at him.

"Piper, I'm not a man to talk about my feelings. I spent

years doing everything I could to suppress any feelings I had so I could do my job and do it well. And I'm not exactly sure how to tell you now, but I thought I had died when I woke up and you were gone."

"I knew you would come for me," Piper said softly as she ran her fingers through his short hair.

"I'm so proud of you, Piper. You were braver and more resilient than most men I know. You didn't need me to rescue you. I love that about you. That and a whole lot more." Aiden held his breath as he waited for Piper to say something. They had talked about dating and about their mutual attraction, but one thing was crystal clear after his night chasing her down. He loved her, and he'd do anything if she'd give him a chance.

Piper took a deep breath as she dropped her hands from his hair. "My brain tells me it's our hormones reacting to each other. It could be smell or the fact that my genes find your genes desirable for human procreation. But that's lust, and I'm way past lust. My dopamine, norepinephrine, and serotonin are in full gear, meaning I'm attached to you on a mental level as well as a physical level."

Piper paused and Aiden saw her look worriedly at him all of a sudden as if she realized she'd spoken in complete science talk and was worried he was offended. "So, you think my genes are sexy?" Aiden's lips quirked. "I think it's sexy when you talk science to me."

"Really? You're not just saying that to get laid?"

Aiden laughed as he wrapped his arms around her waist, letting his hands cup her ass. "Really, Piper. I love you as you are, and that includes your brain, heart, and sexy bits," he said, squeezing her ass.

Piper took a step back and Aiden dropped his hands

from around her. Had he pushed it too far? He knew it was early, but his job required him to know his mind and make split-second decisions. Falling in love with Piper Davies was the easiest decision he'd ever made.

Piper reached up slowly and with a single tug, the towel wrapped around her fell to the floor. "Wow, Piper. You're perfect," Aiden said, his voice low and graveled as his throat had suddenly gone dry. That's when he saw it, the hidden sexiness he'd only caught glimpses of underneath her scrubs. When Piper felt comfortable to be herself, she was a confident vixen.

Piper sauntered toward him, her hips swaying, her breasts bouncing, and Aiden's mouth went dry. He wanted to take her hard and fast, but he knew this wasn't the time. Instead, he kicked off his shoes as Piper began to slowly unbutton his shirt. When she'd stripped him bare, he scooted against the pillows and reached for a condom as he let Piper take control. There was something about them together that was explosive. Every touch, every kiss, and the way her legs slid against his. Aiden bit back a groan as Piper explored him with her fingers and lips. She was going to kill him, and he'd die a happy man.

With their lips fused together, Aiden flipped Piper onto the bed. She'd had her fun. Now it was his turn. Every hitch of her breath, every time she tried to stay quiet but couldn't, he'd only push her further to a delicious point of tension. Her body trembled as his ached, and when he finally slid on the condom and they began moving together, it was a lot more than oxytocin binding them together. They were bound fully— heart, mind, and soul.

PIPER LAY CURLED against his side. Her head was on his chest, her arm was on his stomach, and his leg was thrown over hers. She smelled as if she'd just cooked an Italian meal and looked like she'd had mind-blowing sex. Aiden smiled with pride as she nuzzled her head against his chest, her eyes closed, and her face soft with sexual contentment.

The windows on each side of the bed were open, but the drapes were pulled and Aiden watched the shadows playing off the far side of the wall. The sun and shadows danced. While he stroked Piper's hair, he saw the flicker of a shadow that didn't belong. Aiden silently grabbed the nearest weapon, which happened to be the gigantic solid silicone dildo of "The Royal Member" as Piper continued her nap. He held it tightly in his hands as the shadow slipped from the drapes.

Aiden made his move. He shoved Piper off the bed and leapt to his feet. Piper screamed, Aiden swung, and the dildo slammed into the side of the intruder's head. The man, covered in desert camouflage fatigues and face paint, grunted and pulled a knife as Aiden grabbed the cock and balls of the dildo as if it were a staff.

"Come on, mate," Aiden taunted. The man made a swipe with the knife and Aiden smacked the detailed dildo's head against the man's knuckles. He grunted at the pain of the solid sex toy smashing against bone. The two men continued to circle in a deadly game of knife versus dildo.

The man slashed and Aiden tried to spin out of the way but felt the blade slice through his upper arm. He knew from past experience the cut wasn't deep, and as he spun around he jabbed the dildo into the man's face. He'd been trying to blind him, but it ended up being more of a smack across the cheek.

"What the hell? Who hits a man in the face with a dildo?" the intruder shouted before lunging forward with his knife. Aiden moved to block the attack and the knife lodged itself in his weapon. The man cursed as he tried to pull the knife from where it was lodged, quite literally, in the king's shaft.

Piper's head popped up from the floor. "Dylan?"

"Why are you naked?" her brother Dylan growled as he yanked on the knife harder, but it wasn't coming out. "I'll kill you," he threatened Aiden. "You kidnap my sister, force yourself on her, and then hit me I the face with a dildo. You're a dead man."

"Dyl!" Piper yelled as she grabbed the sheet from the bed. "Aiden didn't kidnap me. He's my bodyguard."

"You slept with your client?" Dylan accused. Neither man was letting go of his weapons. Aiden was trying to pull the dildo toward him as Dylan was trying to pull the knife out as well.

"I'm not her bodyguard anymore. I called in backup when I knew I was emotionally compromised. But Piper was kidnapped before he arrived," Aiden grunted as they circled each other with the knifed dildo between them.

"Piper?" Dylan asked. Her name conveyed all the questions he had.

"It's true. Eddie should be here in an hour. He's flying in from Rahmi, and in the meantime, Draven said if we left the palace we could take his guards with us."

"But he's been with you, what three days, and you're falling into bed with him?"

"Don't you dare question your sister! Who she makes love with is none of your business," Aiden said, dropping the dildo and taking a swing at Dylan. Dylan grabbed the royal dildo and swung it. Aiden ducked, ramming his shoulder into Dylan's stomach, shoving him to the floor.

"Stop it!" Piper yelled, but the two men were already at it.

"I know who you are, but I obviously missed something in your history," Aiden said and he tried to get a handle on his opponent. "What are you?" He was well trained as they went hit for hit. Well, it was more hit, block, hit, block. It was like they had the same playbook.

Dylan smirked at him, and not kindly either. "Wouldn't you like to know? You better not touch my sister again or I'll shove my knife into the real thing instead of a plastic mold."

"Dylan! If you don't stop right this instant I'm going to tell Mom all about that night I caught you and Jackson—"

"Okay!" Dylan said, leaping off Aiden and staring accusatorily at him. "But you're not only a bodyguard either."

"SAS. You?" Aiden replied.

"Something like that."

"Ugh," Piper said with a roll of her eyes. "Why are you here? Why are you sneaking into my room through the window?"

Aiden grabbed his pants and stepped into them while Dylan put one foot on the head of the royal member and his other foot on the balls and tried to yank his knife free. "Royal Member?" Dylan muttered with disgust as he read the inscription. "I never thought I'd need to get my knife tested for STDs."

"Dylan," Piper said with impatience.

"Uncle Miles told me you were in mortal danger and sent me the last GPS coordinates before your GPS tracker was destroyed, which was this room."

"You mean Draven doesn't know you're here?" Aiden asked with amusement.

"I thought he was aiding—" Dylan stopped talking with a smile and a shake of his head. "I think the uncles were having some fun with us."

"My uncles placed GPS trackers on me and then sent you in thinking Aiden had kidnapped me with Draven's help. I'm going to kill them," Piper said with a stomp of her foot.

"Hey, it's what we do," Dylan said with a shrug.

"I'm really starting to like your family more and more," Aiden said as he pulled his shirt on. "To be fair to your uncles, they might have given me the GPS trackers. I'm the one who put them in your bras and various other bags, shoes, and clothing."

"You're not half bad yourself," Dylan said, trying to wiggle his knife free from the large replica of Draven's dick. "But you touch my sister again . . ."

Aiden rolled his eyes as the door opened and Aiden reached for his gun as Dylan brandished the knife-dildo weapon.

"Hey, as you can tell I'm already circumcised," Draven said at the horror of seeing his shaft dangling off the knife.

Piper was about to blow. She was furious. "Get out! Everyone get out!"

"If you want the real thing, I'm happy to comply," Draven winked. Piper growled. Not cute either. She looked like she was about to rip his prick right off.

"Fine, fine," Draven said, holding up his hands. "Hey, when did you get here?"

"Just a couple minutes ago," Dylan said as he casually tried to work the knife from the dildo again.

"You've got to cup the balls if you're yanking on it like

that," Draven told Dylan as he stared at the man trying to work the knife free.

"Dylan, get out." Piper was about to lose it.

"What? I just got here," he said, crossing his arms over his wide chest and grinning. He knew Aiden was about to get it for the GPS trackers.

"I'm not going to apologize for putting trackers on you. It's how I found you."

"Dylan, out!" Dylan didn't budge and Piper turned red. "Or I'll tell Mom about that time you and Jackson—"

"You already threatened me with that."

"No, the other time," Piper said smugly.

Her brother was up and out of the room in a split second, pulling Draven with him.

Piper turned to Aiden. "How dare you put trackers on me without telling me?"

"I dare because it's my job to keep you safe. It wasn't like I was tracking your movements because I thought you were out on a date with someone else."

Piper was fuming. Miles had warned him she wasn't used to being tracked like the other Davies cousins. "Babe," Aiden started but then a pillow smacked him in the face.

"Don't *babe* me. You could have told me!" Aiden crossed his arms over his chest and gave her a yeah-right look. "Okay, so maybe I wouldn't have allowed it."

"Have I ever done anything to put you in danger?"

Piper deflated. "No. You haven't. But don't ever do that again!" she said, hurling another pillow at him.

"About that . . . I'll be needing to put some more trackers on you until Phobos is caught."

"Aiden!"

The door opened and Dylan stuck his head in. "Did you say Phobos?"

Piper flung up her hands. "I've lost this discussion, haven't I?"

Aiden grinned at her. "Babe, it's not about winning or losing. It's about being together. And make-up sex."

A knife went flying past Aiden's nose and landed in the headboard. "There will be no make-up sex with my sister."

"I don't stay around long enough for make-up sex. It is worth it? I guess I could have sex, get in a fight, and then have make-up sex all before morning," Draven called from the hall.

"Do you give them all a copy of the Royal Member as a parting gift?" Aiden asked.

Dylan covered up a laugh with a cough and turned to his sister. "He's in. I won't even give him shit at the family dinner."

"I do. How did you know that?" Draven asked.

"Just a guess," Aiden said, trying to keep a straight face as he and Dylan looked at each other. He could tell they were both imagining a closet in Draven's room lined with Royal Members jutting up from where they rested on their balls, ready to be handed out like party favors.

"Was there something you needed?" Piper asked, sounding remarkably similar to her mother about to lose her temper. Dylan took a step back and gestured with his head for Aiden to do the same.

"Zain is set to call in five minutes. And now that you don't smell, I thought you might want to reward me." Draven wiggled his eyebrows as he peered around the door.

"Dylan, do you have another knife?" Aiden asked, staring down the sovereign.

"Fine," Draven said with a roll of his eyes. "Come on. We need to take this call." Draven turned and began walking away with Dylan. Aiden grabbed the clothes for Piper and helped her dress.

"We still need to talk," Piper said as sternly as she could.

"Yes, dear," Aiden said before placing a kiss on her lips. He loved how she melted under him before playfully swatting him. It was time to get back to work.

22

Piper sat down in the office and let Dylan and Aiden take the lead as they talked with all the uncles and Rahmi security at her parents' house. She was still a little peeved about having GPS trackers all over her. But at the same time, she understood. Piper didn't want to remember Dylan seeing her naked. First Jace saw her in her bra, and then Dylan saw her naked. At least he wasn't wearing a helmet cam and broadcasting his invasion of Draven's palace to Keeneston.

"How are you doing, sweetie?"

Piper looked up and saw her parents. At some point, Nash and the rest of the security experts had left, and it was just her parents on the video. Her mom was as big as a house and there was no way Piper was going to upset her. She sat in her favorite chair rubbing her belly. And her dad, while not always the overprotective one, was looking between her and Aiden with suspicion.

"I'm fine. Looking forward to getting a good night's sleep."

"You hear that, Aiden. Sleeeep," Dylan said, dragging the word out.

"Dylan!" Piper smacked her brother who just laughed. "Mom! I forgot to tell you this funny story about Jack—" Piper started to say sweetly before Dylan took her to the ground, covering her mouth with his hand, and pinning her there. She wrestled with her brother as they rolled along the floor.

"That's kind of turning me on. It would be better if it were me down there rather than your brother and we were naked, but whatever," Draven interrupted.

Piper shoved off Dylan and rolled her eyes at Draven, but Aiden was already leaping across the desk toward his laughing face. "Mom, what are you doing?"

Her mother's face was buried in her phone. "Nothing, dear."

"Are you placing a bet on me?"

"No," her mother said scandalously. "I'm placing it on Aiden."

Aiden looked thrilled as he sat back down. Piper just shook her head. "So, what did y'all decide is the plan?"

"Spend the night here and then we'll head back to Kentucky," Dylan told her.

"But I wanted to stay away from Keeneston," Piper told him.

"We will. Dylan, Eddie, and I are taking you back to the Burnstines' farm," Aiden told her.

"Jackson and his gang will help Aiden and Eddie keep you safe while a small group goes out looking for Phobos," Dylan said.

"Small group as in you," Piper said with concern.

"It'll be taken care of, and you'll be away from Keeneston but still close at hand. Wheels up tomorrow at ten in the morning. We'll be home for dinner. Well, I will. You'll be somewhere without the Blossom Café nearby."

Piper rolled her eyes at her brother again as her dad finally spoke. "Did you have any ideas for FAVOR? Or have you been too preoccupied?" He stared daggers at Aiden as he asked.

"Pierce Davies!" Tammy smacked her husband's arm and then smiled and batted her eyelashes at Aiden. "Piper is doing just fine."

"Actually, I am. Aiden helped me talk it out, and I have a few ideas."

"Eddie is bringing everything from Rahmi, so you should be able to work on it when we get to Kentucky. That is, if you can find some lab space."

"That shouldn't be a problem," Pierce said, "but Piper needs to be focused."

"Pierce Davies, I swear if you don't close your mouth right this second I will get pregnant again the second after I have this child."

Her parents began a whispered argument and Piper must have looked ready to lose it because Dylan stepped in. "Dad, Aiden's been great. I won't let the uncles give him any crap. You'll be able to compete for biggest badass son-in-law with this one."

"Badass son-in-law?" Aiden whispered to her.

"The uncles are in competition over who has the biggest badass for a son-in-law. I think Walker and Nash are in a dead heat. But Layne did beat up Nash, so who knows?"

"Oh, that is a good point," her father said. "Well, um, carry on."

"We'll see you tomorrow. We love you," her mother said before they ended the call.

PIPER WANTED to die of embarrassment. She hated being the center of attention and right now everyone was looking at her.

"Yeah, I'm out. I have one badass penis, but I'm not getting married to you," Draven finally said as he stood from behind his desk. "But all this talk of my penis has me in a certain mood. Excuse me. I'll see you at dinner at seven." Draven walked out the door and was already setting up an assignation with one of the many women on speed dial.

"I'm sorry," Piper said to Aiden. "No one is expecting a marriage. I know I'm not."

"Actually, I'd say forty percent of Keeneston is expecting one in the next three months," Dylan said as he put away his phone.

"Did you just bet on me?" Piper asked with horror.

"Hell yes, I did."

"Dylan!"

"You're the one sleeping with him."

Aiden chuckled as he put his hands in his slack's pockets. "When do you think this blessed event will happen?"

"I said within the week. I know that life-and-death situations accelerate the, um, passions," Dylan said with a wide grin.

"I'm seriously going to die now," Piper muttered as she fell back onto a couch in the office.

"Come on, babe," Aiden said with a knowing smirk on his face. "Let's go take a walk around the gardens and plan our wedding."

Piper took his offered hand. "That's not funny."

"Who said I was joking?"

Piper and Aiden spent the next hour walking through the beautiful gardens talking about Keeneston and Lynton. They didn't mention marriage, but Piper noticed when talking about the future, Aiden said *we* a lot. In that moment, it was easy to forget the realities of their situation. They were safe in a picture-perfect palace, and her lab and work were far away. Their real lives were pushed to the side as they pretended everyday could be like this.

And then there was the kissing, the touching, and the almost sex behind giant rose bushes. By the end of the hour, Piper's head and heart were spinning circles. She loved him. She wanted him. She couldn't have him. There would be an ocean separating them. There was also someone trying to kill her.

"Piper, stop thinking."

"What?"

"I can see you thinking and freaking out. Don't borrow trouble. We have enough as it is," Aiden told her as he pulled her against his side while they walked back inside.

"How can I not think about the future and the problems we face?"

"Because I'm an expert problem solver. And let's live in the moment. We don't have to plan our whole lives right now."

"Boss." Piper heard a deep English voice behind her. She turned to find a tall, muscled man with a shaved head standing about fifteen feet away. He was wearing the same outfit as Aiden—slacks and a button-down shirt.

"Eddie." Aiden grinned before quickly introducing them.

"I'm sorry I wasn't there—"

Aiden cut him off, and Piper felt horrible. This man blamed himself for Piper's kidnapping. The two men continued to talk, and Piper learned her things had been put in her room. Dylan joined them, then Piper excused herself.

"Wait, Dr. Davies," Eddie called out before hurrying to catch up with her. "I'm sorry, we usually have these meetings away from the client. We like to all be on the same page."

"It's okay, Eddie. And please call me Piper. I just thought to jot down some ideas I had. I'll let Aiden fill you in. And thank you for coming on such short notice. I hope your family isn't upset."

"It's a pleasure. My wife divorced me after my second tour of duty and remarried. I'm raising our daughter, but she's at boarding school right now, so the house is pretty quiet until she comes home for Christmas."

"How old is your daughter?"

"Sixteen. She's into science too. If she finds out I am protecting you, she'll be so jealous."

"I'd love to meet her," Piper said as they approached her room. Eddie held out his hand to stop her from entering.

"Give me a minute to make sure everything is clear." Eddie disappeared into the room and a couple minutes later came back out. "Now, if you promise to stay in this room until dinner, I'll finish my briefing. But if you need me, I can put it off until tonight."

Piper smiled gently at him. "I promise to stay here. Thank you, Eddie."

Piper closed the door and took a deep breath. She had so much to think about, but her mind kept wandering to Aiden. Live in the moment. Be in the moment. She could do that. It was against her nature, but she should at least try. Her cousins always rolled their eyes at her and her ten-year plan. Maybe she did need to live more. And if that meant having Aiden in her life, surely that wasn't a bad thing.

WITH A ONE-WEEK PLAN IN MIND, Piper pulled out the things Eddie had brought from the lab and went to work. Before she knew it, Aiden was knocking on the door. "Come in," she called out.

Aiden pushed open the door carrying his bags. "I hope this isn't presumptuous of me, but Eddie should be nearby and I was hoping to spend the night with you so I gave him the room next door."

Piper's heart answered for her. It flipped and she felt her pulse race. "I'd like that."

She bent her head into her work as Aiden set his things down. "It's time for dinner."

"I'm not hungry. I think I'm onto something. It's like I said . . ."

Piper trailed off and didn't even realize she'd done so until a plate of food appeared in front of her. When she looked up, the room was cast in evening shadows, and Aiden was quietly slipping through the open connecting door where Eddie was sitting watching her from his room. How long had they been like that?

"I thought it was time for dinner?" Piper called out, stopping Aiden's progression into Eddie's room.

"It was, two hours ago. I knew you must have been in the zone so I brought you some food. I'll stay out of your way until you're done." Unlike past boyfriends, Aiden smiled and meant it. In the past, they'd been upset if she'd ignored them while absorbed with work.

"Are you sure?"

"Of course. I'm not a young chap who needs constant

attention. I am a grown man with my own interests, you know." He winked and Piper felt her face blush. Oh, she knew he was a grown man.

"I'm so close to figuring this out. I can't wait to get my sample back and get into the lab. I can do some of it in Lexington, but I'll need my sample."

"That's great. I'm proud of you. Now, eat and work. And when you're done, we'll play." Aiden's voice dropped for the last part and Piper licked her lips. She could play forever with him, but his praise gave her the extra motivation to get back to work.

EDDIE HAD GONE to bed three hours earlier. Aiden sat propped up in bed reading as Piper scribbled away. Her fingers flew over a calculator, her mouth moved without words coming out, and her hair was now pulled half out of her ponytail. She was beautiful. It was something to watch her work. He could see her brain connecting the dots, filling the information in, and calculating like no other brain could. Aiden felt honored to be able to watch such brilliance at work. Soon his girl would save the world. Aiden smiled with pride and went back to reading.

It was three in the morning when Piper screamed and jumped up so fast she knocked her chair over. "What is it?" Aiden asked, dropping the book and leaping from the bed.

Piper jumped again, then giggled.

"Oh, yeah, I sleep in the nude. I can grab some shorts."

"No!" Piper said, giggling again as she ran over to him and jumped.

Aiden caught her in his arms but had to lower her because she was a ball of energy. "I got it! At least I'm almost positive I got it. I think I know how to fix it. It was there all along," Piper said so quickly Aiden struggled to hear her as she began to pace. "I mean, it was the nanoparticles—it's like baking. Vary the ingredients, temperature, baking time, and it affects the food. Same thing here. I wasn't *cooking* them long enough and that led to them being unstable. Once they're stable, I'll add in the antiviral component, and I think they'll be able to be delivered into the host. I just have to test out my theory. I can't believe it was this easy!" Piper stopped pacing and her face fell. "Maybe it's not this easy. Maybe this isn't it at all."

Aiden grabbed her and pulled her to him. "You have a good idea, and you're going to try it. I bet it works. I'd bet my life on you and that magnificent brain of yours. You were mesmerizing to watch work."

"What if it doesn't work?"

"Then you'll try something else. But you have an idea and I think you should run with it."

"Phobos," Piper cursed.

"Will be caught soon. In the meantime, I think we should celebrate. All your bouncing around has given me an idea." Aiden's idea was poking her excitedly in her stomach.

Without warning, he wrapped his arm around her waist and fell back against the bed, pulling her on top of him. "I like this idea," Piper said with a mischievous grin. She ground her hips against his, sending his eyes rolling back in his head. When he opened them again, she was straddling him. She reached down and slowly stripped her shirt from her body and tossed it on the floor. Her breasts brushed his face as she leaned for the drawer and pulled out a condom. Oh yes, his Piper was something else all right.

23

The plane ride home was not what Piper was expecting. First, Draven had insisted they take his private plane. He'd told his bodyguards he was going to his regularly scheduled orgy and ditched them at the palace, assuring them that the royal member would be in safe hands. Dylan, Eddie, and Aiden didn't like the implication, but Draven winked as they boarded the plane and Eddie asked if Draven really did have a scheduled orgy.

Once on the plane, the men laughed and told stories as if they were old buddies. The food was excellent, the drinks delicious, and Piper actually enjoyed herself. She even discovered there was a funny, nice man under Draven's horniness, but only after a couple minutes of him complaining about missing an actual orgy.

"We're on our descent," the pilot told them over the intercom. Piper looked out the window at the sun setting over the Bluegrass Region. It made everything glow a warm orange. The rolling hills, the bare autumn trees, and the miles of fences all glowed. Piper watched horses gallop through their pastures as the plane flew closer to the airport.

"Dylan said your cousin Jackson is meeting us at the airport," Aiden said, sliding onto the couch next to her. He put his arm around her shoulder, and she leaned into him. "He's an FBI hostage rescuer?"

"Yes. He's very good at his job too. And his two main partners are hilarious. Talon Bainbridge is Australian. Lucas Sharpe is from northern Alaska and says he grew up playing with polar bears."

"Just when I thought I couldn't love your town more," Aiden said with a chuckle as his phone rang. "It's your mom," he said to Piper as he accepted the video call.

Only it wasn't her mother on the other end.

"Phobos!" Piper gasped. Dylan and Eddie moved quickly and silently toward her so they could listen better.

"I figured you'd run to your boyfriend. Where are you, Piper? It's not polite to run out like that." Phobos's voice was mocking but deadly. She'd angered him.

"Where are my parents?" Piper asked instead.

The phone was turned and Piper stopped breathing when she saw them. "You tied up my mother?" Piper screamed. "She's nine months pregnant!"

"And she and her baby will die if you don't bring your work to me now." Piper saw a man put a knife to her mother's belly, a man she recognized as Royce. Her mother would have cussed him a new one, but her mouth was covered by tape. Her arms and legs were bound together, but at least they'd put her feet up in the recliner. Her father was similarly bound and gagged on the couch next to her.

Piper didn't dare look at Dylan. She could imagine the way his eyes went from twinkling with laughter to flat with death in a split second. There were times her own brother scared her, but she'd never been more relieved to have him with her.

"What formula?" Aiden asked Piper. "What does this man want with you?"

Piper was too stunned to talk at first. But then Dylan kicked her foot out of range of the camera and gestured for her to play along. "I made something this man wants."

"Something? Like a new drug?"

"Yes, something like that," Piper said as her mind couldn't tear itself away from her mother and father held hostage. Rage and fear battled as her heart felt like it would explode before either emotion won out.

"Then give it to him!" Aiden practically yelled.

"That's right. Listen to your boyfriend," Phobos grinned as if he'd just won.

"It'll take time. It's not here right now."

"And where is here?" Phobos asked casually, but she knew it wasn't casual. He wanted to know, and she was at a loss for what to say.

"We're about to land in Rahmi. Piper was found dehydrated in the Surman desert."

"Then you have ten hours to get here with your work, or I'll start killing. I'll start with your unborn sibling and move to your mother, father, and then your little sister. She sure is cute." Phobos held up a family photograph and set it down. "Don't think about calling in for help either. I have people hidden all over town. One move from your cousins or from the Rahmi guards and I start killing. And I won't stop until the formula is here. Do you understand?"

"I understand," Piper said as she slowly nodded her head. "Please, just untie my mother."

"No can do. The bitch almost ripped one of my guys' eyes out. See you soon, Piper. And only Piper."

"But I can't bring it all myself. My brother can help me," Piper said, trying to find a way to get Dylan into the house.

"I don't think so. I've seen pictures of your brothers. One is a crack shot, even if he's a doctor, and the other looks like a tank. He can come. The scientist. Royce said he was boring as hell. You're lucky he only drugged him and didn't kill him."

Aiden looked affronted but kept quiet. "Okay. Can I have twelve hours? The stuff is hidden, and I'll have to pack it up real well. There's lots of it," she lied. It was really only a few vials and her notes and there was no way she was going to be able to get to them in time.

"I'll give you eleven hours. Not a second more." Then he disconnected the call. Aiden held up his finger to stop them from talking until he had completely disabled his phone. It sat in three pieces on the table before anyone talked.

"I'll kill them," Dylan said simply.

"I'll help," Aiden said.

"Me too," Eddie put in.

"Not me. I'm too important to get in a shoot-out."

Piper punched Draven. His head snapped back and Piper yelped as she shook out her hand. "You can't compare to my parents."

"I didn't say I could. I just said I can't die. I'm a king, not a soldier. Plus you haven't met my cousin who would take over the crown if I die. He's a complete asshole. But I can hire a mercenary army in a heartbeat for you."

"No need. We'll handle this ourselves," Dylan said as the plane touched down in Lexington. "We have Jackson, Talon, and Lucas. That's six trained men."

"And one pissed-off woman," Piper said as rage won out over fear. She'd always been the passive one, but not now. She wanted to kill someone badly. Someone named Phobos or Royce who dared put a knife to her mother. And she knew how to do it.

"No, you're staying at the farm," Aiden told her. Piper spun at him and glared. Aiden glared back.

"I'm coming."

"I'll make a deal with you. You can come, but you have to stay in the car and promise to leave if we tell you."

"Fine. Give me your phone," Piper said, turning to Dylan.

"Who are you going to call?"

"Give me the phone," she said with a new seriousness.

Dylan quickly handed his phone over. He'd never seen her this way. Emotional, sure. But deadly calm? Nope, and he was probably as scared as she should be if Piper could feel anything right now.

"Dudley, this is Piper. Want to earn your way back into my good graces?" Piper waited as Dudley quickly agreed. "Good. I need you to bring some things to the private jet wing of the airport right now. I expect you there in thirty minutes."

When Dudley said he was ready, Piper rattled off the list of things she needed and hung up. Her mind was flying a mile a minute as chemical formulas flashed before her eyes.

"Um, luv," Aiden said slowly. "You do know that some of those things can be made into a bomb, right?"

Piper just nodded as she grabbed a napkin and started scribbling. She had a plan. First thing was to get bulletproof coats for her and Aiden. The others would have vests. But now she had work to do while the guys made their plans.

Draven directed the pilot to taxi straight into the rented hangar. The plane came to a stop, the door opened, and Draven exited the plane first. Piper was the last one out as she was still jotting down formulas. When she walked down the steps, she found Jackson, his dark hair cut short and his silver eyes hard as steel, talking to Dylan. It was clear introductions had been made and the group of soldiers was getting down to work.

Jackson saw her first as he strode over to her, his face hard and impenetrable. "We'll get your parents. I swear."

"I know, because I have a plan."

Jackson's eyebrows rose as the men began taking over a large steel table in the hangar. "Piper, hostage rescue is kind of my thing. I think we'll go with my plan."

"We'll see," she smiled as she took a seat in the corner of the hangar, grabbed some paper, and got to work.

"WHAT IS SHE DOING OVER THERE?" Talon asked as they all stared at Piper spread out across the floor. Papers were scattered. Dudley was pulling tons of supplies from his car and laying them out on the floor in front of her.

"I don't know, but she hasn't talked to us in thirty minutes and lots of those chemicals can be made into a bomb," Aiden said, watching now as small vials were set out.

"I know, but she wouldn't blow up our parents or their house, so I'm not really sure what she has planned. But I know that look. I've never seen it on Piper, but when my mom gets those crazy eyes, you just back the hell up and do whatever she says," Dylan told them.

"Thanks for the advice," Aiden said with a smirk.

"Whoa," Jackson said, looking back and forth among Aiden, Piper, and Dylan. "Are you two together now? What's happened in the past week? And how are you okay with this? I'd kill any man who touched my sister."

Aiden's smirk turned into a full-sized grin. "Want to tell them how we met, mate?"

Dylan shot him the finger and turned to his sister. "Piper, um, do you need any help?"

"Nope, this will only take a little bit," Piper said, not looking up.

"I'm pretty good with explosives. There's not much to do in the wilds of Alaska during the long winters," Lucas said with a shrug. "Want any help?"

"Really?" Piper asked, looking up.

"Babe, I'd wager to say all of us know how to build a range of different bombs," Aiden said, looking at what she had laid out.

"This isn't your normal bomb. What do you know about triggers? I have the chemistry down, but if you all know detonators, then yeah, I could use the help."

Aiden and the guys walked over to where she and Dudley were working. "Do you want to hear our plan and then you tell us yours?"

"Sure," she said, not looking up as she measured out something from a vial.

"We were going to surround the house, throw in some flash grenades, and storm in. Kill everyone who isn't a Davies," Dylan told her.

"Well, I think my plan is better. I feel like making a statement. A big one."

"I'd say all that magnesium will do the trick. It's a flashy way to go," Talon said, looking at what she'd rigged up so far.

"I didn't have any C4 at the lab. I guess you all probably have some," Piper said sheepishly as if thinking about what they did for the first time.

"Got some right here," Lucas said, pointing to a duffle

bag. "But magnesium is fun too. It adds a real flare to the bomb."

"I think blowing up their cars, drawing most of them away from my mom and dad, and then hitting them with this," she said, holding up a vial.

"What's that?" Eddie asked, but Aiden was afraid he already knew.

"Something very bad. It's called C1B3. It takes about two minutes for the effect to kick in, and then you won't need to worry about them anymore," Piper said smugly. But then her smug smile dropped. "But that doesn't take care of the people inside. I could drop the virus down the chimney, but that puts a quick timetable on getting to my parents and delivering the antidote. The antidote is safe for a pregnant woman, but I wouldn't want the baby to be exposed to the virus for more than a moment. Preferably not at all, so that's why I came up with this plan instead of fumigating the house with a C1B3."

"What about the guys outside?" Jackson asked.

"We release it like a smoke bomb, right off the patio. They should come out to investigate. There's still cover there so you wouldn't be able to get a clear shot. But my virus can live for five minutes in the air and they won't even know it's there. That five minutes is enough time to infect those sent outside to check out the explosion. More will come out since magnesium burns so brightly. It's not what they would expect. Then wait five minutes and go in. They'll be down in numbers for sure," Piper explained.

"What if the air drifts inside? Will Mom and Dad get sick?" Dylan asked.

"They're in the back of the house, so it's possible but not likely. They could, but death isn't immediate. It takes forty-eight hours to actually die and by then we can get them the antidote. If they do get infected, the first symptom is debilitating cramping, followed by vomiting. After your body gets completely dehydrated, the organs begin to shut down. That's where it gets even more painful. That's why Mom especially needs to get the shot immediately. I don't expect it to take fifteen minutes for you to breach the house. I'm hoping more like a minute or two after people start falling down."

Aiden and the rest of the guys looked down at the vials and took a step back. "Roll up your sleeves. I'll give you the antidote now. It's what we've been making. That, and the viral bullets. You'll be safe from the virus if you are exposed to it."

"Isn't it easier to shoot them?" Talon asked.

"Well, yes and no. Here's my thinking," Piper said, jabbing a needle into Aiden's arm. "Magnesium explosion, no attack, then a couple minutes later, men start dropping like flies. They're going to be completely confused and maybe Mom and Dad could escape in the confusion. If they do, then you can go in shooting anything that moves. If they don't, then the next part is up to you. But also, if Phobos is infected, it's a very painful death. He'd tell you anything not to die after the virus kicks in."

"You were so sweet and kind growing up," Dylan said, shaking his head before smiling. "But I've never felt closer to you than I do now, Sis. I like it."

Aiden rolled his sleeve back down and examined the jacket Piper had given him. It was lightweight, which made it so much easier to move in than a bulky vest. He checked the weapons as Eddie got his injection.

"It feels good to be back in the saddle, doesn't it?" Eddie asked as the men began to go through all their equipment.

After everyone had their shot, Lucas helped with the

detonator while Jackson and Dylan called neighboring farms to have them go into the café for dinner. "Should you be doing that?" Aiden asked after Jackson hung up.

"They won't say anything on the text loop and it's only two houses that are quite a distance from Uncle Pierce. They've staggered their leaving thirty-six minutes apart. They'll also keep quiet because they'll want to be the ones to break the gossip when the magnesium lights up the night sky and people start shooting."

"We'll leave here in two hours. I have a friend in the FAA who filed a flight plan and shows the arrival of a private jet along the time frame Piper gave them. They shouldn't expect us until much later," Dylan announced.

Piper nodded and looked at her stuff. "Want me to make another bomb?"

"You are now my favorite sister. Don't tell Cassidy," Dylan joked.

The two siblings talked as Jackson, Lucas, and Talon sat down with Aiden and Eddie. Soon they were telling war stories as Draven and Dudley talked while sitting in some folding chairs. Draven had been quiet during the planning. He offered to get whatever they needed, but Piper had reassured him she had all she needed.

"Where do you want us?" Dudley asked when it was time to start loading up.

Dudley and Draven looked as if they were going to join them, but Aiden knew that wasn't in the plans.

"They can come with me," Piper said. "Dudley, can you bring the virus and the antidotes and keep them safe?"

Dudley nodded and went to make sure everything was carefully packed.

"Sis, they don't need to come. You don't need to come."

Piper rolled her eyes at her brother and promptly

ignored him as she went back to work. "I'll drive Dudley's car and be right behind you all. Draven is always handy if we need a distraction."

"I could grab this one girl, and we could have sex in the front yard," Draven offered up.

"He's talking about the slag, right?" Aiden whispered to Dylan.

"Nikki isn't a prostitute. I'm assuming that's who you mean," Dylan said as Aiden nodded.

"Really? She's not?" Aiden asked for clarification.

"Nikki, right?" Jackson asked Draven.

"Who?" Draven knitted his brow in confusion.

"The woman you slept with. Nikki Canter, right? Huge, ginormous breasts and equally inflated ass," Jackson supplied.

"Oh, no. She scares the royal member. She might break it."

"It's not Poppy, is it?" Lucas asked.

"Or Zinnia?" Talon asked right after.

"Who?"

Talon and Lucas let out a breath. "They work in the café," Talon supplied.

"No. Cute though," Draven said, giving them a thumbs up.

"Are you finally going to ask them out?" Piper asked the two FBI agents.

"What? Why?" Lucas asked.

"We were just curious," Talon filled in as Piper rolled her eyes.

"Wait, then who from Keeneston is your girl?" Dylan asked the king.

Draven smiled wide. "A king doesn't kiss and tell."

"But apparently he'll shag with her in the front yard," Eddie whispered and Aiden had to fight laughing.

"Okay, y'all. It's time." Dylan announced.

Aiden headed for Piper and grabbed her hand. "I don't like leaving you unguarded."

"I'm not. Draven and Dudley are with me. And I'll only be unguarded for thirty minutes while we drive to our meeting spot in Keeneston." Piper leaned forward and Aiden kissed her as if they had been doing it forever. It was so natural to kiss her goodbye, even when they were only going to be apart for a short time.

"I'll see you soon," Aiden whispered to her as he squeezed her hand. It was hard for him to drop it and walk away. But her parents were in danger, and he knew he needed to be with his team for this. Piper would be safe, he told himself, because he would take out the entire Phobos crew before they could find her.

24

The Blossom Café was busy that night as the Rose sisters ambushed Cady Woodson, the new and very young master distiller of Barrel Creek Distillery. She'd just lost her father a year before and was spending every moment she had renovating the ancient distillery on the outskirts of the county. Reagan and Carter had been lucky enough to get married there and that had offered the town their first glimpse of the revitalized grounds.

It was built of old limestone and had been empty since Prohibition. Cady might only be twenty-three, but she had grown up with a father who was a famous master distiller who had taught her everything he knew. She'd bought and made the distillery functional enough to get the first batch of bourbon barreled and stored recently. Now she was slowly using her inheritance to upgrade machinery, plumbing, and electrical. She handled all the cleaning and what renovations she could do all by herself. She'd turned a grand open space with pine floors and large windows into a reception hall. Cady said she would start giving tours of the facility three days a week in the spring.

And it was Cady the Rose sisters needed to speak to. They needed this young, shy, and somewhat reclusive woman's help.

"Hello, dearie," Miss Lily said, taking a seat at Cady's empty table in the back of the café. Her sisters followed suit and soon Cady was surrounded and looking quite nervous about it.

"Hello."

"Do you believe in love?" Miss Lily asked.

Cady's face turned bright red, and she choked a little on the sweet tea she was drinking. "Excuse me?"

"Do you believe in love?" Miss Violet repeated.

"I mean, I loved my dad. But I haven't had any time for love myself."

"But you believe in it, right?" Miss Daisy pushed.

"Yes," Cady answered nervously as she looked from sister to sister. "But I'm too young and have too much to do to get married, so please don't bet on me," she pleaded.

"Oh goodness no! It's not your time yet," Miss Lily said with a smile.

"But there is a couple long overdue, and we want your help to give them a little push," Miss Violet explained.

Cady looked relieved. "Well, sure, I guess. What do I need to do?"

"After the wedding, Gemma Davies ran a great article about how romantic your venue is," Miss Daisy began.

"And we want you to offer a giveaway for a romantic evening at your distillery. A private tour followed by a candlelight dinner with music sounds good," Miss Lily told her. "We envision it before Christmas with the room filled with decorations and glowing in the candlelight."

"I can do that, but I don't have the money for a band and

such. I can cook, but it's not as good as y'all's food," Cady said, and the Rose sisters just smiled and sat back.

"Don't worry about a thing. We'll cover all the costs and provide the dinner. We just need you to pick the most romantic spot and then make sure you draw a certain name when the time comes," Miss Lily said as she grinned in victory.

"That's cheating," Cady whispered as if someone would tell on her.

"It's not cheating. It's helping fate along," Miss Daisy said, waving at Poppy who nodded and then came back a few minutes later with a gigantic bowl, pens, and little pieces of paper.

"Here you go," she said, setting it on the table. "What's this for?"

"Cady is having a drawing for a super-romantic tour and dinner for two at her distillery," Miss Violet told her.

"Oh! I want to sign up. I don't have a date, but I'd find one for a tour of the distillery."

That was all it took. The Rose sisters sat back and watched as the news spread and everyone signed up for a chance to win, including the one person who was destined to win.

~

"*Squawk*, you're too old," sang Gus, Pierce's now forty-year-old blue-fronted Amazon parrot from his perch in the living room. "Too old, *squawk*."

"Gus," Tammy hissed as she narrowed her eyes at her husband who looked sheepishly away.

"Can I borrow your gun?" Tammy asked the man in charge, the same man she'd seen before when Sophie and

Nash saved the missile from going off. He'd said he was with the Department of Homeland Security. Nash had said he was having trouble following leads to find his true identity yesterday, and really, Tammy didn't care who he was just as long as her daughter did the right thing and stayed far, far away.

"Aw, that's a good bird," Gus cooed as he cocked his head and looked at Tammy.

"Bad bird!" Tammy argued with the bird to the amusement of the men there.

"Too old, too old," Gus started singing as he bopped along his perch.

The men guarding them broke out into laughter. They'd made themselves at home since they'd stormed the place and taken the husband and wife hostage. Tammy looked at the clock. It was time for dinner and one of the men was cooking in the kitchen.

"Where did he learn that?" the main man, who she assumed was Phobos, asked, taking a seat across from where she was tied up.

"I'll give you a guess," Tammy said, glaring at her husband. Bless his heart. Right now, anger was the only thing keeping her together. Anger that her husband kept telling her she was old. Anger at this man for tying them up. Anger that her loved ones were in danger. And most importantly, anger at the threat the man at the window across the room made against her unborn baby. Royce was his name, and there wasn't a doubt in her mind that if she could, she would kill him. The thought of losing any of her family made her angry. She was a mother and a wife and she was going to kick some ass. Well, first she was going to pee, then she was going to kick ass.

"I need to use the bathroom, and my feet are swelling to

the size of watermelons. Is it possible to let me walk around a little?" Tammy asked, looking sadly at her swollen ankles.

Phobos looked at her and Tammy looked pitifully at her feet again as she rubbed her very pregnant belly and felt a kick. She rubbed on her unborn child, telling him or her she'd take care of them no matter what. Sometimes moms just needed to do whatever it took to get things done.

The man picked up his walkie-talkie. "Is everything clear?"

"Clear in back."

"Clear out front."

Phobos looked around at the men stationed in the living room as the men from other parts of the house checked in. All clear. Thank goodness. Piper better stay away if she knew what was good for her.

"Okay, but you have to keep the door half open."

"At this point y'all could watch me, because if I don't go now I'll be peeing right here." Tammy struggled to sit up as Phobos came over and untied her feet. He pushed the recliner down as Pierce tried to help push her up with his tied hands. Since her hands were still tied, Phobos had to heft her up.

Pain shot through her feet and Tammy almost embarrassed herself by falling. Phobos steadied her as he looked at her. "You're not going to have this baby right now, are you?"

"No, I'm not due for another week. But I am going to pee right here if you don't help me to the bathroom."

Phobos helped her to the bathroom in the little hallway between the kitchen and the living room. "Watch her," he ordered to the man cooking as Phobos headed to the front of the house. Tammy didn't care where he was going. All she cared about was relief and a chance to think of a way to escape. Maybe she could light a fire in the bathroom and then run. She looked at the small window and knew crawling out wouldn't work. Her belly wouldn't fit.

She had to think of something and fast. She had a husband, a parrot, and her unborn child to save. There might be ten men there, but they were no match for a pissed-off mother.

25

“Be very careful with this,” Piper said for the tenth time as she handed the homemade chemical balls to Jackson. They looked like marbles but were actually rigged out of condoms. Thanks again to Draven.

“I’m a crack shot, Piper. I’ll make it,” Jackson said for the tenth time as he loaded the condoms of death into a paintball gun they’d rigged to get more distance. Piper had five of them ready to go, and Jackson was going to shoot them along the porch. Piper held back a sixth ball in case of emergency. She had two syringes on her with different color ribbons tied to each to indicate they held the virus, a small vile of antidote, and several hypodermic needles at the ready.

“We’re all set,” Aiden reported as he joined them in a field behind her parents’ house. A quarter mile or so of woods separated them from the house. “Dylan has the bomb in place on a very nice black SUV and is in position. Talon and Lucas are ready as well. Lucas will blow the car when we are all in place.”

Eddie strapped on his vest and checked his weapons one last time. "I'm all set too."

Piper gave two doses of the antidote to Aiden. "Inject my parents immediately, even if they have no symptoms. This will prevent them from getting it."

The plan was for Jackson, Dylan, Talon, and Aiden to do what was needed to allow Eddie and Aiden to rescue her parents. If all went to plan, everyone on the team could waltz right into the house and get her parents out without a single shot being fired, but that was too much to hope for. Not all the men would come out to investigate, but those who did would no longer be a threat.

Jackson leaned over and gave Piper a quick kiss on the cheek. "We'll get your parents, Cuz. Don't worry about a thing."

And then he took off. He was going to have to run about a mile in the growing darkness to stay wide of any guards and to make it to the front of the house. Eddie had taken some steps away and Piper realized he was giving her and Aiden some privacy.

"This isn't what you signed on for. You don't have to do this," Piper told him as he wrapped his arms around her and pulled her close.

"I'm not doing this because of a job. I'm doing this because they're your parents. I'm doing this for you. And I would do this to help anyone in need. It's why I went into the profession I did. But this time I have you to come back to."

"You'd better come back to me," Piper said, her throat tightening as she willed herself not to cry.

"Nothing could keep me away. I have a first date to plan and a woman to make fall in love with me," Aiden smiled down at her. He slowly leaned forward and kissed her. What scared her was this kiss felt like goodbye.

As Piper watched him head off into the woods, she wished she'd told him she was already in love with him.

"I could take your mind off him," Draven called out from where he was leaning against the side of the car with his arms crossed and a cocky smile on his face. He winked and Piper laughed.

AIDEN AND EDDIE ran silently through the woods. He might be retired from the British Army SAS, but you didn't forget your training. He and Eddie both trained regularly with current members and kept up with the physical standards. But more than that, it was a mindset: how you moved, how you thought, how you processed your surroundings.

He and Eddie fanned out. Though they were both coming from behind the house, they would be coming from two different directions. Aiden dropped silently to the ground and pulled out his gun. He was fifteen feet from the backyard, still in the shadow of the woods as he scoped his surroundings.

"I have two men back here, walking back and forth across the back patio," Aiden said into his coms.

"Clear on the north side," Lucas replied.

"Clear on the south side," Talon added.

"Two men out front," Dylan said. "Waiting for slowpoke Jackson."

"Bite me. You're not running with a deadly chemical gun," Jackson said over the coms, not even breathing hard. A mile was nothing to them. They trained under far more stressful and changing circumstances.

"Try running in hip-deep snow with a polar bear

chasing you," Lucas said with a chuckle. "Fun times. Man, sometimes I miss home. Bertha is a real sweetie. She probably wouldn't have killed me."

Aiden shook his head as he struggled not to laugh and blow his cover. While his training made it possible to easily fit in and work with similarly trained men, and despite the fact that he'd worked with some real characters in their own right, he'd never encountered a team like this before.

"I'm in position and taking aim," Jackson said as everyone got ready. Aiden attached the silencer, then flipped the safety off on his gun. His body relaxed as he got into position. His muscles twitched with anticipation, ready to react to whatever came next.

"Ready. On your mark," Lucas said more seriously than Aiden had ever heard him.

The coms were quiet for a moment. No sounds were heard until the coms crackled. "Mark," Jackson said and a second later a blinding light lit the night sky, but Aiden didn't look. He kept his eyes on the two men out back.

~

TAMMY WAS WALKING out of the bathroom when a blinding light shone through the windows. There was yelling as Phobos ordered men to check it out. They turned their backs on her and Pierce and raced to the windows and the front door. Even the asshole in the kitchen ran past her, knocking her against the wall, dropping the pan he'd been using.

Tammy glanced around before sneaking into the kitchen. She wrapped her hand around her favorite pan, a gift from Miss Violet, and then looked around and decided to grab a knife. It was awkward with her hands tied together, but she fumbled them into position and headed to save her husband, bless his heart.

"What the hell is that?" Phobos yelled as men ran out of the house to investigate. "Watch for an ambush," he warned before turning to Royce. "Check to see where the plane is."

The man was pulling something up on his phone as Tammy took a seat next to Pierce. She hid the pan under her leg and pulled the knife out and went to work on Pierce's ropes. Keeping one eye on Phobos and Royce checking on Piper's plane, she sawed through the bindings on Pierce's ankles.

"Hurry," Pierce whispered as she moved to start cutting the bindings at Pierce's wrists. Her heart pounded, her hands were sweaty, and she almost cheered out loud when the ropes gave way. Pierce grabbed the knife and started on her bindings when Royce began to turn.

"Stop," she whispered, but Pierce had already tucked his hands and the knife between his legs.

The man looked at them briefly before turning back to Phobos. "It says they're over the Atlantic. Their flight is scheduled to land in five hours."

"Can they verify who the passengers are?"

"Yes, Piper Davies and Aiden Creed. Plus two pilots. That's it, and my source is in the FAA. It's solid."

Phobos turned to them and Tammy froze. "Do you know anything about this?"

They both shook their heads. "Could it be one of your enemies?" Tammy asked. "I mean, if you're good at your job, which it appears you are, you've probably made enemies. A rival group or something that might want to take you out?"

Phobos turned around, no longer paying them any attention. The front door opened and one of the guards hurried inside. "There's no one out there."

"Check again," Phobos snapped, sending the man running back outside. "Could it be Zhao?" he asked quietly to Royce.

"It could be, but why not attack? And how would they know we were here?"

Pierce turned and began to quickly saw through her bindings. From outside they heard screaming, moaning, and even crying. Phobos was pressed against the window, gun in hand as he tried to see out front. Tammy's ropes snapped when the front door opened and a man stumbled into the living room. His face was white, sweat poured from his brow, his walking was stiff as if his legs had cramped before he fell to the ground writhing in pain. "We're all down," he said through clenched teeth as he grabbed his stomach and howled in pain. He wrapped himself into a small ball of pain on the floor.

Instinctively, Tammy covered her mouth with her hand, only realizing too late that she'd shown her hands to be untied. Her eyes clashed with Royce's whose eyes widened. He lunged forward and Tammy screamed. She wrapped her arms around her unborn child and rolled from the man, giving him her back. Instead of the pain of his touch, she heard the sickening sound of a knife ripping through cloth and sinking into flesh.

"Pierce!" Tammy shouted as she spun in horror.

Only it wasn't Pierce who was stabbed. It was the man who had threatened her child. Her husband's face was set in stone as he slowly pulled the blade from the man's chest and held out his other hand for his wife. "We're leaving," he said, grabbing her hand and squeezing it to so tightly Tammy thought he might break it.

Tammy grabbed the pan in her left hand as Pierce pointed the knife at Phobos with his right. "And you're not going to stop us," her husband said to Phobos as he tried to walk them by him.

"I don't think so," Phobos said with confidence. "Didn't anyone tell you never to bring a knife to a gunfight?"

Pierce whistled and Gus squawked before flying from his perch. Tammy didn't stop to think as Phobos raised his gun. Gus stomped his claws on Phobos's head, ripping hair and skin. Tammy swung just as Pierce whistled again. Gus flew up a second before Tammy backhanded the cast iron pan into the side of Phobos's head.

~

AIDEN AND EDDIE held still as the men searched the area. When they reported the all clear, Aiden made his move. He ran from the shadows, and in less than a second, he'd shot both men dead. Eddie, on the other hand, shot him the finger for taking out his man. Aiden grinned at him as he vaulted the back railing and landed quietly on the porch.

Both men flattened themselves against the back of the house on each side of the door. They counted down and Aiden shoved the door open, rolling inside as Eddie took aim and would provide cover if necessary. Instead of having to take down men, Aiden found a very pregnant Tammy swinging an iron skillet as if it were a baseball bat.

There was a thud and the man crumpled to the ground at the same time Tammy screamed. The skillet dropped from her hands as she grabbed her stomach a second before the sound of a water balloon popping was heard.

"Mr. and Mrs. Davies," Aiden said, lowering his weapon as he could hear Lucas, Talon, Jackson, and Dylan surrounding the house. "I was here to save you, but I think you did a good job on your own."

Aiden looked for the source of the water sound but didn't see anything except a puddle under Tammy. "Oh, bloody hell," he muttered a second before Tammy grabbed her husband's hand and squeezed so tightly Pierce went down to one knee.

26

Aiden rushed forward, pulling the needles from his jacket. "You have to have these." Not bothering to explain, he pulled the top off with his teeth and jabbed the first needle into Tammy's arm. Her eyes went wide, and she growled at him before he injected Pierce with the second needle full of the antidote.

"One man is dead, the other is just unconscious," Eddie reported before stopping to stand in front of the man crying out in pain as his muscles cramped. "Do we save them or shoot them?"

"Babe," Aiden said calmly into his coms. "How much antidote do you have?"

"Two more needles from the ones you have. Jackson has them. Why?"

"I'm thinking we should probably save the few that are left. There's one inside and"—Dylan and Jackson walked in—"how many still alive out front?"

"All of them. We didn't have to shoot anyone," Dylan said with a frown.

"Five," Jackson answered shaking his head at his cousin.

"Six infected men. Possibly seven, but your mother took him out with a pan. Speaking of your mother, can you call an ambulance? She's in labor," Aiden said as Piper screamed on the other end of the coms and Dylan went white.

"You're having the baby?" Dylan asked his mother who looked exactly like a woman having a baby. "You can't have the baby now."

"Too old," Gus squawked.

"Someone give me the gun. I'm making parrot stew as soon as I have this baby," Tammy said as she narrowed her eyes at the bird.

"Aww, who's a good bird?" replied Gus.

Aiden blinked at the battle of wills between the pregnant woman and the parrot. "Get everyone detained," Aiden ordered as Eddie went to help Lucas and Talon tie everyone up. "As soon as everyone is detained, question them and then call it in. Or I can since you all shouldn't even be here."

Dylan stripped out of his vest and ran upstairs. A minute later he was in street clothes. "I'm just here to meet my new brother or sister."

The sound of a car busting through a fence had Aiden armed and at the window. Through it he saw Piper driving madly toward the back of the house with Draven clinging for dear life in the front seat. "Oh good. Piper's here."

"Hospital. I need a hospital," Tammy said as she reached for Aiden. "Pierce, get my bag. You," she said, digging her fingers into his arm. "This is Phobos. Question him or kill him. I don't care. Pierce got blood on the rug when he killed that man so I have to get a new one anyway. Do whatever, just do it on this rug."

"This is Phobos? You took down Phobos?" Aiden asked.

"You don't mess with my family. Now get me to the damn hospital."

"Yes, ma'am," Aiden said, pulling out his phone and calling Nash. "Tammy's in labor, and she knocked Phobos unconscious."

"What the hell?" Everyone in the room heard Nash yell.

"Long story, but Phobos was holding Mr. and Mrs. Davies hostage. All's well now except the baby is on the way. Phobos and his men are apprehended. Royce is dead and two others in the back." Aiden hung up after Nash said some choice words. "Um, everyone will be here in a couple of minutes."

Piper burst into the room through the back door and scanned it, making sure everyone she loved was safe. "Mom! Dad! Did Aiden give you the antidote?"

"I don't know, he jabbed me in the arm with something." Tammy paused and took a deep breath. "Pierce, get my bag. Piper, drive me to the hospital before I have this baby right here."

"Thank goodness. You and the baby will be all right. The chemicals have dissipated, but still, let's go out the back," Piper said.

"Chemicals?" Pierce asked, taking his wife's other arm. "Ah, the men writhing in pain. That was you?"

Piper nodded. "It made it easier for everyone to get to you."

Aiden followed her to the car as Dudley was looking toward the front of the house where the howls of pain were coming from. Draven was still sitting in the front seat playing on his phone as if he were completely bored. "Is that King Draven?" Tammy asked, and Piper nodded as she was already running everything that needed to be done through her head.

"Dudley! Can you make four more doses of the antidote? Do it just like I showed you. In fact, just make as many as you can in the next thirty minutes. There're supplies in my old workroom and ingredients in the trunk," Piper said, pointing to the shed out back.

"So, now that everyone is safe, I'm hungry. Can we go to the café?" Draven complained. Tammy reached through the window and grabbed him by his shirt collar as another contraction hit. She let out a low groan as she grasped Draven.

"Never mind. Not hungry anymore," Draven gasped as he tried to pull Tammy's fingers from his shirt.

When the contraction passed, Aiden helped her into the back of the car, and Piper leapt into the driver's seat.

"I'll meet you at the hospital after everything is wrapped up," Aiden said, leaning through the window and kissing her. "I love you."

Piper kissed him back and then took off with Tammy screaming, Pierce looking ready to pass out from the pain of a broken hand, and Draven asking if the baby could be named after him.

"You love her, huh?" Aiden turned to see Dylan grinning.

"I do," Aiden replied.

"Good. I like you. I was afraid she'd wind up with some lab geek like Dudley. And then what kind of fun could we have together? You, on the other hand," Dylan said, looking around, "*you* I can have fun with."

"I second that," Jackson said, joining them. "We're going to be cousins after all, and cousins in this family have something called a cousin special. It's when we get a boon and no one can ask what for. I have a feeling we'll get some help from you on that front."

"Help, how?"

"Invading armies." Dylan shrugged.

"Weekend trips overthrowing countries," Jackson added. "And even harder, keeping secrets from nosy parents."

"And don't forget trying to get the inside scoop on the bets. Speaking of which," Dylan pulled his phone from his vest, "when are you thinking of proposing to my sister?"

"I have to get her to fall in love with me first," Aiden muttered, but it wasn't soft enough. The two men heard him.

"She's already in love with you," Dylan said with surety.

"Definitely," Jackson said. "Plus you saved her parents. Total bonus points there."

"Here comes everyone," Dylan said, looking out the driveway as Eddie joined them. "Did you learn anything?"

Jackson nodded. "Got all their names and the names of all their associates not here."

"I got a list of locations of storage containers and warehouses with everything from drugs to weapons," Eddie added.

"Good job," Dylan told them. "Jackson, take Eddie and the guys to the car. We'll meet at the café."

Jackson put his fingers to his lips and whistled. Lucas and Talon trotted toward them. "Ready to go?" Talon asked.

"I can't wait to get back to the café. Have you been there, Eddie? There's these two sisters," Lucas began explaining to Eddie as they walked into the woods.

Dylan waved at Nash, then at the unmarked FBI cruiser, and finally at the two sheriff cars pulling into the house. Nash, Nabi, Ryan, Matt, and Cody got out of their cars and looked at the six tied-up men screaming in pain. Nash simply raised an eyebrow as he looked at Dylan and Aiden.

"They must have caught something," Aiden shrugged.

"Luckily we have a doctor here looking out for them," Dylan said loud enough for his cousin Ryan Parker to hear.

"What are you both doing here?" Ryan asked as he joined them. "Is this something I need to leave for a little while and then come back to?"

"Nah, we're good," Dylan said, patting his cousin's shoulder. "How's Sienna?"

"About to pop, but she's still three weeks from her due date. It's horrifying. She's so calm. It's freaky."

"Speaking of popping, I'm officially here to welcome my new brother or sister into the world. Just arrived and the timing couldn't be more perfect. Mom went into labor so I'd better get going. Aiden's joining me since Piper, his *girlfriend*, is driving Mom and Dad to the hospital."

"Wait, what?" everyone asked at once.

"And you're okay with this?" Nash asked.

"Sure am," Dylan said, grinning at Aiden. "Of course, he knows I would hunt him down and slowly tear him limb to limb if he hurts my sister."

"I'd start with the nails first. Very effective torture technique," Aiden told him.

"Oh," Ryan, Matt, and Cody said together again as if they all got it at once.

"This makes sense," Ryan added.

"Yup," Matt agreed. "Welcome to the family."

"Not so fast. Lover boy here has to get my sister to fall in love with him." Dylan looked as if he were having way too much fun with this.

"Have you gotten naked? Works for me every time my wife gets naked," Ryan advised.

"No," Dylan said, shaking his head. "Just, no."

"Grand romantic gesture," Matt told him with surety.

"I did save her parents."

"You can't get grander than that," Cody said with a smirk. "Unless it's a huge diamond ring."

"I don't see Piper being a huge diamond ring kind of girl," Aiden said.

Dylan grinned as he slapped Aiden's shoulder. "See. Perfect guy for her."

"Romantic dates, then," Nash suggested. "Picnics, hikes, horseback riding. That kind of thing."

"I could do that," Aiden said as his mind started coming up with romantic gestures. Just because he'd never done romance didn't mean he couldn't.

"Excuse me," Dudley said, pushing up his glasses. "I have the—"

"Medicine," Dylan finished for him. "Good. Start giving it to them." They watched Dudley walk off and Dylan let out a breath. "So much better than him for my brother-in-law. He's a genius, but there's no way he'd go shooting with me."

Ryan tried to hide his laughter, but Nash lost it. "And who Piper marries is all about you?" Ryan asked.

"I have to live with him too," Dylan said as if it were common sense.

"I'm not going to touch that. Should I walk away from this?" Matt asked as he and Cody looked around. "Is the FBI going to take jurisdiction?"

"Actually," Aiden announced, "Rahmi is claiming jurisdiction."

"Say that again?" Ryan asked, his face losing the traces of humor.

"I'm on a diplomatic mission for Prince Jamal to do whatever it takes to retrieve Piper Davies and secure the Rahmi International Nanotechnology Laboratory."

"You're shitting me?" Ryan put his hands on his hips. "You have proof?"

Aiden handed him the papers Jamal had given him. "But I'm sure it could become a joint operation."

Nash got the hint and walked off with the phone to his ear. Five minutes later, he was back. "A press release will be out from the king commending the local FBI office for their assistance in a raid that captured Phobos and nine members of his gang."

"I know how this works. In return for what?" Ryan asked.

"I need thirty minutes with Phobos before I hand him over. You try him here, but then immediately extradite him to Rahmi for trial as well."

Ryan's lips pursed as his phone rang. "It's my boss," he said, walking off for a moment.

"This is the virus used to do that to the men," Aiden said, handing the needle to Nash. "And this is the antidote. I thought you might want them. Death doesn't come for forty-eight hours, but Phobos doesn't need to know that."

Nash pocketed the needles as Ryan came back. "The deal is done. I'll wait out here. You're on the clock, Nash. And Nash, he'd better not end up dead."

Nash didn't say anything as he disappeared into the house.

"Here's the information we've gotten so far from the men outside," Aiden shot him a text with the notes. "And you might want to question them before they get their medicine. They seem very talkative right now. Oh, and Royce, the dead man inside, was the man who threatened Tammy's unborn child with a knife and kidnapped Piper in Rahmi. Let's just say his death was a result from crossfire."

"What really happened?" Matt asked.

"Pierce killed him. Let's keep that and everything about Mr. and Mrs. Davies out of the public record as much as possible. I don't want any chance of retaliation against them," Aiden told them.

"Got it," Matt said as Cody nodded.

"No problem. This appears to be a field in central Kentucky," Ryan replied.

"Well, I think our time is done here. I have a brother or sister to meet and Aiden has my sister to win over. We'll see you all later." Dylan pulled the keys from his pocket and pointed Aiden toward the garage.

"Tell your mom we're thinking of her," Matt called out as they began to walk away. "And romance Piper. Preferably by two weeks from now."

"Why two weeks?" Aiden asked Dylan.

"That's when he placed his bet on you proposing."

"And when did you place your bet?"

Dylan just smiled as he opened the garage door to reveal a minivan, a truck, and a sports car. "I think this is a Corvette moment."

"If only it were an Aston Martin," Aiden said as he opened the passenger door.

"Here I was just beginning to like you and you pull that English car crap on me," Dylan said with a shake of his head.

27

Piper floored it as her mother's panting increased. The screams of pain from her father came every two minutes now as her mother squeezed his hand with each new contraction.

"Draven, call my sister and let her know Mom's in labor," Piper said as she rattled off the phone number.

"She's the hot little one, right? Who's good with her tongue?"

Piper's hand shot from the steering wheel and smacked him at the same time her mother hit the back of his head. Cassidy was just a baby in her mind, but in reality, she was about to turn twenty-one, which was just a couple years younger than Draven in his mid-twenties. She had a knack for picking up languages and was still trying to decide what to do with that talent.

"Hello, sweetness, it's the man of your dreams."

"Draven!" Piper's mother screamed as another contraction hit. Oh, they were getting closer. Piper sped into Lexington, passing cars left and right.

"Yes, that's your mother. She's having the baby and is being incredibly rude as I try to invite you to view the royal member."

This time it was Pierce who reached forward to hit Draven.

"I'm a king, you know. You'd die in my country for that."

"Well, in my town you'll die for bad manners," Tammy said between pants.

Draven rolled his eyes. "Anyway, your mom is in labor and your sister is driving us all to the hospital and wants you to let everyone know."

"Why am I here?" Draven repeated. "I came to save your parents' lives, and I can think of the perfect way for you to repay me."

Piper shoved the side of his head, causing Draven to bonk against the window. He rolled his eyes at her as Piper sped up to the emergency room doors. Draven hung up with Cassidy who had said she'd call Jace and Dylan and alert the town via text to meet them at the hospital.

"Draven, could you get a wheelchair for my mom?" Piper asked as she grabbed the overnight bag from her father and moved to help her mom from the car.

Minutes later, there was still no Draven and no wheelchair. Her mother was slowly waddling her way inside with Pierce on one side and Piper on the other. She was going to kill Draven. He was probably hitting on a nurse.

When the doors opened and they stepped inside the ER, Piper and her family froze. Draven was running around and around a section of chairs as a nurse chased him.

"I really am a king!" he yelled.

"The doctor will find that very interesting. Just let me give you something to calm you down," the nurse responded.

Draven caught Piper's eyes and stopped running. "There," he said, pointing to Piper. "She can tell—" The nurse injected the needle into his arm and Draven went down.

Her mother let out a low groan and nurses swarmed her. "He really is a king. But you might take advantage and castrate him like a dog who humps your leg too much." Tammy panted as she sat down in a wheelchair.

Piper pulled up the headline about the King of Bermalia signing a treaty in Keeneston. Under the headline was a big picture of Draven. The nurse who had given him a sedative went white. Her eyes were huge as she looked at the picture and at the man now snoring at her feet. "Just put him a private room and we'll say he slipped and hit his head." The nurse looked relieved as two other nurses helped to get him onto a gurney and wheeled him away.

"Good luck, Mom!" Piper called out as her parents disappeared down the hall. Piper turned to sit, but the nurse who had tranquilized Draven approached her.

"Thank you. I would imagine he could get me fired. I can take you to the labor and delivery waiting room if you'd like."

"Please," Piper told her as she followed her down the same hall that her parents were taken. She took a seat on the pale blue padded chair and waited. There were a few other friends or family members waiting for their loved ones to deliver their baby and it made Piper think of when each of her siblings was born. For every child born after her, Piper had always been with Grandpa Jake. Grandma Marcy was always one of the first people at the hospital. Piper and her grandfather would fix farming machinery, go horseback riding, or do something else that always made her feel special. Grandpa Jake always made each of the kids feel special, even in the moments that weren't their own.

Aiden made her feel special too. Piper took a deep breath and looked toward the door. Would he come? Some guys got weird about women having babies. Especially single men, so maybe he wouldn't come. Piper looked back down at her lap. Her hands trembled from relief, adrenaline, worry, and for once, not having a plan. She'd always known what she wanted, what the next step was. But right now she didn't. There were more questions than answers about her feelings for Aiden.

Piper groaned and put her head in her hands. She should have told him she loved him. And what was happening to him back at her parents' house? Would Ryan or Matt actually arrest him? Her hands started shaking more. She didn't like this uncertainty. She had thought love would be a slow, gradual build. You become friends, you talk for a year, decide to go out on a date, and over time feel a companionable love. She should have known better. Piper saw how her friends and cousins had fallen in love. Some quick, some over time, but one thing was sure. They all knew they were in love, and it wasn't companionable and comfortable. It was so much more intimate and passionate.

Piper didn't notice the people coming and going from the waiting room. Her thoughts were on Aiden. To live in the now. To be with him. Just the thought of it was enough to make her heart pound and her lips twitch into a smile. And then she had her answer. Love wasn't scary. It wasn't a leap of faith because Aiden would always catch her. They would hold each other up so they'd never fall.

"Where's my grandbaby?"

Piper was pulled from her thoughts as her grandmother shuffled in with the Rose sisters and Aniyah right behind them. Aniyah was weighed down by baskets of food. "I brought them as soon as my Sugarbear told me Miss Tammy was in labor. How is she doing?"

Piper grabbed a basket of cookies from her as the four elderly women began walking straight to the nurse in charge. The nurse smiled at them and happily took the apple pie Grandma Marcy handed her. Everyone in the hospital loved when a woman from Keeneston had a baby. They were bribed with homemade treats to get up-to-the-second information.

The nurse hurried off to see how Piper's mother was doing as the four moved to the nearest seats. Aniyah looked Piper up and down. "What's the matter?"

"You mean besides being kidnapped, stowing away in containers of fish, having to ask King Draven for help, sleeping with Aiden, having my brother walk in on us naked, my parents held hostage, releasing a deadly virus, having men risk their lives to save my parents, my mom going into labor, and having to leave my brother and Aiden behind to maybe be arrested for killing a couple of bad guys?"

"Yeah, that's kinda par for the course around here. What's really bothering you?" Aniyah pulled Piper down into the nearest chair and dug around a basket for a cookie. "Here you go. Tell Aniyah all about it."

Piper gave up. No one could resist Miss Violet's cookies. "I love him."

"Isn't that good news?" Aniyah asked, taking a bite of her cookie.

"It should be, but I'm too worried about the future."

"Ah. Have you talked to him about it?" Aniyah cocked her head in a don't-lie-to-me look.

"Not exactly."

"My Sugarbear and I share everything. If there's something bothering me, or something that I'm worried about, we talk about it. Two minds are better than one, especially when two hearts have become one."

Piper flung her arms around Aniyah. "Thank you."

The double doors opened as Dylan and Aiden stepped into the waiting room. Dylan was in his normal clothes and Aiden still wore his military gear, minus the weapons and bulletproof jacket. His stubble was slightly darker than normal and his eyes . . . they were glued to hers. Dylan held balloons and Aiden had a small teddy bear in his hands.

"Girl, if you're not about to jump him right now, I will. All this talk about babies and love has me fired up," Aniyah said, pulling out her phone and texting her Sugarbear.

Fired up was one way to put it. Piper melted. He was standing there with a teddy bear for her little brother or sister and a smile on his face that told her so much more about how he was feeling than the "I love you" he'd told her earlier. Especially when his eyes dipped to her midsection and his smile softened. In a flash, her future hit her. Walking down the aisle to him, standing there in a tux. To nights of laughter and lovemaking. To years of love and growing together. To walks along the shore in Lynton. To horseback riding in Keeneston. To his hand resting on her own swollen belly filled with their child. Aiden laughing as he played with their children. Their hair turning silver. Their wrinkled hands clasped. It all flashed before her in that one split second that left her racing toward him.

Aiden's arms opened as Piper flung herself into them. "I love you, Aiden. I love you so much."

Aiden's arms closed around her, holding her tight as her feet dangled inches above the ground. He looked down at her with so much love that Piper's heart almost burst. Everything felt right—felt perfect. Aniyah was right. Together they could conquer anything. They'd already proven that.

"I love you too," Aiden said with such sincerity Piper didn't care she was in the middle of the waiting room with the biggest gossips all watching avidly. She kissed Aiden with everything she had. Their lips came together to seal their love and unspoken promise of a future together.

"Davies family?" a nurse asked, breaking their kiss.

Aiden put her down, but didn't drop his hands from her sides as she turned in the circle of his arms, pressing her back to his chest and resting his clasped hands on her stomach.

"Yes?" half the waiting room replied.

"Mrs. Davies is doing well. She's progressing rapidly, and the baby should be here any minute," the nurse said as Aniyah handed her a cookie. "I'll be back shortly with another update."

"Aiden, I'd like you to meet my grandmother."

"I'd be honored to."

Piper led Aiden across the waiting room and stopped before her grandmother, who had the biggest smile on her face as she sat with the Rose sisters.

"So, you're the lucky one to scoop up my Piper," Marcy said.

"Grandma, this is Aiden Creed. Aiden, my grandma, Marcy Davies."

Aiden lifted Marcy's hand and kissed her knuckles. "It's a pleasure to make your acquaintance, Mrs. Davies."

Miss Violet moved to grab him again but Piper blocked her. Miss Violet crossed her arms and pouted. "It's his accent. It does it to me every time." Aiden grinned and her grandmother blushed. "Oh my," she whispered as Aiden pressed a soft kiss on Miss Violet's cheek and whispered something in her ear. "Oh my," Miss Violet gasped as she smiled wide. "He's a keeper."

"Now, young man, take a seat next to me and tell me all about yourself," Marcy said, patting the empty seat next to her. Aiden took the seat with the teddy bear still in hand and began talking to Piper's grandmother.

"Piper!"

Piper turned to see Jace and Cassidy rushing through the doors. Cassidy had a bag of their mom's favorite fast food and Jace had a bottle of wine in hand.

"How's Mom?" Jace asked.

"Doing well. Baby should be here really soon."

"I can't believe I won't be the youngest anymore. I don't know if I like this," Cassidy said jokingly.

"Now you know how I felt when each of you were born."

"Hey," Cassidy said, tapping Piper on the arm, "who's the hottie talking to Grandma?"

Piper saw her sister straighten up and fluff her hair. Nope. No way. "That's my boyfriend, Aiden."

"Boyfriend?" Jace and Cassidy questioned at once.

"I thought he was your bodyguard," Jace said as his eyes narrowed to where Dylan was now talking to Aiden and Grandma Marcy.

"He could guard my body anytime," Cassidy muttered as Piper smacked her. "Sorry, but he's totally hot. And not that you aren't or anything, but you've always brought home those nerdy guys. And not the hot nerdy type, but the kind that probably secretly picks his nose and wipes it on his clothes."

"Cass!" Piper looked to Jace for backup, but he just nodded his head in agreement.

"Dylan seems to like him." Jace changed the subject.

"He was British Special Air Service," Piper said, noting how Dylan and Aiden were talking with the Rose sisters and Grandma Marcy, completely at ease with them and each other. All four women looked like they were in heaven. All they needed was a new baby to hold.

"Oh," Cassidy and Jace said as if that explained everything.

"That makes him so much hotter. I swear, if you don't marry that man, I will," Cassidy told her seriously.

"That's a little shallow. You haven't even met him yet."

"He has an English accent and looks like that. That's enough for me." Piper rolled her eyes at her sister. "Come on, introduce me."

"You flirt with him, and I'll shave your head again while you sleep," Piper warned as they made their way over to Aiden.

"I wouldn't do that. I'm just happy for you. For us. We have a hot, badass, possible future brother-in-law. That will make family dinners even more interesting. Remember that last guy who thought he was so much better than we were because he invented some chemical reaction?"

"He was the worst," Jace agreed. Piper silently agreed too.

"Aiden," Piper said, drawing his attention away from the older women, even though he'd been watching her since she stepped away to go talk to her brother and sister. "You know my brother, Jace. This is my little sister, Cassidy."

"Pleasure to meet you," Aiden said, shaking her hand. "Piper has told me a lot about you."

Cassidy turned to Piper and mouthed *marry him* before

turning back to Aiden. "I know I'm looking forward to hearing more about you and how you and my sister met and started dating."

Piper didn't have a chance to respond as the nurse came hurrying back out. Everyone stood and waited. "Your newest Davies is here!"

28

Piper looked down at the sleeping bundle in her mom's arms and for the first time in her life she wanted one of her own. She looked up and caught Aiden looking at her thoughtfully.

"She's beautiful, Mrs. Davies," Aiden said, handing her the teddy bear. Tammy squeezed his hand and smiled up at him and Piper as if she knew something they didn't.

"Oh Mom, she's adorable," Cassidy gushed.

"I did play some part in making her, you know," Pierce said.

"I know, sweetie. And you did good," Tammy said, holding out her hand for her husband to take. Piper saw the strong bond between them and felt Aiden shift so he was standing behind her with his hand on her shoulder.

"The doctor said your mother did better than any twenty-year-old," Pierce said with pride.

"Honey, why don't you take her and introduce her to her family?" Tammy said as Pierce bent and gently placed the newborn in his arms. He turned to his mom, Marcy, first and knelt down to place the baby in her outstretched arms.

"Mom, meet your granddaughter, Cricket Davies."

WITHIN THIRTY MINUTES, the entire town of Keeneston had bribed their way into the room with pies, cookies, cornbread, and casseroles. Aiden never asked to leave. He was having too much fun. Instead, he spent the time talking to everyone, laughing with Jace and Cassidy, telling stories with Dylan, who somehow never told one of his own, and hanging out with the rest of her extended family. Grandpa Jake laughed at the stories of the Lynton goats as he cradled his newest granddaughter in his arms.

Piper put her hand on Aiden's arm as he talked to her cousin Sophie. "I'm ready to sneak out and let my mom get some rest."

"Whatever you want, babe," Aiden whispered back. He turned and said goodbye to Sophie. Before they left, they made the rounds once more. "Mrs. Davies, Cricket is perfect. Congratulations."

"Thank you, Aiden. Why don't you hold her?"

Pierce didn't give him a chance to say *no*. Piper's little sister was placed in his large arms. Her sleepy eyes batted open, and she grabbed his finger. How could someone so small change your whole life? But he saw it. He saw it in the way this child had an effect on everyone in the room. She was born into something big. Something loving. Something filled with people who wanted to help her live her best possible life. And he'd be damned if he didn't feel the same way. He wanted to be a part of this kid's life too. And when he looked at Piper, he knew he wanted to experience this with her as well. Someday he hoped to be holding their daughter in his arms.

"Hello, poppet," he whispered to her. "You be a good girl

tonight and let your mum rest." He kissed her forehead gently and handed her back to Tammy.

Piper kissed her mother and father and started out the door before Tammy called out to Aiden. "Yes?" he said, turning back to her.

"You're part of the family now. You have all the blessings you need. But most importantly, treat my daughter well. Don't make me get out of this bed and smack you for blowing the best thing that will ever happen to you. I expect an engagement, a wedding, and a grandchild. Little Cricket needs family to play with after all."

"I'll see what I can do about that," Aiden said with a wink.

"What the hell happened?" Aiden turned to the door to see Draven holding his head and leaning against the door.

"You slipped and hit your head. The nurses took excellent care of you," Piper said with a straight face.

"Is little Draven here?"

Tammy grinned and called Draven over. "Meet Cricket."

"Oh, a girl! Dravina would have been good too, but Cricket is cute. Like a little insect she is." Cricket chose that moment to spit up some of the milk she'd just had all over Draven's shirt.

DRAVEN COULDN'T BELIEVE he was wedged in the back of a car between three old ladies. And not one of them grabbed his royal member. What was wrong with them? It would be worth the humiliation, though. He was twenty minutes away from seeing the one woman who blew his mind. Or at least he hoped he'd see her. The Rose sisters assured him that everyone would be at the café. And when they pulled up, it did seem that most of the town was still there.

Through the large windows he saw the two FBI guys from earlier talking to the waitress and the cook. Then he saw the nerdy guy with his eyes staring at Nikki's enormous boobs. He remembered her name. When she'd leaned in and talked dirty to him, his royal member had shrunk and gone into hiding.

The car stopped and Aniyah got out and went straight into the arms of her Sugarbear. Apparently he was some kind of law enforcement. The Rose sisters gingerly emerged from the car along with Marcy. Draven was finally able to get out of the car and get a good look inside. There she was. He didn't know what this feeling was. His royal member wasn't the only thing pounding. So was his heart.

Draven opened the door to the café and Nikki shoved the poor nerd out of the way and stuck her body on his like a leech. "Oh, your majesty."

But Draven ignored her. The woman who made him feel things he'd never felt before wasn't paying him any attention as she sat at a table of her friends. She didn't pay him attention last time either. It's what drew his attention to her. And when he'd tried out his best lines on her, she'd rolled her eyes and turned her back on him. But not tonight. Tonight would be different.

Nikki's hand cupped his member, and she purred as she rubbed her body against his. "I'm sorry, that's not for you," Draven said, pulling her hand away. "But you're the lucky woman tonight sitting with him."

"Dudley?" Nikki replied.

"Yes. Didn't you know? He saved everyone tonight with his chemistry genius."

"He's a nerd," Nikki said as she reached down to grab his butt. "I don't do nerds. I do kings."

Draven lowered his voice. "You don't know about nerds?"

"What about them?" she whispered back.

"They're very attentive lovers. So much so, I've had lessons from them in the oral arts," Draven lied. Until that moment, he'd always been a very selfish lover. But looking at the woman across the room made him want to get on his knees and pleasure her all night long. Their last encounter had been brief and accidental, but it had left an impression on him.

"Really?" Nikki asked as she looked back at Dudley.

Draven shrugged. "Don't take my word for it."

"You're really going to pass this up?" Nikki asked, pressing her mammoth mammaries against his chest.

"I am. But I'm doing you a favor since I consider you a friend. The nerd will worship you instead of you worshipping me."

Nikki looked back at Dudley once more. "I didn't think about it like that. I like the idea of being worshipped. Thanks, buddy."

Draven let out a breath as Nikki rushed back to the table and ran her hand down Dudley's chest. The man looked as if he'd expire on the spot with pleasure. Draven smiled to himself. It looked like all those diplomacy tips Queen Suri and Princes Mo and Zain had given him really did work. Feeling unsure for the first time in his life, Draven walked to the table of women. They stopped talking as he smiled down at her. "Hello."

~

AIDEN AND PIPER moved as one. They didn't say anything

as their eyes locked. Aiden brushed aside a strand of her hair as he moved above her and kissed her. They'd made love every night for the past couple of days. Well, night, day, it didn't matter. What mattered was they were so in sync it should be frightening, but Aiden found it exhilarating.

Sometimes they were fast, hard, against-the-wall encounters when they just couldn't stand another second apart. And others, like now, he enjoyed savoring every achingly sweet and slow moment. They had helped her mother get settled with Cricket. Answered all the questions about Phobos, who was currently being held at a secret government location as Rahmi and US agents worked to bring down the rest of his organization. And now it was time for Aiden to go back home later tonight. He was flying out at midnight.

Only this time he wasn't going alone.

Piper clutched his arms as her whole body convulsed, triggering his own orgasm.

"I love you," Aiden said, resting his forehead against hers.

"I love you too.

Aiden slipped from the bed and looked at the clock. "I'm sorry, love, but I have to run out real quick."

"Again?" Piper asked, sitting up and leaning against the headboard.

"Yes, hopefully for the last time."

"Are you going to tell me about these mysterious disappearances?"

Aiden smiled as he headed to the bathroom. "Not yet," he called out to her. He heard her protest, but he had a plan and he was sticking to it.

"I guess I'll pack while you're gone."

"Good idea, luv," he said, kissing her after he walked nude into the bedroom.

"Does this have anything to do with your refusal to talk specifics about our future other than saying you think it'll work itself out?"

Aiden didn't answer as he stepped into his jeans and pulled on a dark green sweater. "I'll be back soon."

PIPER LET out a huff of annoyance. They were so happy, she didn't want it to end but it must. They were flying into London and then driving to Lynton to get her virus. She had notes of things she wanted to do to fix it. Now she just needed to be here in her lab and run tests on it. Dudley and Sada were meeting her in three days at the Lexington lab and together they were going to solve the problem and launch the most revolutionary medicine known to man. Epidemics wouldn't stand a chance against her nanotech cure.

Piper's phone rang and she answered it as she started packing.

"Is it true?"

"Is what true?" Piper asked Abby Mueez.

"About his penis. What else would I want to know about?"

"Every story you heard is completely false."

"Oh," Abby said with disappointment.

"There's no way they could grasp the full size of it and his ability to use it."

"Sweet magnolia," Abby sighed and then giggled. "So, it's going well between you two?"

"Sure is. The future is still up in the air, but he did agree to go to the Daughters of Elizabeth Ball with me for New

Year's Eve. We're heading back to England in a couple hours. He'll stay there, and I'll come back to my project."

"Maybe you can get a mold of his penis before you leave," Abby snorted.

"Oh my gosh! Who told you?"

"Both Jackson and Dylan told me. I guess Dylan told Jackson and Jackson called me and then I couldn't help but call Dylan to rub it in." Abby cracked up and Piper did too. "That he took a dildo to the face. Oh my gosh, I will forever be in love with Aiden for that."

Piper talked to Abby as she packed and finally it was time to go. She was showered and waiting for Aiden when he returned. Much to her annoyance, he wouldn't talk about where he'd been . . . again. Instead, he hurried her from her house and they drove to the airport. With a sigh, Piper took her seat on the plane next to Aiden.

"Get some sleep, babe. Tomorrow is going to be a very busy day."

WHEN PIPER OPENED HER EYES, they were landing in London. She was cramped from sleeping on a plane but luckily well rested as they made their way through security and out to the car Eddie had dropped off for them. And soon all her worries were cast away as he drove them toward Lynton. Once they left London, the countryside was beautiful. They talked the entire way and when they pulled into the airbase, Wick was waiting for them.

"No one has come looking for your—what is it exactly?"

"A deadly virus that could wipe out the world."

"Funny," Wick said with a roll of his eyes. The commander happily handed off the virus and accepted her thanks for trusting him with it. Probably because several higher-ups in the government had also called to thank him for his vigilant work.

Mrs. Creed greeted them at the bar and handed over her notes. Now with everything in hand, Piper started to get the itch to get back in the lab. And she would be soon enough. She'd be leaving tomorrow. Alone.

"Lovey, do you want some fish and chips?" Mrs. Creed asked.

"Yes, please. I'm starving."

"I hope you don't mind, but I asked Eddie to meet us here for our meeting."

"Why would I mind?" she asked Aiden.

"I told him he could bring his daughter."

"Of course! If I can inspire just one woman to join the science ranks, I'll feel as if I accomplished something."

"You'll inspire more than one as soon as the world learns what you've done." Aiden chimed in. He put his arm around her as she leaned against him. His mother brought out the food and the three of them talked, told stories, and laughed for an hour before Eddie and his daughter showed up.

"Oh my gosh! Dr. Piper Davies!" The girl screamed as she looked back to her dad for reassurance.

"Surprise," Eddie grinned.

"You are the best," she said, hugging her dad.

"Eddie and I have to talk so you two enjoy yourselves," Aiden told her.

Piper watched as Eddie and Aiden walked across the bar to an empty table. She turned to the young girl and smiled. "Come, sit. Let's talk about my favorite subject in the world —science."

AIDEN SHOOK Eddie's hand before the two men joined the

women at their table. Piper and his daughter were in an animated discussion about mutations when they arrived.

"It's time to go," Eddie told his daughter who groaned.

"Do we have to?" the young girl whined.

"Here's my number and email. I expect to hear from you often," Piper said, sliding a piece of paper to her.

"Thanks!" she said excitedly as she left talking so fast to her dad that Aiden couldn't make out her words.

"Are you ready?" Aiden asked.

"Aren't we going to wait for your mom?"

Aiden shook his head. "If I only have a night with you, we're not spending it at my mum's. I rented a little cottage for us."

THE COTTAGE WAS BESIDE A STREAM, surrounded by wilderness. The owner already had dinner cooked and waiting for them in the cottage along with some champagne and wine. And when Piper gasped in pleasure at the cottage, Aiden knew he'd made the right choice.

"Oh, Aiden. This is perfect," she said, looking around the cottage. The stone fireplace was lit, dinner was warm in the oven, and the bedroom windows didn't even need curtains since they were completely alone out here.

But then her smile fell. "What is it, Piper?" Aiden asked, reaching for her.

"I'm going to miss you. New Year's seems likes forever when it's only six weeks away. Am I silly?"

Aiden pulled her close and kissed the top of her head as he held her. "No, it's not silly. I'm going to miss you too."

And for the rest of the night, Aiden showed her how much he'd miss her with every caress, kiss, nip, lick, and thrust.

29

Five days later . . .

PIPER STARED at the computer results. Was it really that easy? After only two days of work? Sada and Dudley screamed and hugged each other. She'd done it. *They'd* done it. They'd taken a look at her notes, made the adjustment she thought of in Bermalia, and FAVOR was perfected.

It would still undergo years of testing, but it was done. She knew it deep in her heart. This would save millions of lives. Sada wrapped her arms around her, and they jumped up and down.

"Dudley, what are you doing? Get over here!" Sada laughed as Dudley typed something out on his phone.

"I'm writing Nikki. If what she did for me helping defeat Phobos blew my mind, I can't wait to see what she does when I tell her this. It is okay, right?"

"Right," Piper laughed. She had no doubt this thing between Nikki and Dudley wouldn't last, but it was giving him a lot of confidence and Nikki seemed very sated. But she also had a roaming eye. Especially for firefighters.

"Okay, here I go," Piper said, sending a secure file to the pharmaceutical company that had provided the grant. She'd already called an armored guard to arrive in an hour to transport the sample to them as well. Piper wanted to scream. She wanted to cry. But mostly she wanted to celebrate with Aiden. They talked or texted constantly, but it wasn't the same.

With her work done, she thought about flying to England for a couple days, but Aiden said he was slammed at work. Soon. They'd meet up in Atlanta very soon. Piper, Sada, and Dudley packed up the samples and broke out a bottle of bourbon as they waited for the guards to get there. By the time guards arrived, Piper had video-chatted with Aiden to let him know she'd accomplished her goal and they might have been a little tipsy.

"Babe, I hate to cut our talk short, but I have to go. Promise me you won't drive."

"I won't. I love you, Aiden."

"I love you too."

Piper pulled up her phone and called her cousin Layne for a ride. Her physical therapy office was nearby and that made her just minutes away and prime to bum a ride. Layne screamed when Piper told her about perfecting FAVOR, and seconds after that a town text went out. Party at the café that night.

Layne arrived minutes after they hung up, the same time as the armored car appeared. Piper might have been a little tipsy, but she compared identifications, called the armored car service, and only once she was sure they were who they said they were did she hand over FAVOR. She watched as the taillights disappeared down the street and sighed. In eight hours, FAVOR would be in the hands of the pharmaceutical company and for the most part, out of her hands. She would stay involved as a consultant and creator, but mass production and testing were now the company's responsibility. In the grant papers, Piper had signed over fifty percent of the ownership of FAVOR, which meant, in ten years or so, she would be a very rich woman when FAVOR hit the market. But instead of smiling, she frowned.

"What's the matter?" Layne asked as Dudley, Sada, and Piper gulped down the last of the bottle of bourbon and made their way into Layne's backseat.

"I miss Aiden. I wish he were here to celebrate with me."

Layne hugged her and Piper rested her head on her shoulder. "I know. But if it's love, it'll work out. You'll find a way to be together."

"I'm thinking of moving my lab to London," Piper admitted. She felt Layne stiffen, but Layne didn't discourage her.

"I'll miss you, but I want you to be as happy as I am. Besides, I've always wanted to tour England. Now I'll have my own personal guide."

"Thanks, Layne," Piper said, giving her cousin a hug.

"But now we party. You earned it."

Piper got into the front seat and soon they were laughing as they drove to Keeneston with music blaring. Even as Piper laughed and sang, a part of her heart wasn't in it. That part was always with Aiden.

LAYNE CURSED and turned down the music. "Something's wrong, y'all. The car just died."

Piper noticed that the car was cruising to a stop just outside of downtown. While only steps from the town center, they were still on a narrow two-lane country road. Layne pulled as far over onto the grass as possible and let out a string of curses anyone from the military would be proud of.

"Can you call for a tow? My phone is dead," Layne said as she popped the hood.

Piper reached for her phone and frowned. She patted her pockets, emptied her purse, and then jumped out of the car and looked all around the floorboards. No phone.

"Can I borrow your phone?" she asked Dudley.

"Here," he said, handing it to her.

Piper would have to ask Aiden to find it for her. She knew he still had a tracker on it. For some reason it made her feel better having that connection to him. She tried to turn on the phone. Nothing.

"It's dead. Are you kidding me?" Piper handed it back to Dudley. "Sada?"

"I don't have international calling. This would cost me a fortune. Isn't the town right there? Just walk."

Yes, it was. It was literally less than a quarter mile away. More like two hundred yards. Piper grabbed her purse and coat to ward off the cold night air. Layne's head was stuck under the hood as she cursed again.

"I'm just going to run to the café. I'll send help," Piper said, annoyed that her happy buzz was wearing off. She'd get some special Rose sisters' tea when she got to the café to help her forget Aiden wasn't here to celebrate with her.

"Okay. Thanks, Piper. Sorry," Layne said sadly.

"It's not your fault. It'll only take a minute."

Piper jogged down the side of the road and around the corner to the beginning of Main Street. The town was awash in the yellow glow of the lights. Thanksgiving was coming and everyone had decorations up. Piper passed the insurance agency, the art gallery, and then slowed. There was a light on in the building that had been for sale. There was talk that Norma from the Fluff and Buff was going to buy it and move down there since it was a much bigger location.

And if it was Norma, she could call her brother who could come tow Piper's car. Piper hurried her steps, but then they stopped. She was frozen in place. For it wasn't a sign for Fluff and Buff on the window. Instead, it read *CREED SECURITY SERVICES, International Headquarters.*

Piper's breathing stopped as Aiden's reflection appeared in the window behind her. "Hello, luv."

Piper put her hand to her head and shook it. Was she that drunk? But then she felt his hands on her shoulder turning her toward him. And when she looked up, it was into the eyes of the man she loved.

"What are you—what is going—are you really here?"

Aiden smiled and Piper didn't care what was going on. She jumped into his arms and kissed him. They'd only been apart for five days, but she had a feeling it wouldn't matter if they were apart for a few hours. Her heart would always skip a beat for him.

"I missed you!"

"I missed you too," Aiden said as he laughed at her eager kiss and kissed her in return. "It seems we've both been busy this week."

"What is this?" Piper asked, turning to the building.

"Something I had to do so I could do this."

"Do what?" Piper asked, turning back around to find Aiden on one knee with a ring between his fingertips.

"To ask you to marry me."

"Yes!" Piper shouted.

Aiden's eyes crinkled with laughter as his lips split into a large grin. "Wait a minute, Piper. I have this all planned out."

Piper shifted from foot to foot, her heart racing, her eyes tearing up as Aiden grabbed her hand. "I never wanted love. I saw how it broke my mother's heart after my father died. But she told me one day a love so strong would walk into my life, and I wouldn't be able to live without it. I thought it was silly until I met you. Until you crashed into my life with bullets flying and a town ready to do battle to save you. I knew I was in danger that first night—in danger of losing my heart to you. And I did, but imagine my surprise when it wasn't trouble, but overwhelming joy and happiness. It was love. I never questioned it because I knew it the second I saw you. I knew then I loved you and I knew I wanted to spend the rest of my life with you."

Aiden took a breath and held the ring close to her finger. "Piper Davies, my love, will you marry me?"

"Yes," Piper said again, this time not screaming because tears ran down her face. As Aiden slipped on the ring, which was a band of diamonds woven into a double helix around her finger, Piper became aware of the sounds of clapping. From the café the patrons stood fanned out along the sidewalk and into the street, and then the group of Layne, Sada, and Dudley were happily clapping from beside Layne's now perfectly operational car.

"You did all this?" Piper asked, looking around. "How did you know I would fix FAVOR tonight?"

"I had faith in you. And I didn't do it all tonight. I've been setting up offices in Los Angeles and New York City. I've also been getting Eddie settled as the head of the London office. It's been a very busy five days. Your father had the lettering for this building ready to go. I bought it the night we left for Lynton. He was keeping me up to date on your progress so I could make it back in time to surprise you. I never doubted you, so I knew I had to move fast."

"You did all of this to be with me?" Piper had never felt so loved.

"I'd move heaven and earth to be with you," Aiden whispered as he covered her lips with his. He pulled her tightly against him as he kissed her with all the promise of the future.

30

"Come on, you two, we have an engagement party in here," Tammy called out. Aiden looked up to where his future mother-in-law stood with his own mother and wrapped his arm around his fiancée. His mother had been right. Finding love changed you. Everything before Piper was just that: the past. But now, now the future held all the promise in the world.

Aiden shook hands and received hugs from all his soon-to-be cousins. It was strange coming from being an only child into this huge family that incorporated more than just family, but a whole town. He thought it would be overwhelming. Instead it was a warm blanket on a cold night.

"Now that you're part of the family, how do you feel about tinkering?" Pierce asked as he held baby Cricket in his arms.

"I tinker with explosives," Aiden said.

"I was thinking more of farm equipment, but I do have an old building that needs to come down. You can blow that up if you'd like."

"Dad!" Dylan complained, joining them as he gently took Cricket from Pierce. "You told me I could blow it up."

Aiden laughed as Dylan gently rocked his baby sister. So, this was what it was like to have a brother.

"You two can do it together," Pierce said with a roll of his eyes.

"And we can go shooting together," Jackson added as he joined them and held out his hands for baby Cricket.

"Now, isn't that a sight?" a woman said from behind Aiden as Dylan kissed Cricket's forehead and handed her over to Jackson.

"Abby!" Piper screamed as she raced across the café to hug her friend. Aiden turned and smiled as he recognized the woman everyone knew of, but so few actually knew anything about.

Abby and Piper joined him. Abby looked straight to his package. "I've heard so much about you."

"Abby!" Piper, Jackson, and Dylan admonished.

Aiden raised an eyebrow at Piper who blushed the truth. He should feel embarrassed, but he quite liked the idea of being worthy of girl talk. His father-in-law didn't look as pleased, though.

"What are y'all talking about?" Cassidy asked as she joined the group. Jace did too, and Aiden just shook his head.

"Nothing!" Pierce practically shouted, drawing Tammy's attention.

"Are you talking about a wedding date?" Tammy asked as suddenly the circle around them grew.

Dylan grinned largely. "I already won the bet on the engagement. Go ahead and make me the winner of the wedding date."

"We haven't talked about it yet. I've been engaged for all of one hour," Piper said with a roll of her eyes.

"Well, you two settle on the date while we attend to some business," Miss Lily said, pulling a reluctant Cady with her to the center of the room. "We have a drawing for a romantic dinner to announce. Cady."

"The winner is," Cade pulled out a card and read it. "DeAndre Drews."

Aniyah screamed and leapt into DeAndre's arms. Of course, she was five-foot-nothing and DeAndre seemed to tower over her, but he sweetly bent down and kissed her.

"So, when do you want to get married?" Piper asked.

"Now?"

Piper laughed and Aiden's heart seemed to expand even more. "Wait, you're not joking."

"I'll marry you as soon as I can get you."

"Right before Christmas would be lovely. Your mother could stay and help plan the wedding," Tammy offered.

"That's brill," his mother said to Tammy as Tammy looked at her in confusion. "Brilliant," his mom clarified before turning to the couple. "But, this is your decision. I wouldn't want to interfere."

"Don't worry about that. You'll learn soon enough how to interfere," the woman Aiden knew as Kenna called out as all the other mothers nodded their agreement.

"It's not interfering. It's motherly love," Morgan, Miles's wife, said with a grin.

"It's motherly love that you ask me every week if I'm pregnant yet?" Layne asked.

Morgan smiled pleasantly. "Yes. I want you to know motherly love too."

"Malarkey," Sydney, one of Piper's cousins, said. "You believe in karma. All y'all want to sit back and laugh as we make our way through parenthood while you get to play the doting grandparents."

The parents took great interest in their shoes and drinks. Piper just shook her head. "Well, sorry, Mom, you'll have to wait a little while until you're a grandmother. But luckily you have a little one to occupy yourself with in the meantime."

"If I can ever get her back," Tammy said with a fake pout. Her daughter was currently being passed around among Sydney, Mila, Sophie, Riley, and Reagan.

"I think a Christmas wedding would be lovely. Your mom can help me pick out a dress, and we can hold the ceremony at Cady's distillery. With all the Christmas decorations, it'll be magical." Piper began to imagine it all as though she were already there.

Aiden pulled out his phone and looked at the calendar. "December nineteenth?"

"Sure. We need to send out invitations right away, though. But I guess most everyone is here right now," Piper laughed.

"So, we have an official wedding date?" Poppy asked.

When Aiden and Piper nodded, Poppy called out, "December nineteenth is the winner."

"Yes!"

"Father Ben?" Piper questioned as the young man jumped up and down and high-fived an older priest. Aiden thought he looked familiar but couldn't remember why.

"He looks familiar, doesn't he?" Walker asked.

"Yeah, but I can't place it," Aiden whispered back.

"I don't know if it's him specifically or if it's his build."

"Definitely his build. Was he Special Forces?" Aiden asked Walker.

Walker shrugged. "No one knows. But he fights like he was."

"Hmm. Well, he's not now unless he's undercover."

"He swears he's a priest."

"Well, he could be both, I guess."

"Witness protection," Cassidy added. "That's my guess."

"Either way, he'll marry us on the nineteenth," Piper told them with a roll of her eyes. "He'll tell us about his past when he's ready."

"Now," Tammy said with Aiden's mother in tow, "what colors do you both love? I see green and gold. You both have the most beautiful eyes." And with that Aiden wrapped his arm around his future bride and planned a wedding as if he were planning an attack. But it turned out Keeneston had a lot of practice, and in less than two hours, his whole wedding was laid out in front of him. Now all he had to do was say *I will.*

~

"OH, SUGARBEAR!" Aniyah gasped as they walked into the uppermost floor of the distillery. A large window overlooked the landscape: the snow-covered fields, the running creek, and the white lights decorating the evergreen trees.

The tour had been so interesting as Cady talked about what she'd done and what she planned to do. The property was so historic and romantic that Aniyah couldn't stop touching her Sugarbear.

DeAndre pulled out a chair at the table set for two overlooking the beauty of nature and Aniyah took her place at the table. A red candle sat in the middle of the table as red, green, silver, and gold candles bathed the entire room in a warm glow. On the far side of the room, three musicians serenaded them.

"I thought you'd like it better if I kept out of the way, so I put everything on the table including a bell. You just ring it when you're ready for dessert."

"Thank you, Cady." DeAndre smiled as Cady hurried from the room.

"Alone at last." Aniyah took her honey's hand in hers and gave it a squeeze. "This has just been the most romantic thing ever. Are you okay?"

"Yeah, I brought a bottle of champagne and forgot it. I'm sorry, baby. I'll be right back." DeAndre hurried from the room and ran into a wall of elderly ladies on the other side of the door.

"Are you ready?" Miss Lily asked as she dug around in her purse for the ring.

"Why am I so nervous?" DeAndre asked as he wiped his palms on his black dress pants.

"Here's the champagne," Miss Violet said, shoving the bottle at him.

"Now, do it just as we practiced," Miss Daisy said with a smile.

"Ah, here it is," Miss Lily said, producing the small black box. "You've got this. We've gone over it again and again."

"Yeah, I've got this," DeAndre said, putting the box in his pocket and psyching himself up.

DeAndre turned and headed back to the table. As the door closed, the Rose sisters exhaustedly slumped against the wall to listen.

"You know I love pink champagne!" Aniyah cried as DeAndre popped the bottle.

"Nothing is too good for my baby." DeAndre took a breath as he lifted his glass to her. "Aniyah, you are a force in my life. A force of love, happiness, and I wouldn't be me without you."

The Rose sisters pushed the door open a little to peer out. "He's doing it!"

"Hush, Lil."

"Don't tell me what to do, Vi."

Daisy smacked them both as they all glared at each other before looking back at the couple at the table who seemed blind to everything but each other.

"Oh, Sugarbear!" Aniyah said, wiping at her eyes. She was beautiful that night in a Sydney-created red dress that hugged her perfect, generous curves. Sydney had called it an early Christmas present, but it was really all part of the master plan.

"I should have done this long ago, but I kept thinking you'd leave me. I wasn't good enough for someone so full of life and love as you. You take care of me, love me, and drag me out of my shell to make me a better man. I only wish I could be the man you deserve," DeAndre continued.

"Do what?" Aniyah asked. "Are you breaking up with me?"

"No, baby," DeAndre said, sliding out of his chair and kneeling beside her. "I'm asking you to marry me."

DeAndre opened the box to show the heart-shaped pink sapphire and Aniyah screamed so loudly the Rose sisters could hear her without their hearing aids. "Yes!" She screamed as she knocked the chair over and leapt up with excitement. "Yes, yes, yes!"

DeAndre slid the ring on her finger, and Aniyah couldn't stop crying as she kissed him. Miss Lily turned to her sisters and dabbed away a tear. "We've still got it, ladies."

Sienna Ashton Parker was sitting in bed reviewing a patient file as her husband, Ryan, cheered on the University of Kentucky Wildcats in basketball. Her dog, Hooch, sprawled on her other side with his gigantic head resting on her unborn baby. Hooch seemed to enjoy the feel of the baby moving beneath him.

"What a play!" Ryan clapped as he reached out with his other hand to hold hers. "Sweetheart, are you okay?"

Sienna shook her head. "No. Not okay."

Hooch's head shot up and he howled loud enough to wake the dead.

"Indigestion again?" Ryan asked as he reached for the chewable tablets. Hooch was frantic now. His wagging tail was clearing the clock and lamp from the nightstand and his nose was pressed to Sienna's belly. He was snorting in and howling out.

"What is the . . . are you in labor?"

Sienna only nodded at the contraction rippled across her belly at the same time Hooch howled.

"I'll call—"

"No! Just us!" Sienna managed to say between gasps. "Holy crap, that hurts."

"Okay, what do I do? I mean, breathe. Good. Now breathe again."

"I know how to freaking breathe! Get the bag and start the car."

Hooch lay down next to her as Ryan went running. The dog's big brown eyes looked worriedly at her as he nuzzled her belly. Sienna ran a hand over his head. "Don't worry, big guy. Soon you'll have a little one to meet." Hooch wagged his tail and whined.

"Okay," Ryan called out as he raced back into the room. Suddenly everything slowed for Sienna. There was no more panic, only joy. Soon they'd be a family of three. "I have the bag in the car, the garage door open, and the car heating. Is there anything else I need?"

"Maybe some clothes?" Sienna suggested with a laugh as her husband stood in the doorway completely naked.

Ryan laughed and Sienna held out her hand. He raced over and took it as he helped her from bed. "I'm excited," Sienna said as she stepped out of her pajamas and pulled on a sweater dress.

"I am too," Ryan admitted before he gently kissed her.

"ONE LAST PUSH NOW," Dr. Emma said from the foot of the bed. Okay, so she had called one person. But Dr. Emma had delivered half of the kids in Keeneston.

"You're doing great," Dr. Ava, Emma's daughter, said with a smile as she held one of Sienna's legs.

Ryan leaned over and kissed her forehead. "One more push and we meet our child. You're amazing, Sienna," he said with tears in his eyes.

Sienna pushed and there was the sound of baby crying. Ava went to assist her mother and Ryan kissed her again as he squeezed her hand. A nurse left the room, but Sienna didn't notice anything except the baby Dr. Emma had lifted up to place on her chest. "Say hello to your son."

"Oh, Paige, we have a grandson!" Sienna heard her mother call out.

Sienna looked to Ryan and shook her head as she heard her mother cry out from the hallway. "Just let them in," she told her husband as Dr. Emma cleaned her up and Dr. Ava weighed her son and wrapped him in a blanket.

As soon as she was ready, Ryan opened the door and her

mother, his mother, and Grandma Marcy burst into the room, full of tears, cookies, and gifts.

Ryan approached the bed as Sienna's mother, Kenna, kissed her and ran a shaking finger over the baby's chubby cheeks. Ryan took a seat on the other side of the bed and put an arm around his wife. Sienna looked up to see a smile so filled with love and pride that her heart melted all over again.

"Oh, he's perfect," Paige, Ryan's mom, said through tears.

Sienna handed the baby to Ryan and looked to where Grandma Marcy sat with silent tears streaming down her face. Ryan carried the baby to her and put him in her outstretched hands.

"My first great-grandchild," she whispered as she placed a kiss on his forehead.

"Can you die happy yet?" a voice from the hallway asked.

"Grandpa," Ryan laughed as Grandpa Jake came into the room with Ryan's father, Cole, and Sienna's father, Will.

"I have a lot more great-grandbabies to hold before I die," Grandma Marcy said as Grandpa Jake ran an arthritic finger over the baby's cheek.

"How did y'all know I had the baby?" Sienna asked.

"Since you're a mother now, we can tell you," Grandma Marcy said, handing off the baby to Kenna. "The secret is to bribe the nurses. I always bring one of my apple pies, so I got a call before you were even admitted."

Kenna nodded too. "Cookies."

"Brownies," Paige added as Kenna passed the baby to her. "Are you crying?"

"No," Cole said, wiping a tear away as the baby reached out and grabbed a finger.

"He has the Davies eyes," Will said to Grandpa Jake, the originator of the hazel eyes that many of the Davies descendants had inherited. Grandpa Jake just nodded, too choked up with emotion to talk.

Finally, after everyone had a turn, his son was back in his arms. Ryan looked down at him and his wife in wonder. She had brought this gift into their lives and he didn't think he'd ever been so happy. As soon as he heard that baby cry, it was as if his whole life changed in that one instant.

Kissing his son one more time, he placed him in his wife's arms.

"What's his name?" Will asked.

Sienna looked to Ryan who nodded for her to tell them. "Ashton Davies Parker. We're going to call him Ash."

At that pronouncement, Will sniffled as Marcy and Paige burst into tears. "What a way to honor the entire family," Will finally said.

"Welcome to Keeneston, Ash," the Rose sisters said from the door as they smiled at the happy family.

EPILOGUE

Piper looked at her reflection. Eight weeks. It had been eight weeks since Aiden had entered her life and somehow it felt as if he had always been in her heart. She placed the veil over her face and took a deep breath.

"Are you ready, honey?" her father asked.

"I am," she said, taking his arm. The wedding and reception were held at the distillery. People were seated at their tables with an aisle down the middle. The dance floor was covered with a red rug and two Christmas trees decorated with white lights, gold ribbon, and red bulbs were on each side of where Father Ben stood with Aiden.

As Cassidy went ahead of Piper as her maid of honor, Aiden broke with the old English tradition of keeping his back turned and looked right at her. Piper's breath stuck in her throat as she looked at him. He was devastating in his black tuxedo, his eyes filled with love and his lips tipped up into a smile. Wick, his best man, winked at Cassidy as she took her spot, and then he whispered something to Aiden.

Piper's heart was so filled with love when she stopped

next to Aiden. That walk seemed to have taken forever to get to him.

"You're the most beautiful woman I've ever seen in my life, and I'm the lucky man who gets to marry you," he whispered to her as he took her hand.

"We come together . . ." Father Ben began and all too soon while not being soon enough, "I give you Aiden and Piper Creed."

~

PIPER DANCED in the arms of her husband as the town joined in. She smiled as her friend Ava, or Doc Ava as everyone had started calling her when she graduated medical school, danced by her with Luke Tanner holding her tight.

"Who's he?" Aiden asked. "I feel like I'm getting to know everyone in town, but I haven't met him yet."

"Oh, he's not from here. He's from Moonshine Hollow, Tennessee. He helped with Reagan and Carter's rescue when her plane went down," Piper told him. "And that," she said, pointing to a tall man with dark hair, "is my cousin Gavin. He's from Shadows Landing, South Carolina. Next to him are his sister and cousins. The one talking to my cousin Colton is Ridge Faulkner. He's a builder and has designed the new fire station for Keeneston."

"I can't wait to meet them. But first, I have a gift for you," Aiden said, leading her from the dance floor.

"What is it? You already gave me this necklace for the wedding."

"Here you go," he said pulling an envelope from his tux pocket.

Piper opened it up and found two plane tickets for the

next morning. "New Zealand!" she gasped. "But you said you didn't have time for a honeymoon right now."

"I lied. I wanted to surprise you. I know you've always wanted to go. We leave tomorrow morning and will fly back to Atlanta right in time for Sydney and Deacon's Daughters of Elizabeth Ball."

"Oh, Aiden!" she cried, flinging her arms around him and kissing him.

"Come on, wife. Let's mingle, and then you're all mine."

Piper laughed as Aiden's fingers entwined with hers and they set off on their happily-ever-after.

TAMMY WATCHED as her son Dylan, so big and brawny, danced slowly with his littlest sister in his arms. It surprised her how her sons had taken to little Cricket. Not just sons, but all their cousins. Jackson had had the last dance, and Jace was waiting for the next. And when they weren't holding Cricket, they were holding Ash.

"I think they're doing it to get women," Tammy said to the table filled with her friends. They looked to the side of the dance floor where tens of women stood practically drooling.

"Good point. Shoot, I'm through menopause, and I can practically feel my ovaries crying out," Katelyn said with a laugh as Tammy smacked her.

"Ladies," Dani Ali Rahman said, lifting a glass of champagne, "to all our achievements this year and to our first grandmothers."

Kenna and Paige gave a mock bow before clicking glasses in celebration.

"Did you know Ryan would be such an attentive father?" Annie asked her sister-in-law.

"Yes," Paige said with a small smile. "He was always such a good big brother. Both he and Jackson loved to take care of Greer." The table looked to where Ryan was now standing with Ash in his arms, talking to his siblings.

"And Sienna is the most peaceful mother I've ever seen," Bridget said, as everyone's eyes shifted to where Sienna stood talking with friends.

"She's taken to it with gusto," Kenna told them. "But now we need to get back to business."

"The next couple we are going to pair up," Dani whispered to the group as she brought out the old notebook the Rose sisters had passed down to her, Kenna, and Paige.

"The way Jackson is with little Ash, I would say he's ready," Paige said.

"I could say the same for Dylan with Cricket," Tammy responded.

"What about Wyatt?" Morgan asked Katelyn.

"I would love nothing more than for my son to be married. Soon, but not yet. He's still struggling to get the farm back on track while running the large animal vet practice. Another year and then he'll be ready. But my daughter better be giving me a grandchild soon, though," she said, looking to Sydney.

"And here I am with two children married and not a grandchild to be seen," Dani added. They all knew Mila and Zain were having fertility issues. But so far Gabe was falling into this diplomacy roll well and Sloane loved working as a counselor at the high school so they appeared to be holding off for a bit.

"I guess I can't complain about Reagan and Carter since I have baby Ash." Kenna grinned.

"I can," Gemma said with offense. "That's all fine and dandy that you don't feel the need for Carter to have a baby, but he's married to my daughter, and I have two daughters married and no grandchildren," Gemma complained as she looked at her twin girls, Reagan with her husband, Carter, and Riley with her husband, Matt.

"Well, I'm thrilled," Annie grinned.

"Of course you are. You're going to be a grandmother next year," Morgan snorted as they all watched Nash hovering over Sophie. "But there is someone without any chance of becoming a grandmother."

Everyone at the table looked to Bridget. Neither of her kids, Abby or Kale, was married.

"Ahmed would lose his mind if Abby got married," Bridget said with a sigh.

"If Cy can get over it, so can Ahmed," Gemma said with certainty. It had taken quite a bit for Cy to get over his baby girls being married, but now he loved Carter and Matt like sons.

"Miles loves Walker," Morgan added. "And you know how crazy protective he was of Layne."

"But is Abby ready?" Dani asked.

Bridget looked over to her daughter standing with her old high school boyfriend, Nolan. Just then Jackson and Dylan joined them. They stood laughing and talking, but there was something in her eyes. Her daughter was closed off. She'd been like that since she graduated college and went to work in a job Bridget knew wasn't personal security as Abby claimed.

"She might not think so, but I do. It's time for her to step out from the shadows and be the woman I know her to be. And that means to find a man who will love all of her, including the parts she doesn't want anyone to see. My husband is going to have to deal with it."

"Bless his heart," the table said as one, as Dani wrote *Abigail Mueez* in the notebook.

"But who do I write beside her?" Dani asked, looking up. "Nolan? Jackson? Dylan? Someone else?"

Bridget looked at her daughter. She could pretend all she wanted, but Bridget knew her and knew her well. "I have an idea, but let me give it a push first to see if I'm right."

Dani closed the notebook and raised her glass again. "To Abby. May she find true love."

AIDEN HELD his wife's hand as they ran through the shower of red rose petals out to their limo for the short drive into Lexington. They were staying in a penthouse suite for privacy and ease to head out on their honeymoon the next morning.

Aiden paused at the door to the limo and bent down. "What's this? Someone's knickers?"

"The panty dropper!" Piper gasped as the town crowded around.

"Excuse me," Miss Lily said as the driver stepped forward to see what was going on. "Did you see anyone out here?"

He shook his head. "I've been staying warm in the kitchen. I came out ten minutes ago to start the car. Why is he holding someone's underwear?"

"Blast! I will find you!" Miss Lily yelled as everyone from the town laughed.

Two people in the crowd laughed, but their laugher was nervous—very nervous. They'd been too careless this time, missing the driver by mere moments. But again, they couldn't keep their hands off each other. This was the last time. Maybe.

~

SHE HELD her husband's hand as they walked into their bedroom. "What a beautiful wedding."

"It was," her husband agreed. "It makes me think of our wedding. You were such a beautiful bride."

"You're so sweet," she said, kissing her husband. "I'm going to take a shower."

"I'll be waiting for you in bed." He wiggled his eyebrows and she laughed. She loved her life.

She turned on the shower, undressed, and then paused as she looked at her naked self in the mirror. One, two, three, four, five, six, seven, eight . . . it had been eight weeks since she'd had her period. Wait? That wasn't possible, was it?

She looked at the door and thought about running to tell him, but it was probably just stress. Since this had happened before, she didn't want to get him excited, so she reached far under the sink for the pink bag she kept there. She unzipped it and pulled out a pregnancy test.

After taking it, she set it on the counter and got into the shower. She thought about it more and knew it had to be stress. That, and her cycle wasn't the most regular. She'd been down that path twice before, only for her to get her period the next week. She turned off the shower, toweled off, and pulled on her robe. Almost not wanting to look at it and be disappointed again, she told herself to just get it over with.

She picked up the test, *Pregnant,* and screamed for joy.

Her husband raced into the bathroom. "What's the matter? Are you hurt?"

She was crying so hard that she couldn't answer as she handed him the pregnancy test. He looked at it, then at her. "We're having a baby!" he screamed as he picked her up and spun her around.

The End

Bluegrass Series

Bluegrass State of Mind

Risky Shot

Dead Heat

Bluegrass Brothers

Bluegrass Undercover

Rising Storm

Secret Santa: A Bluegrass Series Novella

Acquiring Trouble

Relentless Pursuit

Secrets Collide

Final Vow

Bluegrass Singles

All Hung Up

Bluegrass Dawn

The Perfect Gift

The Keeneston Roses

Forever Bluegrass Series

Forever Entangled

Forever Hidden

Forever Betrayed

Forever Driven

Forever Secret

Forever Surprised

Forever Concealed

Forever Devoted

Forever Hunted

Forever Guarded

Forever Notorious (coming January 2019)

Shadows Landing Series

Saving Shadows (coming October 2018)

Women of Power Series

Chosen for Power

Built for Power

Fashioned for Power

Destined for Power

Web of Lies Series

Whispered Lies

Rogue Lies

Shattered Lies

ABOUT THE AUTHOR

Kathleen Brooks is a New York Times, Wall Street Journal, and USA Today bestselling author. Kathleen's stories are romantic suspense featuring strong female heroines, humor, and happily-ever-afters. Her Bluegrass Series and follow-up Bluegrass Brothers Series feature small town charm with quirky characters that have captured the hearts of readers around the world.

Kathleen is an animal lover who supports rescue organizations and other non-profit organizations such as Friends and Vets Helping Pets whose goals are to protect and save our four-legged family members.

Email Notice of New Releases
kathleen-brooks.com/new-release-notifications
Kathleen's Website
www.kathleen-brooks.com
Facebook Page
www.facebook.com/KathleenBrooksAuthor
Twitter
www.twitter.com/BluegrassBrooks
Goodreads
www.goodreads.com

CPSIA information can be obtained
at www.ICGtesting.com
Printed in the USA
FSHW012255161218
54523FS

9 781722 833206